The Popularity PROJECT

Joddie Zeng

authorHOUSE®

AuthorHouse™
1663 Liberty Drive
Bloomington, IN 47403
www.authorhouse.com
Phone: 1 (800) 839-8640

Published by AuthorHouse 5/5/2015

ISBN: 978-1-4969-6941-5 (sc)
ISBN: 978-1-4969-6940-8 (e)

Printed in the United States of America by BookMasters, Inc
Ashland OH
June 2015

To my parents, for giving me this incredible opportunity, and to my cat, Rosie, for being the best companion an introvert like me could ever ask for.

Prologue

I never believed in happily-ever-afters. Most girls tend to dream of their Prince Charming coming and sweeping them off their feet. I never bought it. What's the point of relationships, anyway? Other than the fact that we need them to keep the human race going. You lead yourself to believe that you love one person more than you could ever love any of the seven billion other people in the world when, in reality, it's not worth it. Relationships equal distractions. That's the truth. They suck you away from what's really important and trick you into believing that that one person is truly worth fighting for. Nothing will matter as long as you have him/her, right? Wrong.

Besides, not only do you become a helpless, love-sick puppy, but you eventually have to deal with the heartbreak. The one that every girl supposedly goes through at least once in her life. When that one person suddenly isn't what you hoped they'd be, and it's really over. When you realize that you've wasted a chunk of your life when you should've been worrying about something much bigger. Like the future. What are you if you don't have a future?

Nothing. That's it. You'll end up being helpless and possibly out on the streets. Love doesn't get you out of a mess like that. A job does. A high income does. You can love all you want, but it's simply a waste. A waste of time, a waste of effort, and a waste of heartbreak. Love doesn't get you anywhere. I never understood why girls let themselves fall in love. Why get yourself into this huge mess when it won't last anyway? Maybe I'm being too harsh, but I just can't wrap my head around it. Maybe I'll never understand why girls choose love over a successful, worthy, and steady future. In all honesty, I don't really mind never understanding.

Chapter 1

I trudged down the hallway, avoiding as much eye contact as possible, and passed a banner for the annoying winter formal, which Easton High had so generously decided to host tonight. I didn't care how many signs they'd nail up, the only plans I had tonight consisted of staying home and rereading my Complex Analysis textbook until I didn't have a single question left. Or maybe the clouds would finally clear out a little so I'd be able to get some quality shots from my special spot. I had heard that Cassiopeia was going to be out at around nine o'clock. Cassiopeia had always been one of my favorite constellations to photograph because when my parents gave me a Canon EOS Rebel for my fifteenth birthday, it was the first constellation I got a decent shot of. Sure, it wasn't the most complex constellation out there, but sometimes simplicity was the ultimate beauty.

But before I could get too excited for the night to come, I still had eight periods and two hours of intense indoor track to plow through. And it definitely wasn't about to go by fast.

As I continued to walk to first period, I could hear a distinct, high-pitched squeal, no doubt coming from Caroline Myers. It was her designated laugh to show that she was interested in a guy and that all the other girls had better back off. When I looked to my right, I saw that my assumptions were correct. *Fan-freaking-tastic.* Caroline was flirting with Parker Andrews, one of the wide receivers of the football team I had yet to go watch. By the looks of it, Caroline's flirting was working. Parker swung an arm around her shoulder as they walked downstairs.

Caroline was one of the many Barbie dolls—at least that's what I called them—in our school. These girls probably had so much potential for success, but it had been wasted on all the mascara and crop tops they'd spend their time shopping for. And it truly disgusted me how much they reeked of desperation for attention. But it really didn't matter what I thought of them because in the end, they were pretty and popular, and guys were going to want to hook up with them.

There were valid reasons I didn't like "the popular crew," one being how cruel they could be. I remember how parts of freshman year sucked big time because on the way to lunch, Caroline and her friends were always coincidentally walking right behind me and oh-so-subtly talking about how I looked like a hobo. That was reason number five thousand and twenty-three I loved being able to take my afternoon classes at Marlin County College.

It's almost like Caroline had nothing better to do than compare the thousands of dollars and time she spent on making herself look good to my cheap T-shirts and makeup-less face. It wasn't like I ever did anything to her. I didn't think I ever said ten words to her. Needless to say, we weren't friends. I didn't hate her though. I didn't know her well enough to be able to say I hated her. I disliked her, yes.

I disliked that she thought school was a Victoria's Secret fashion show.

Her friends thought that too.

But I couldn't act surprised, because Easton High was a private school in Cercis, Maryland. Cercis was certainly not a city that was lacking money, so clearly a lot of people were going to be more interested in the newest trends than their next test.

I just had to stick with my plan for the rest of junior and senior year and then I'd hopefully be going to Columbia. Columbia. I had started thinking about going there in sixth grade. The big city where so many successful people lived. Of course, I'd have to fight my way to the top. Starting with a good job in the business industry and then—I hoped—creating my own business by my late twenties. New York was a place that either meant great success or huge failure, and I wasn't about to let myself fall into the second category. I know. A seventeen year old who knows what she wants to do with her life? Shocker, isn't it?

I sighed with relief as I dropped my books on my desk. Career Workshop was my favorite class. Since my high school credits were met, I was technically supposed to have a free period, but instead the school had created this class. There were a total of six people in Career Workshop, including me. Many of the other people in the class specialized in one subject for which they had completed the credits, so they had a free period. Me? I was lucky enough to be taking all college classes.

The class was all about life. It was a mix between college preparation and life preparation for success. I took a seat at my usual desk in the front row, twiddling my thumbs as I waited for the bell to sound. Occasionally, I would push my droopy glasses back to their original spot on my face. My eyes wandered around the room but froze as I saw the newly written words on the white board.

A New You project due May 31. I blinked a few times, making sure the date was right. Nothing changed. I even yanked a strand of my hair but it was useless. The words didn't disappear, and my scalp kind of hurt when I yanked my hair. But it was only November 26th. What could possibly take six months to complete? And a "new you"? That sounded like something from an anger management course.

When the bell dinged, I waited attentively to find out what on earth was going on. "Good morning, class," Mr. Kinsey said, clapping his hands. "I see some of you have noticed that I have a new project for you all. I shall explain. As you all know, you have been put in this class because of your outstanding grades. Every single one of you specializes in an academic topic and/or topics, and you do exceedingly well in those topics. However, the school and I have finally been able to find a way to test your ability to handle something out of your comfort zone."

I really liked Mr. Kinsey, to say the least. He was also my AP French Five teacher in freshman year and when he noticed a tiny little ninth grader in his class, he went out of his way to make me feel as comfortable as possible in a room full of seniors. But at the moment I had mixed feelings. When I looked around at my other classmates, I saw confusion etched onto every single one of their faces.

Well, at least I wasn't alone.

"Lincoln Bay has teamed up with three nearby public schools to give you all a once-in-a-lifetime opportunity. Based on how successful this year is, we will decide whether or not this will be a yearly thing. I will be sending every single one of you to a different public school where you will be altering an aspect of yourself to fit into a different social group from the one you are in now. You will act like a new student who has moved from another state. You will be taking the classes that normal juniors take. The teachers know not to give you homework unless you or they feel it is necessary for the project. The teachers understand that you will not be required to take any of the tests. They will, however, be giving you all the work so you don't blow your cover.

"Unfortunately, there is only one flaw that we hope to fix next year. Regrettably, you will all have to sit through some of the classes you have already taken, but since you have all taken your SATs, you shouldn't feel terribly stressed about it.

"Each of your teachers now will be giving you a packet compiled with all the notes and work you will be expected to learn this year. With that, your teachers have very kindly prepared videos with concepts they feel need an explanation or think you may struggle with. Your grades for the next six months will be based mostly on the work you do on the material in these packets.

"In addition to the packets, you will be required, to come back after school once a month, to be tested on

7

certain concepts in these packets. This is mainly to make sure you don't cram everything at the last minute. Your teachers will be e-mailing you frequently, asking if you have any questions, and informing you what will be on the quiz or test you are taking that month."

Three hands shot up, and Mr. Kinsey waved to show that he wasn't finished.

"Now to what you will really be doing at this new school. You will act like a regular student, but you will behave according to your topic. From there, you will expand your knowledge of the people from your assigned group, as I assume they will become your friends. You must find out what makes each person tick, why they act the way they do, and so forth. To help you, the principals and I have designed each one of your schedules to be the same as that of one other person in your social group. You do not necessarily have to get to know that person, but, considering that the two of you will have all your classes together, it will be a lot easier. You all are basically assuming a new identity for six months. Eventually you will come across something that will change how you see the world. It may be just a tweak but I am sure that there'll be something. When the time is up, you will return and write up your experience and what you've learned as a school project."

"Of course, this is a graded project, so I will need to set some guidelines. I would like to see a picture slideshow somehow incorporated into your presentation. You are allowed to be creative, but I do need proof that you are doing what you're supposed to be doing. The teachers to whom you will be assigned are good friends of mine, so they will be watching to see that you're doing what you're supposed to be doing. You will also need to write down your oral presentation, whether on note cards or PowerPoint. I will need that turned in as well. I would like to see that you have taken on these new identities and are committed to doing your best. And I know some of you guys will want to come back early if you've completed the project, but the other principals and I have decided that if you do complete it early, then you should devote all the remaining time to your real school work.

"Before we can get to the fun stuff, I must give you these permission forms, as your parents or guardians need to be okay with all of it. The paperwork has all the information in it, and if they have any questions, they can always e-mail me. I would like these permission forms to be turned in Friday since tomorrow is Thanksgiving, so I know how many people will be participating. If you won't be doing this project, I will be giving you large amounts of schoolwork that certainly won't be as much fun as trying out this project. Any questions so far?"

From the corner of my eye, I could see a hand fly up.

"Yes, Matt?"

"Um … So if our parents agree to the project, when does it start?" Matt's voice was definitely uneven, but he was one step ahead of me, since I could barely say a word at the moment.

"Ah, I was just getting to that." Mr. Kinsey smiled an all too comforting smile. "The reason I need your permission slips Friday is that the project will begin on Monday. I know, it's fast, but we just worked out the logistics, and this is the only reasonable time possible. If you have any trouble, you can always talk to me. Oh, and I will be e-mailing each one of you a rubric. If you need a hard copy, see me at lunch. This project will be more or less one hundred points." Matt nodded. "Any more questions?" The room was quiet.

It felt like I was having a huge brain fart, and all I could think about was how this would all happen. Surely it couldn't be that bad, could it?

"All right, after careful consideration, I have chosen your topics according to what I believe will be suitable for you. Now let's get down to the fun part." Mr. Kinsey rubbed his hands together like an evil villain plotting an attack. "Ariel, you will be assigned to Lincoln Bay High School." His warm smile barely eased my tense muscles, but at least it was something. *Sounds like a decent school, I suppose.* It certainly wasn't Easton High, but it couldn't be too bad. "Your topic will be popularity. You will change your image to fit your way into the popular crew. From then on, you will befriend the people of that group and learn about their perspectives. You must have full faith that you will be entirely successful and that this will be an experience to remember."

Of course. I would get the topic I can't stand.

Well, at least I could pray that Aunt Stella would think that the project was preposterous and wouldn't allow me to do it.

Ha! Fat chance.

At that moment, Mr. Kinsey was dethroned from his position as my favorite teacher. I hadn't even had enough time to take in the information when he moved on to the next person.

"Bella," Mr. Kinsey began. Bella Butler was the science expert of our little class. She knew everything from minerals to compounds to anything else science related. I was pretty sure she was two levels above me in science. "You, my friend, will be learning all about the art of theater at Herbert High. You will be the leading lady in their school play. Lucky for you, I've spoken to the theater teacher, and the role is already yours. She will be spending a lot of time with you, helping you immerse yourself into theater. Herbert High has an excellent program, and I know you will make some great friends there as you break out of your science shell."

I turned around in my chair to look at Bella, whose jaw had dropped. She looked horrified. The truth was that I was horrified for her as well.

The theater geeks were a rather eccentric bunch of people, and the thought of Bella being one of them was crazy. But of course before Bella could say anything, Mr. Kinsey moved on.

"Matt," Mr. Kinsey began, but he was interrupted by Matt's loud groan. Matt Brown was the history-obsessed boy in the class, which was what I liked to call him. I never understood how someone could adore history so much, but he did. He constantly had a book with him, and it almost always included something with world history. Matt wasn't the fittest person—in fact he was a bit chubby—but he was a genius.

"You, sir, will be having some fun on the football field at Westbank High. I want you to take on the sport of football. The coach knows you are a beginner, so he will be giving you some one-on-one help. You will get on the football team and learn every aspect of the game. I am sure you will make loads of friends, so don't you fear."

I didn't even have to look at Matt to know that he was shocked and pissed. We all were. Eventually, I just zoned out, hoping that the class would just end already.

Soon enough, the bell rang, and I gathered my books

and walked up to Mr. Kinsey's desk. He must have been expecting me as he waited for me to speak. I got there first only because I sat in the front. When I turned around, all six of us were lined up wanting to talk about the same thing as me. I smiled innocently, but that was only because I was majorly confused. And it was impolite to glare at teachers.

"Mr. Kinsey? I'm sure you have made a small error. Are you sure popularity is my topic? I mean, don't you think that's a bit unreasonable?" I asked. I could never let myself be one of them.

"Ah, yes. Ariel, I have not made a mistake. When deciding on your project, I tried to give you a topic that is completely out of your comfort zone, which is the social aspect of high school. I do apologize, but I have noticed that this aspect is your weakness. I am positive that this is good for you, and I have no doubts about your success." Mr. Kinsey's reply was firm and confident. He patted my back, signaling that I should leave because of all the other students waiting to talk to him.

"Very well. Thank you, Mr. Kinsey," I forced out. But I wasn't thankful. If anything, I was the exact opposite, considering that turning into a brainless, attention-seeking brat was not on my bucket list. There wasn't anything to learn. My project would end up thirty seconds long.

Mr. Kinsey handed me the permission slip. I turned to leave, but I stopped when he called my name.

"Ariel?"

"Yes?" I said, turning back to face him.

"This will be a good experience for you," he assured me. *Ha! Good experience, my ass.*

I gave one last nod to Mr. Kinsey before rushing out the door to AP Physics. My eyes were nailed to the tips of my shoes so I suppose it was partially my fault when I was slammed onto the ground. My butt hit the floor with a thud, but luckily enough, my backpack broke most of the fall. I had never been more grateful that the school let us carry our backpacks around. When I looked up, I saw Marcy McLean, one of Caroline's best friends. I swear, if she put any more mascara on, her eyelashes would have been too heavy to open her eyes. I had had the good fortune to have known her and the rest of the popular crew since first grade.

"Watch where you're going, geek," she sneered as she walked away.

Thanks for the help.

I sighed and picked up my books, walking quickly to second period so I didn't have to encounter any more people. At least I didn't run into one of the guys. *Now that would've been embarrassing.*

The next two periods felt like days. And to say the least, I couldn't focus. All I could think about was how different life would be in just a couple of days.

By the time there was exactly five minutes left of third period, my eyes were practically glued to the clock. I resorted to mentally counting down the minutes and seconds until lunch.

Three, two, one … ding, ding, ding.

When the bell rang, I couldn't get out fast enough. I jogged to the cafeteria as I pulled out my lunch from my backpack. Slipping through a small space between a guy and a couple making out, I stepped into the cafeteria and took a seat at Flora's and my table. Normally, we ate outside but it was getting too cold for that. I tried to ignore the couple who was very publically showing their affection as I began to peel an orange.

13

One day, they'd regret doing all that publicly. This was high school. When it was time to go to college, they'd say bye-bye. Possibly they'd try to go long distance, but it wasn't going to work; high school relationships rarely did. Then she'd end up crying her eyes out, and he'd end up moping around. Eventually reality was going to hit, and they'd crash and burn. Life wasn't always like a romance novel with a perfect ending.

I rarely expressed my thoughts out loud, though. For one, no one would listen, and second, that was kind of dark, in a way.

I barely even talked to Flora about it. I never understood why she still stuck with me, considering that, physically speaking, we were polar opposites. The way her chocolate-brown hair cascaded down her face made it seem impossible that she could ever have a bad hair day. She had brown eyes that always sparkled. I didn't know such a dull color had the ability to be so spectacular—until I met her, that is. But then when she smiled, she flew to a whole new level of captivating. She'd flash those perfect pearly whites, and any guy would be down on his knees begging.

So, what differentiated her from the Barbies wasn't any lack of beauty; in fact, she could have hung around with them, if that was what she had desired. Even though, on a scale from one to ten, she was a solid fourteen, she also had a kindness that not many people possessed. There wasn't a nasty bone in her body.

Every one of Flora's features was the opposite of mine, and I knew it the moment we met in sixth grade. My dirty-brown hair always stayed limp. When my hair decided to be curly, it was always just one stringy curl that would sit there just to piss me off. My plain, brown eyes didn't sparkle in the slightest. They represented the color brown perfectly. Dull. Boring.

I called them my poop eyes.

For some weird reason, Flora thought it was hilarious.

I never quite cared about my appearance as Flora did. No, she didn't dress to impress. She said it made her feel good, and I couldn't complain. I couldn't even judge, because even though she spent a lot of free time not studying, she had a perfect GPA. Smart and pretty. She was the perfect combo.

When I finally spotted Flora, I realized that she wasn't alone. A boy was talking to her. I didn't know who it was, since he was walking backward while facing her, but I could see the number 14 on his football jersey.

"Hey, Ari!" Flora said when she was a couple of feet away. She had given me that nickname when we met. The boy turned his head to glance at me, and I mentally gagged. Those famous green eyes belonged to Tanner, Easton High's most popular boy. Quarterback of the football team and popular with most of the girls. I swear he had been trying to get a date out of Flora for two years. And by "date," he meant "fuck." He'd made that pretty clear the first time he hit on her. In freshman year, Tanner had taped a note on her locker that said "Hey there, cutie, if you ever need a tutor, I'll be your guy. I'll teach you a whirlwind of things. Yours truly, Tanner."

At first, I thought he meant he actually wanted to help until I saw another girl with the same note in her hand talking about how Tanner really helped her.

"Um, hi."

"Oh yeah, you're Ariel, right?" He scratched his neck, obviously irritated that I had screwed up their conversation.

"Yeah."

"Well, Flora, talk to you later, then. You know my number." And then he was gone.

Once he was out of sight, Flora's arms were around me. "Thank you, thank you, thank you. He wouldn't leave me alone."

I rolled my eyes. "Just tell him to back off."

"Like I haven't tried. I am this close to taking his offer and then dyeing his pants pink. The boy won't take a hint."

"Has he ever?"

"Good point. So how has your day been? I don't want to think about Tanner anymore."

"Okay, I suppose." *Awful, horrendous, depressing ...*

"What's wrong?" Flora's toothy grin slowly faded. "Get an A- on your test?"

"Why does something have to be wrong? And no, I did not get a bad grade on a test. I'd have to take a test to get a grade like that, and it looks like I won't be doing that for a while," I grumbled. She rolled her eyes.

"What? Oh, and you should probably turn that frown upside down because I think gravity is working a little too well at the moment."

"Bitch," I scoffed. "Why are we friends again?"

"Because you love me." She leaned in and whispered, "Are you on your period?"

I shoved her back. "You know, I consider that to be very offensive."

"What has your panties in a twist, then?" Her smile was growing by the second, and it was getting harder and harder to keep a straight face.

"Guess who gets to go to Lincoln Bay for six months and pretend to be popular?" I grumbled.

"Huh?" Her eyes grew.

"Kinsey's making us go to different schools for six months to try to pretend to be something we're clearly not." I pulled out an apple from a Ziploc bag.

"Explain." She grabbed my apple and slipped it back into my lunchbox.

When I finished explaining, she didn't have the same face I had had when I heard about the project. "Why are you smiling?" I pulled my apple back out and took a bite.

"That's so cool. You get to be someone you're not for the next six months!" Flora peeled her banana, and I wanted to shake her and tell her that it wasn't cool at all.

"Let's switch places, then. I don't even know where to start."

"Your appearance. You have to look like you care even if you don't. Besides, you get to be popular at a brand-new school. And if you don't like it, it's only for six months."

"That sounds like torture," I said blandly.

"It's really quite nice, because I've wanted to help you show off your beauty for literally about six years."

"Pft! Beauty, my ass."

"Please, you've actually got a really nice body. You just don't show it off so people won't notice you."

"This is getting too sentimental," I rubbed away a fake tear.

"Fine, I take it back. You're annoying and chubby, and I hate you."

"Thanks, best friend." I swung an arm around her neck. "Because a lot's about to change, and I need you every step of the way."

"Of course, we'll go shopping this weekend and glam you up."

"Please don't use that phrase ever again." I unwrapped my sandwich and shoved it into my mouth. "And who knows, maybe Aunt Stella won't let me do it."

"Don't hold on to that because I am almost one hundred percent sure Stella is going to love this."

"Thanks for shattering my dreams."

"We need to start getting you prepped now. First, stop inhaling that sandwich. You look like you haven't eaten in days."

"Don't comment on my eating habits. Food is a very nice thing, and I didn't have breakfast."

"I just can't wait until we get you out of these sweats. How does it not get old?"

I "inhaled" another bite, chewing as loud as I could just for Flora. "I like my fashion. It's comfy."

"Oh please, Ari, you're wearing clothes five times your actual body size," she said dramatically.

"That's an exaggeration."

"Well, you're not wearing clothes that fit your size."

"And your point is?" I tapped my foot impatiently, but I was sitting down so it didn't work too well.

"You have a great figure, and now you're finally going to be showing it."

"Ew."

"Oh, suck it up."

"Thanks, loving and caring best friend," I said.

"Oh, go cry about it." She laughed. And that was when I couldn't sustain a pout on my face, so I gave up and laughed with her.

18

When I got home from track, it was six o'clock, and I was exhausted. I fell onto the couch and shut my eyes for a few moments until I was interrupted by the sound of Aunt Stella coming down the stairs.

Aunt Stella was living with me because in August, Mom and Dad got a call from my grandma, who was extremely sick. I wasn't going to be that daughter who whined and pleaded for them to stay because obviously I shouldn't have been the priority. Grandma was the priority.

They had offered that I go with them, but that was unrealistic, since I had to stay in school. That could've ruined my plan to attend Columbia. So they called Aunt Stella, who had been traveling, and she gladly came to stay. I didn't complain. I loved Aunt Stella. She was more of a friend than an aunt, and I loved that.

"Look at you, haven't even made it to your room, and you already look like you could pass out for a whole month." Stella's cheery voice was right above me. I opened one eye and saw that she was hovering over me.

"Hey there, Stella." I grinned and sat up.

"Well, hello to you, too, Miss Sunshine." She plopped down next to me.

"How was your day?"

"Oh, it was just fine, but wait, I made spaghetti. Here, why don't I grab two bowls while you go turn on *The Bachelor*, and we'll talk then?" Stella scampered into the kitchen as I grabbed the remote. Reruns of *The Bachelor* had been on the entire week, and she was addicted.

I flipped to *The Bachelor* just as Aunt Stella returned with two bowls of pasta. She handed me a bowl, and my mouth watered when the scent reached my nose.

"So how was your day, darlin'?"

I started spinning my fork, piling on as much spaghetti as I could. "Not the greatest. I was hoping you could maybe help me get out of a project," I hinted as I placed the delicious heaven of pasta into my mouth.

"What kind of project is it? You normally love doing projects."

I explained the project for the second time that day, making it sound as awful as possible, but by the look on her face, it didn't sound that bad.

"That sounds like so much fun! And I bet it would get you out of that room of yours once in a while." That wasn't what I was hoping for.

"I get out of my room," I protested.

"Not to be social, you don't."

"Well, I'm doing pretty great, aren't I?" I pointed to my face, since I was smiling.

"Yeah, but I think this project will be good for you."

I pulled out the permission slip from my backpack along with a pen and handed it to her. "So there's no way I'm getting out of it?"

"Nope." She read the form and signed her name on the "yes" line.

"This is betrayal."

"Oh, quit being so over-the-top." She handed the paper back to me, and I reluctantly stuffed it back into my backpack. "Now, what season is this?"

"I think this is season one. I guess we're starting with Alex." I shrugged.

"I've always like him."

After about an hour, I put my bowl in the dishwasher and went upstairs. I said goodnight to Aunt Stella, who was still attentively waiting to see who Alex was going to give the rose to, even though she already knew. Today was one of those days when I had finished my homework during the breaks I had during track, and all I had left to do was shower and, I hoped, take a few nice photographs.

I had some time to kill first, so I plopped onto my bed, picked up my sociology textbook, flipped to page fifty-five, and started reading. When I had reached page 200, it was around nine.

I grabbed my towel and headed into the shower for about fifteen minutes. I never understood the point of taking a long shower. It was honestly just wasting studying time, in my opinion. I dried my hair and put on a sweatshirt over my pajamas. I unlocked my phone to check the time. *9:20. Perfect.*

I poked my head out the window, and the moon was glistening. I happily picked up my camera—a.k.a. my one true love—and opened the window fully. When I crawled out, and my foot reached the "half roof," as I liked to call it, I was met with a slight breeze. I breathed in the fresh air and slowly scooted to the middle of the roof.

The house had been built so that there were four levels overall. The basement, a living room, a level that held only my parents' room and the guest room, and the highest level, where my room and a bunch of other rooms were positioned. Luckily, I had the room that was right above my parents' room, so I was able to crawl onto the roof, which just happened to be the perfect location for spotting constellations.

It had become my special place since I first set foot there when I was fifteen. I'd sit on the roof with my camera, snapping away until I'd get a photo that would just blow me away. There were no streetlights, which just made the stars pop in the camera once I was able to set it so that there was just the perfect amount of exposure. Capturing these moments became my getaway, my escape hatch, when I'd get too stressed. Just the sight of the constellations and the stars in general was magnificent.

The only decor in my room was photographs of some of the best constellations I had caught on camera. I had gotten them printed and framed and then hung them on my wall. It was a reminder every day of how breathtaking nature was, especially when no one was watching. I leaned back so the back of my head was pressed against the slate of the roof. I searched around for the starting point of Cassiopeia. With my finger, I slowly traced the W shape until I saw it clearly. I turned on my Canon EOS and slowly brought it to my eye.

I'm pretty sure that, when I had first gotten the camera from my parents, I fainted. But after that, I read almost every article on how to get quality shots at night.

When I had found Cassiopeia through the camera, I steadied my hands as best I could and began rapidly taking shots. If I wanted more professional-looking photos, I could've used a tripod, but I loved the feeling of having the camera in my hands. Besides, I probably wasn't going to become a professional photographer anyway. And the only thing I was really good for was capturing these moments at night.

Once I had taken about fifty shots, I brought the camera away from my eye and began to look at the photos. I had used just the right exposure to make Cassiopeia stand out from all the other stars. But out of those fifty shots, there was one that stood out from the rest. That just completely took my breath away. The moon was peeking into the corner of the shot, glowing. The stars weren't bright enough to outshine Cassiopeia, but they were bright enough to bring out its beauty. It was a photo that made Cassiopeia seem like one of the most magnificent constellations ever, even though it was rather common.

I deleted all the other photos and headed back inside. I put the lens cap back on, turned my baby off, and put it back into its case. I crept into bed, and that's when reality came flooding in, and I realized that my life was about to change. And not for the better.

Chapter 2

I didn't have a single pair of jeans that fit me.

The last time I actually purchased jeans was in the middle of seventh grade when I was trying to, "find myself," as my mom described it. But after I had worn them to school for a full eight hours, I stuffed them in the back of my closet and never wore them again.

It wasn't that I looked bad—not at all. The reason I had bought them in the first place was because I liked the way they looked.

What I didn't like was how uncomfortable they were. When mom was helping me pick a pair out, she opted for skinny jeans. I had been so blinded by how nice they looked that I didn't realize that they were cutting off the circulation in my legs. And if I forgot my gym clothes, then I was completely screwed.

After that day, I stuck to yoga pants and sweat pants, so anyone could probably understand my reluctance to go shopping with Flora when buying jeans was inevitable.

"Come on, Ariel! We still have to get a haircut!" Flora said as she dragged me through the mall.

I had originally thought I would have Saturday off and do everything Sunday, but it seemed like Flora couldn't wait. For the past five hours, she had hauled me around the mall looking for outfits.

I never knew that shopping was this tiring. Running a 5k would have seemed easier than this.

We ended up going into American Eagle, and I basically had a cringe attack. *Short, short, and shorter* I thought as I saw the clothes. Each time she found a frilly top or a pair of jean shorts, I found a reason not to buy it.

My reasons included:

"It's too expensive."

"It's not my style."

"This makes me look fat."

But she and I both knew that I didn't care if I looked fat. We both also knew that none of these clothes made me look fat.

Even I knew I was stalling.

I knew she didn't care that the color of the shirt could fade in the washing machine even though it wouldn't. I didn't care either, but it managed to get me out of buying quite a few shirts.

It wasn't entirely my fault for acting this way. Instead of easing into the entire thing by first getting a frozen yogurt, once we got to the mall, she started by dragging me into Forever 21. I had never gone in there before, but I knew it was one of her favorite shops. Our conversations went like this:

"This is adorable," Flora cooed as she lifted up a frilly, pink top. I faked a gag. She rolled her eyes.

"That pink is too pink," I attempted. I sounded like an idiot.

"Are you being serious right now?" she deadpanned.

"I genuinely don't like it." I said, having barely looked at it.

She put the shirt back, and I nearly high-fived myself.

Eventually, Flora just ignored me and piled a bunch of shirts in her arms for me to try. And to piss me off, Flora put that stupid, frilly, pink top in the stack too. *Asshole.*

After hours, I finally agreed and ended up buying everything because I was tired and hungry. I bought a bunch of sweaters and jeans because it was winter, but Flora had also chose some shorts and shirts for when it got warmer. *These clothes better be worth it, because they sure were expensive.*

We had also stopped by the Sephora because she said it was, and I quote, "Sooooooo important" with an emphasis on the "so." And Flora insisted on going to Sephora because apparently it was one of the best stores in which you could get a variety of brands.

Since Flora was quite the expert—well, more of an expert than I was, at least—I allowed her to choose my makeup so we could leave quicker. She tried on different types of eyeliners, mascaras, and lipsticks as I sat there like a mannequin. I could've sworn that Flora was drawing on my eyeball with that eyeliner. I was also extremely confident Flora would end up poking my eye with a mascara brush, but thankfully she didn't.

Sometimes, you just had to believe that your best friend wouldn't think it was funny to poke you in the eye.

All I could say was that I was doing a lot of trusting.

"I'm coming! These bags are so heavy!" I complained. I had to have been holding at least ten jam-packed bags.

Haircuts had always been awful for me. I had never really bothered to choose a hairstyle, so I just allowed the stylist to do whatever she desired. It never ended well, but it was just hair, anyway. It would grow back.

Except for bald people's hair.

I was pretty sure that bald people's hair didn't really grow back, but maybe it was just at an extremely slow rate. I never asked because it would probably have sounded really offensive if put into words.

I stepped into the hairstylist's shop just as Flora checked in with the girl in the front. Flora pointed at a chair in the back of the store, motioning for me to take a seat. I scowled, and reluctantly and shamefully sat in the black chair. I let the bags drop on to the ground as a sigh of relief went through me. I rubbed my palms together, attempting to get the marks on my hands to a point where they were not noticeable anymore.

Of course it didn't work, but I still tried.

Flora pulled up a chair and sat next to me. "Oh, it's just a haircut. Don't look at me like someone just ran over your precious camera."

"Why couldn't they wait until next year to grace us with this amazing project?"

"I don't know, but I do enjoy watching you freak out." She beamed from ear to ear as she looked at the hair dressers' catalog. The hair dresser finally arrived, and my stomach flopped a little.

"Hello, dear. My name is Sandra, and I'll be helping you look more fabulous today, even though you're pretty enough as it is. Is there any specific hairstyle you would like?" Sandra asked with a soft smile.

I assumed that she was in her late thirties. Sandra had dirty-blonde hair that was cut to just beneath her shoulders. I was pretty sure she had highlights, and I noticed that her hair had quite a lot of volume. But it wasn't technically frizzy. It looked nice on her— something that I never could've pulled off. She wore dark-blue skinny jeans and a white blouse.

I opened my mouth to reply, but Flora cut me off. "Could you do this one for her?" she asked, pointing to a picture I couldn't quite see. I strained my neck to catch a glimpse of the picture, but Flora noticed me looking and turned the book away so I had no chance of seeing it. Period. I guessed that it would be a surprise.

Sandra only smiled. I guess it couldn't have been horrendous. "Of course I can. Good choice, by the way. Now darling, just sit back, relax, and let me work my magic."

I pointed a finger at Flora. "I'm putting a lot of trust in you today."

"Oh, just shut up and do as Sandra said."

As Sandra snipped at my hair, Flora whipped out what looked to be my phone.

"How do you have that?" I lifted my hand to grab it but Flora merely slapped it away.

"I'm a ninja." She said while scrolling through who-knows-what.

"Can I have it back?"

"No, I'm getting you an Instagram."

"Why?"

"I guarantee all the people you hang out with will have one and they'll want to see yours."

Social media had always been Flora's strong suit in our friendship. I must've been the only girl in school who had never bothered to download Instagram or Twitter. Even Aunt Stella had a Facebook account. But I just never bothered. It always seemed like an unnecessary waste of my time.

"But it'll have no pictures, and I won't have any followers. At most, they're going to think I'm a loser."

It wasn't like I was Chloe Grace Moretz, and millions of people would jump at the opportunity to follow me.

"That's where I come in."

There was a five-minute silence during which I just sat there watching strands of hair fall while Flora tapped my phone.

"There, most of these people will follow back by the end of the day so you should have at least four hundred by seven o'clock. Before we left, I made sure to take a cool picture so your account wouldn't be blank."

She handed my phone back, and I marveled at how fast she did all that. My username was Ariel_Winters, and I was thankful that she hadn't put it as something mortifying like pizzalover1234, because that was something that she'd totally do. I only had one follower— most likely Flora— but I already followed six hundred people. I scrolled, and it was filled with people from Easton.

The picture she posted was of one of the framed photographs in my room. She chose Virgo probably because she was a Virgo. Still, it wasn't a bad picture. It was kind of artsy. She captioned the picture, "Sometimes, you just gotta stop and look at the stars. You might be nicely surprised by what you see." She added a star emoji to the end.

"We just gotta post some more stuff before you go. And I also made you a Snapchat in case some people ask. You don't really have to use it, but it's best if you just have one."

"Thanks. If you weren't here, I'd probably still be trying to figure out how to create an account."

She flashed a grin.

"I don't doubt that."

"Voilà!" Sandra sang.

"What do you think?" I turned to Flora.

"You look like a serious badass, Ari."

"Not exactly the look I was going for, but thanks."

"But I want you to see the finished look, so sit back, let me do your makeup, and then you can look."

"That's so stupid," I whined. "It's just hair."

"Really fabulous hair, that is."

Flora pulled out a makeup kit from her bag as I pulled off my glasses. Right as I set them down, she began attacking my face with different sized brushes. I didn't feel any different. The only difference was that I could feel the thin layer of makeup coating my face. That was a huge reason why I hated makeup. No matter how subtle it was, I could always feel it on my face.

Finally, Flora sat back and motioned for me to take a look in the mirror. Hesitantly, I grabbed my glasses and staggered to the nearest mirror to examine my complexion. I almost didn't want to see it, but then I noticed how idiotic I sounded, so I looked.

Holy ball sack.

Now, I know what you're thinking and the answer is no. It wasn't like I got a new haircut, put on some makeup, and changed clothes then I was suddenly this perfect human being. I didn't switch from hobo status to model status in the blink of an eye. I just looked a bit different … better. Nicer. Like maybe I had a chance at surviving at Lincoln Bay. My long, brown hair flowed down into big curls, which had replaced my messy ones. Not much had been cut but a lot of styling had happened in that hour. The mixture of black eyeliner and mascara made my eyes pop, and they were no longer poop-looking, which was one of the biggest changes that had taken place today. My gaze traveled to my outfit. I had on a pair of black skinny jeans. I guess the pain of getting into those stupid pants was sort of worth it. Okay, very worth it.

But seriously speaking, for a moment, I thought the jeans would cut off my circulation. I was prepared to call a paramedic and make her cut the pants off. I could practically see the situation unfolding. Aunt Stella would get a call informing her that her niece had suffocated in really tight jeans. Man, would she make fun of me.

I had on an adorable winter sweater that Flora had insisted on buying. I thought it was a bit too form-fitting, so I had wanted a larger size, but Flora wasn't having it. My new chestnut Uggs were really quite nice with the rest of the outfit. They were the only part of the outfit that I didn't mind buying. Uggs were comfortable, anyway. I could use them for years. I pulled out my small, portable Canon camera and decided to take a picture right there. I had brought it just in case I felt the need to take a photo, and I was happy that I had.

I smiled as Flora strolled up behind me, her expression saying, "I told you so."

"See, it didn't take much for you to look absolutely stunning. Just don't let those Lincoln boys screw you over."

"Like that'll happen."

"Now we are officially single and ready to mingle!" She crooned.

"Never say that again."

"Come on, let's go get you contacts and then you'll be completely prepared for Monday."

I skipped over to the chair and picked up my bags, thanking Sandra. I left the hairdresser feeling a little more confident than normal. Flora and I strutted around the mall looking for the contacts store. One the way, a group of boys who looked about our age stared agape at the two of us. We smiled and strolled past them.

Well, Flora's smile was more flirty. I kind of did this weird, lopsided smile that didn't quite work, but it was okay.

We stopped at the contacts store and walked in. My confidence flew away. Of all the changes that had occurred, contacts were my worst nightmare, even since I was a child. Why would I poke my eyes every day when I could simply wear glasses? Flora noticed my frown and gave me a reassuring smile.

"It'll be fine, Ari."

Pft! Coming from a girl with perfect vision.

After a bothersome hour, I ambled out of the shop with brand-new contacts. I let out a groan of annoyance. If looks could kill, those contacts would have been burned up and buried at the bottom of the ocean.

"Stop it. This'll all be worth it when you have every guy eating from the palm of your hand." Flora smirked. "I just wish I could be there."

"That's not the point of the project."

"Yeah, yeah, become popular. Learn something new, blah, blah, blah."

It's for the A+. It's for the A+. It's for the A+.

"Hah, I beg to differ." I scoffed. "And jabbing my

eyes every day doesn't sound like the most fun. What if they, like, move and cause problems? I could become blind."

"Oh, just thank me already," Flora said, completely ignoring me.

"Thank you." And I did mean it. "Who knows what I'd be doing if you weren't here?"

"Oh, probably still cursing the entire mall." She winked.

"Thanks for ruining the moment," I snorted.

"You know I love you."

It was certainly an interesting day, but it eventually had to end. At about 5:00 p.m., I drove Flora home, and we went our separate ways. As I pulled into the driveway, I saw Aunt Stella's cute, yellow buggy car. Compared to my beat-up black Sedan, Aunt Stella's car was definitely a lot cuter.

I had thought she would be home later. Aunt Stella was one of those art teachers who came to your house and had one-on-one sessions with people who wanted to learn. She also did a lot of sculpting. And painting. And drawing. Come to think of it, she basically did everything and she did it well. Normally, weekends were her busiest times, so I hadn't expected her to be home until around 9:00 p.m.

When I walked in, she was lounging on the couch, watching *Keeping up with the Kardashians*. I snorted, and she looked up.

"How's it going, sweet pea? I swear they need to stop making these reality shows so addictive—wow! When you said you were going to the mall with Flora, I hadn't expected all this." Her eyes widened, and she stood up from the couch.

I didn't know whether that was a compliment or an insult.

"Gee, thanks Stella."

"No, I mean you look dazzling. Is this for that project you made me sign the permission form for yesterday?"

"I know. This sucks, right?" I pointed to the bags in my hands.

She raised an eyebrow. "What the hell are you on about? This is amazing. The Lord has heard our prayers."

"You're ridiculous."

"Have you eaten yet?" she asked, changing the subject. I shook my head, and she gave me a toothy grin. "Well, I got a pizza, so why don't you sit down, and we can have a little Stella and Ariel time."

"Keeping up with the Kardashians, really?" I stared.

"Hey, why not?"

I could easily have thought of ten reasons why she shouldn't have been watching *Keeping up with the Kardashians* on a Saturday evening.

The worst part was that I knew I would eventually get really into the show. It was a guilty pleasure. I gave in and took a seat on the couch next to Stella. I grabbed a slice of pizza and got comfy. It felt like my last day of normality before everything would change.

For six months, at least.

Chapter 3

I believed that everyone in high school has a specific style to help define them. Whether it's leather jackets with skinny jeans or cute, flowery skirts, I always noticed a pattern in the overall look of a student.

Me? I never really figured out my trademark style, and, because I never really cared about finding it, I kept it simple. Yoga pants were my life. And big T-shirts. They were comfortable, affordable, and perhaps borderline hobo-looking, but they passed the checklist of what clothes had to be.

Over the years, in events and 5k runs, they'd give out free T-shirts. Once, I happened to have received a T-shirt that was just a little too big. But it was free, and it fit, which meant it was going in my closet to be worn to school.

Going to Lincoln Bay meant a whole new style. It wasn't necessarily going to become my new style, but at the very least it was going to be my fake style, and I felt very uncomfortable in it. Shopping with Flora made me see how big of a role clothing had in our society. If I had walked into Lincoln Bay with sweats and a T-shirt, I probably would've gotten a completely different reaction as opposed to if I wore a leather jacket and ripped-up, black jeans. It was kind of screwed up, really.

Sunday passed in a blur as I read some random book I had already forgotten the name of and then it was Monday.

I stepped out of my car and stared at what was going to be my school for six months. It didn't look that different from Easton, other than the massive sign that had the words Lincoln Bay High School plastered across the front of the facility. And it was a lot bigger than Easton.

The trees were mostly bare, and I could see limp branches swaying to the right. I grabbed my deceivingly small Vera Bradley bag, which was annoyingly expensive, and checked my appearance one last time.

The thing was that I looked exactly the same as when I had checked ten seconds ago. Man, I was turning into a girl who was constantly aware of how she looked, and it sucked. I pulled out my camera and snapped a photo of the front of the school.

I had curled my hair so that it flowed down my back into soft waves. But no matter how hard I tried, I could never get my hair back to how it had looked when it was cut, which was another thing I hated about haircuts.

My makeup wasn't too severe. Although I needed to be popular, I still didn't want my face to look like I drew it on with crayons. Plus, Flora only showed me how to do one simple look, and I never bothered to go on YouTube to find more ways to do makeup.

I wore a light-pink blouse that cut right under my

belly button, as well as a pair of high-waisted, navy-blue skinny jeans. I had put on my chestnut Uggs, and if I'm going to be honest, I felt pretty.

I strutted into the school feeling prepared and confident. Well, as prepared and confident as I could be, which most likely wasn't enough. As I walked through the halls, pairs of eyes were slowly looking me up and down.

It was expected, considering that most students didn't enter in the beginning of December, but that didn't stop me from wanting to run. Lincoln Bay's social groups were even easier to distinguish than Easton High's. On my left crowded a group of five or six students, some with nose piercings, others with dyed hair. On my right, I found the group I'd be spending my time with for six months, and my stomach dropped.

It was roughly about ten people, half girls and half boys. What surprised me weren't their faces; it was the fact that the girls were all wearing shorts that barely covered their asses. It was the beginning of December, for God's sake. Weren't they freezing yet?

The guys were a little bit better. They were dressed appropriately, for one. I had to admit they weren't bad-looking, but their gelled hair and polo shirts reminded me that they knew it, too.

I figured they were the guys who could get any girl wrapped around their finger in the blink of an eye, but of course they would want nothing to do with them after about a week—maybe a month if they were feeling frisky. Clearly, none of these guys would ever be able to maintain a decent relationship. Why couldn't they focus on school instead?

If they had as much passion at school as with girls,

they would all have perfect GPAs. But I was judging too quickly. *Who knows? Maybe they're nice and smart and kind and all have straight A's. Hah! That would be a dream come true.*

I must've been staring too long because one guy was smirking at me. *Oops.* I don't know why I decided to do this, but I winked at him and turned to go to the main office. *And it begins.* I found the principal's office, and, before I could control it, my hand knocked on the door.

"Come in," a voice bellowed.

I slowly opened the door and walked into the small office, where I saw a woman in her fifties. She was wearing a business skirt and a formal white blouse. Her oval glasses hung around her head, reminding me how I was being forced to stab my eye while she had the luxury of glasses. She gave me a pleasant smile as she motioned for me to take a seat.

"Hi, I'm Ariella Winters. Mr. Kinsey told me to come here."

I hoped that I was in the correct school. Otherwise it would have been rather uncomfortable and hard to explain. Her smile didn't fade, which I took as a good sign.

"Yes, dear, I have been expecting you. I'm Principal Calder. Mr. Kinsey has told me many wonderful things about you. You are welcome to complete this six-month project, and I wish you the best of luck. I only wish my school had a social project like this back in the day. Also, if you have any trouble, my son knows of your presence, so he may be able to help you," Mrs. Calder reassured me. "I have a feeling you will bump into him, because he's one of those hooligans you're befriending."

I tentatively took the schedule she presented me with

and thanked her. I left her office, my head bowed, staring at the schedule that I would follow for six months. *1st period: Honors precalculus with Mr. Blair, room 101B. Damn, not that class again. Been there, done that, and hated it.*

And by the way, it was boring as hell. If I had to choose classes to take again, it certainly wouldn't have been precalculus.

I wandered around the hallways, trying to familiarize myself with the school. So far, all I knew was that first period was downstairs. I passed room after room, finally reaching 101B, but not before accidently wandering around the entire level three times. Through the small window on the door, I could see the teacher already beginning his lesson.

Late. This was just a perfect way to make an impression. I took a deep breath and walked into the classroom. I was basically walking into my life for the next six months.

Suddenly all eyes were on me as though I were an alien from another planet. Mr. Blair looked confused for a second, but then I suppose he remembered I was coming because he greeted me with a smile. I scanned the classroom, which just made me more uneasy because I didn't know a single face. At least it was only first period so everyone was half-asleep. Instead of hyperventilating from nerves, I kept my eyes locked on Mr. Blair's chin. It seemed that he hadn't shaved in a couple of days. But I couldn't miss the group of guys in the back fooling around.

"Hello, dear. You must be Ariella. Welcome to Lincoln Bay." Mr. Blair had to have been in his late twenties. He had jet-black hair that was combed over to the side and dark yet welcoming eyes.

"Sorry I'm late. I got lost." I explained.

"No worries. Class, this is Ariella Winters. She is a new student here. I expect you all to be kind to her. Is there anyone who would be willing to show Miss Winters around the school?" Mr. Blair asked.

One hand shot up from the back of the room. The boy raising his hand gave me a smug smile and called out, "Mr. B., it would be my pleasure to show Miss Winters around the school."

Cocky, great.

Mr. Blair rolled his eyes and scanned the room to see whether any other students would offer. I snickered. *Guess he's not a teacher's pet.* When no one else raised their hands, Mr. Blair sighed. "Very well, Ashton. Ariella, you can go take a seat next to Mr. Walker over there. He will show you around and help you find your classes."

Oh look, there just happens to be an open seat right next to him. My luck is uncanny.

"Thank you."

"You are certainly welcome. And Ashton? I have no tolerance for any funny business." Mr. Blair looked Ashton straight in the eye.

I took my seat, leaning as far away from this Ashton boy as I could without it seeming suspicious.

I tried to scoot my chair over the slightest bit, but the screeching sound that the chair made put me to a stop. I guess that wasn't an option.

I studied Ashton's face as he turned to watch Mr. Blair. Well, he certainly wasn't ugly. In fact, he was much more than not ugly. He had chocolate-brown hair that was shaken to create a messy yet perfectly neat look, long enough to cover his forehead but not long enough to poke his eyes. He had these ocean-blue eyes that I could stare at all day. The color, I mean. My hand twitched a little in my lap, which could've been worrying. He was wearing a gray-and-white speckled sweatshirt and black jeans. He had on worn-out black vans that shouldn't have been cute but were. It wasn't hard for a girl to fall for a guy like that.

At that moment, two thoughts flew into my head. One: I really wanted to go home.

Two: *Please don't share a schedule with me.*

He was one guy I didn't need to be wrapped up with.

"Take a picture, gorgeous. It lasts longer," Ashton whispered, a smug expression plastered all over his face.

Asshole. I focused my attention on my thumbs.

Wait, that's too nerdy.

I looked up, giving him what I hoped was a cute face but in reality probably made me look constipated. Although he was hot, Ashton was unmistakably a hopeless candidate to befriend.

Just don't fall for his tricks, and it'll be fine. Avoid as much physical contact as possible. Work on your facial expressions so you don't look mutated.

I already had a mental checklist on the first day of school.

Taking a deep breath, I looked him square in the eye and scoffed, ready to start acting. "Don't get cocky on me now, pretty boy," I replied.

Pretty boy? That's the best I can do?

Ashton smirked and eyed my body up and down. Starting to feel self-conscious, I turned to watch the teacher, but Ashton snatched my schedule. On the inside, I was hyperventilating, and I could only pray that I didn't look how I felt.

"Well, gorgeous, looks like we have all our classes together."

Damn it.

I stared into his eyes, hoping to find something worth being happy for, but everything was blocked by that stupid, classic smile. I rolled my eyes, rotating my body to listen to Mr. Blair speak. I had two options. Pretend to focus on a class that I had already taken or pretend to be enjoying someone's company.

Precalculus it was. Hands down.

Throughout the class, I didn't dare to glance at Ashton, but I could feel his stare burning holes into the side of my face. It felt like he was examining me to decide whether or not I was worthy.

God, I hated the way that he looked at girls. It was as if Ashton saw them as fresh meat. Like a new challenge, and it was his responsibility to complete it. And I was the new challenge. But this challenge wouldn't be very easy to complete, especially considering that I was aware of the rules. *Not fair? Maybe.*

But you know what else wasn't fair?

The fact that I had to be in this school for six months.

"Come on, Ashton, we have to get to class. We're already late." If I could look him in the eye and say, "Don't touch me," I would have an hour ago.

Being late to class, being social, and dealing with a boy I wanted to stick in a box and mail to Australia wasn't the most enjoyable thing in the world. My tolerance levels were plummeting. Ashton, however, seemed to be extremely amused. I groaned as we reached an empty hallway. He touched my hand. I pretended to see something interesting and swiveled away, but he was too fast and spun me around so I was facing him.

"So, gorgeous, what brings you to this school?" Ashton asked with that same vain smirk.

I froze. What was I supposed to say? *Oh Ashton, I'm here because I am pretending to be popular to find out your biggest secrets for a school project.*

"Oh, you know. I moved to town and this was the closest school." I winked at Ashton. What was I even doing? Why did I think it was cool to wink after everything I said? I had no clue. I couldn't wink anyway. It probably looked like my eye was twitching. Or that I was emphasizing a blink.

Either way, it was nowhere near attractive.

"Well, I'm glad you're here."

"Thanks?"

Suddenly, he pressed me against the lockers and leaned real close. His hands were pushing up against the lockers on each side of my face. "Really glad." He whispered. His nose touched mine, and I could feel his minty breath hit my face. "You know, we could always skip. I got soccer practice later, but I'm one hundred percent free after that."

"Er, thanks but no thanks. I have no intention of catching a STD." *Wait, you're supposed to be nice to the guy.* "Sorry, that was rude—"

"You're in luck because I'm clean. Coach makes us get tested every year." He was so close that I was completely dumbfounded that our lips hadn't accidently touched.

Too close. Way too close.

His eyes began to shut and it became clear that he was going for the kill—in this case, kiss—but instead

43

of letting them touch, I swiveled my head to the side and received a feathered kiss on my cheek. In one quick motion, I wriggled out of his grip, grabbed my schedule out of his hands, and turned so I wasn't facing him. I rubbed my cheek with my hand. Why did humans like to show affection with their mouths? It was just plain weird. *He's just a project, Ariel. Stay calm. Just play along.*

But before I fast-walked to class, I turned my head and said, "Oh come on, pretty boy. I can't skip class on my very first day. That's naughty."

I didn't catch Ashton's reaction, but I took it as a good sign when he took a couple of seconds too long to follow me. By the time he caught up with me, I had already opened the door to the classroom. I walked in, feeling slightly victorious. Maybe acting wasn't so hard after all.

Wrong. So wrong. I couldn't even comprehend how wrong I was to have thought that.

Throughout the entire class, I could feel Ashton's heavy gaze on me to the point where I wanted to dig a hole and burrow in. Every time I'd turn around, Ashton would be staring.

Why did he have to sit right behind me?

"Hey, you're Ariella, right?" a girl whispered. I snapped my head to my right and nodded at the girl. I almost cringed. She had bleached blonde hair that ran down to her belly button. But it wasn't the hair that made me cringe. For one, her hair was longer than her shirt, which probably wasn't good. The shirt was tight, too. Almost like another thin layer of skin. Her navy-blue shorts were so short that her ass was hanging out of them. Her face looked like she had dipped her entire head into a pot of melted makeup. Her eyebrows were darkened to the point where they looked jet-black, so when I looked at her face, all I could see was the two thin lines that were her eyebrows. Her fake lashes and black eyeliner definitely did not brighten her face any more than those eyebrows did. Her cheeks were bright pink, and it looked like she was constantly blushing.

But maybe she'd be nice, right? I hadn't been taught never to judge a book by its cover for no reason. I put on a fake smile and twirled my hair because that's what they did all day, right? She seemed satisfied with my actions, as if this were a test, and I had just passed with flying colors. This would count as the easiest yet stupidest test I had ever taken.

"Yeah, I am. It's nice to meet you."

"Right back at ya. Since you're a newbie and you're superpretty, would you like to sit with us at lunch?"

"I'd like that."

No, I don't like that. At all.

"Erika, quit talking to Ariella and listen, or you will get detention." The teacher, whose name, I believe, was Mrs. Goldberg, screeched.

Erika, however, rolled her eyes and sat back down, chewing her gum noisily. I watched Erika for a couple more minutes, but all she did was play with her hair. Every so often, she'd take notes.

"Oh, and by the way, my name's Erica." She beamed at me, and I fought the urge to tell her that it was kind of obvious.

At least she was easier to understand than Ashton. I suppose Erika and I were friends. I couldn't say I minded being her friend, but I certainly didn't have any interest in hearing her talk for the next six months.

After a painful forty-five minutes, the bell rang. "Come on, Ariel!" Erika whined as she pulled me out of the classroom. Her fake nails were beginning to dig into my arm. And it really hurt. Damn, they were like weapons. And the jewels glued onto the nails didn't help.

"I bet Tara wants to meet you," she squealed.

"Who's Tara?"

"She's awesome. You'll love her. Everyone loves Tara Cunningham."

Somehow, I just didn't find that one hundred percent accurate. She pulled me toward a hallway I had never seen before, and that's when I realized that we weren't eating in the cafeteria. *Of course, you idiot! Most people don't eat in the cafeteria.*

We turned left, then right, and I spotted a group of people sitting against the lockers. *Time to not trip or fall or do anything stupid. You have to belong.* As we got closer, I realized there were only four boys including Ashton.

The first boy had dirty-blond hair and crystal-blue eyes. He winked at me, and my eyes immediately transferred to the second boy. He had jet-black hair that was gelled upward, giving him an extra inch, not that he even needed to be taller. He had hazel eyes, and until now I hadn't realized how pretty that color really was. The third boy was even better-looking than the last two, and I wanted to slap myself for even thinking thoughts like that. He had emerald eyes and disheveled, sun-kissed blond hair. When he smiled at me, I could see his two deep dimples, which couldn't've been missed by any girl.

Let there be a decent guy. Let there be a decent guy. Mother of all that is holy, please let there be a decently nice guy.

Still, the Lord did not hold back on making them good-looking. If they had six-packs, I was pretty sure they could be models. *Note to self: buy a device to shock yourself with when you think thoughts like that.*

My gaze traveled to the girls. There were five girls, not including Erika. One girl struck out more than the others. Her bold lipstick and brown highlights didn't match in the slightest. She had on a purple V-neck T-shirt that just clung to her body and so much foundation that if she had wiped her cheek with her sleeve, there would have been a huge stain. She had these light-brown eyes, but I could've sworn they darkened when she saw at me.

Suddenly, I was having trouble comprehending what confidence was. I never knew it was possible to intimidate someone within the first five seconds of meeting them, but there were firsts for everything. I guess a new girl wasn't exciting for everyone. I could've been hallucinating, but it was pretty hard to miss a stare like that.

The girl didn't hold her stare long and wasted no time before jumping into Ashton's arms, planting on his cheek one of the sloppiest kisses I had ever seen. It couldn't have felt too great, and my ideas were confirmed when Ashton not so subtly pushed her off him.

Too much PDA. Way too much. PDA no bueno.

"Ashy poo, I missed you. Where were you Friday?" she cried, slinging her arms around his neck. For once, I felt bad for Ashton. He had found quite the catch.

"Yeah, Ashy poo, she missed you," I whispered to myself.

"That's Tara." Erika pointed to the girl.

Deciding to take charge, I marched up to Tara when she wasn't attached to Ashton.

Sticking my hand out, I tried my best to make a flattering face. "Hi, you must be Tara. I'm Ariel."

Meeting Tara could only be described in one word: craptastic.

"You're the new girl."

Well hello to you too.

"Yeah, nice to meet you."

"So you like this schoo—" She paused, took a step to her right, pursed her lips, then stepped back to face me. I turned my head to see Ashton smirking at me in a way that made me want to elbow him accidentally in the ribs. "Any guys you like?"

"Oh, um not really, why?"

Tara stepped right beside me and slung her arm around my neck. Jeez, we had known each other for five minutes, and we were already this close.

"Just in case you don't know, I've got dibs on Ashton."

Since when do people still call dibs on guys they like?

"That's cool. I don't like him." I didn't think I had ever been surer about something in my entire life.

"I like you. And I love these shoes. Come on, I'm hungry."

Tara let go of my shoulder and began walking to where the other girls sat. I was right behind her but a tap on my shoulder stopped me.

"Ah, so you're the famous Ariella." The boy with sandy blond hair said.

I nodded before turning my fake flirtatious mode on perfectly aware that I looked ridiculous. He seemed more amused than interested in my games.

I didn't know exactly why I thought that flirting with this boy was a good idea. It wasn't.

"Hi, there. How do you know my name?" *And I ruined it.*

"Everyone is talking about you." He paused. "And you know you kind of just introduced yourself to Tara."

Oh, God. Everyone knows who I am. Wait, no, that's a good thing. No, it's bad for Ariel. Good for the project.

But I just smiled and twirled my hair. "That's just wonderful."

"You don't have to act around me, darling. I actually thought we could be friends." He grabbed my hand and hauled me out of the hallway before I could complain. "By the way, my name's Elliot."

He knows. He knows. He knows. I knew my acting was bad. There's a reason I'm not starring in a movie.

"What's the matter? Cat got your tongue? So, do you want to tell me the full story, or shall I just tell you what I know, and we'll go from there?"

Not a time waster, I see.

But I didn't get it. I had never broken character during the four classes that I had had, even though I didn't talk a lot. And that had certainly been an achievement. I didn't trip, and I didn't stutter. I didn't do anything wrong. And I hadn't even seen him until now. *What a bummer.*

"I have no idea what you are talking about," I said, attempting to deny his accusations, but he merely chuckled at me.

Smart guy, I see.

"Quit lying already. But I have to give you credit. Ashton's bought your act," Elliot said.

He may have known, but I couldn't give it to him quite yet. There was no doubt that he was like the others. Elliot must have expected me to confess, because he looked stunned when I gave him the meanest glare I could muster.

But it probably didn't even look like a mean look. I probably looked like a puppy upset that she didn't get a treat.

Curse my baby face.

I stood up and grabbed my lunch. I was about to leave when I turned around and spoke to him. "How dare you accuse me of lying?" With that, I stormed off, back to the rest of the bunch. I knew exactly what Flora would say. It would go something like, "You go, girl! Show him who's boss."

It wasn't until I stopped in the hallway that I realized how rude I had been to Elliot. I had never been so discourteous to others before, let alone talked to a boy alone. I felt a slight prickle in my toes urging me to go apologize, but instead I stomped my feet a little louder. I was going through my list of firsts faster than a mouse running from a cat. Well, it had to be pretty easy, considering that I was sort of hiding under a mask. I had the ability to do anything.

It was sort of like *The Purge* except without all the murder and the crime.

And it was during a six-month period.

And this was real life.

I finally found my way back to the popular hallway, not before getting lost first, and I saw that Elliot was already talking to Ashton and the others. When he saw me, he just smiled. My eyebrows weaved together in exasperation, and I rolled my eyes.

I wish I could've just wiped that smile off his face like wiping a bug off a windshield.

Erika patted the floor next to her, so I just took a seat. When no one was paying attention to me, I took out my camera and quietly snapped a few pictures of Erika and the rest of the crew.

I avoided Elliot and Ashton for the rest of lunch. When the bell rang, I nearly dashed out of the hallway. However, I was yanked back by a strong hand on my shoulder. "Don't worry, Ariel. Take all the time you need," Elliot leaned over and whispered in my ear. His grip loosened, and he walked off in the other direction, leaving me completely dumbfounded.

Chapter 4

I had never thought I would ever be yearning to go home from school, but here I was, practically dancing around because the first day of this project was done. I didn't think to call Flora right away, but I guess I didn't have to because at five o'clock she decided to grace me with her presence. I was hoping to persuade her to go on a run with me but alas, she doesn't "run voluntarily."

Instead, she decided to bombard me with things I had zero interest in. We were in the living room. I didn't live in the largest home, but it was just small enough to be real cozy. I certainly did not live in one of those giant mansions that made up a huge part of Cercis.

I could buy hundreds of thousands of tacos with one tenth of the cost of those houses.

The cream walls and tan sofas made the room comfy. The living room was a real catch for movie nights. We had a rather large TV in the room for when my parents and I had family night. It was also great when Flora and I just decided to hang out.

But today, there was a constant glint of curiosity in her eyes as she fired questions at me. I thought this was just going to be a normal hang out.

"Ariel! Are those Lincoln boys drooling over you yet? Was I right? Oh, of course I'm right," Flora gushed.

After an endless day of avoiding Elliot, the last thing I wanted to do was talk about how everything sucked. Aunt Stella was still working, so I dodged a bullet there.

"Are you hungry? We still have some ice cream, I think."

She waved a hand dismissively. "Just answer the question already, smart-ass."

"Why can't we talk about your day?"

"Nothing interesting happened," she said nonchalantly. "Come on, this is like a TV show come to life. Now answer the damn question."

. "Well, jeez. No need to be so demanding." I trailed off. "Fine. Well, sort of. Well, not exactly. I don't really know. Uncomfortable, I guess."

"You kind of just avoided my question, but okay. Any cute boys? Because the only guy who I've spoken to all day is Tanner."

"I am so sorry I wasn't there."

"You can pay me by telling me if you met any supercute guys. I can sense that someone's gotten under your skin." She scooted a little closer.

"How?" I stared at her with a blank expression.

A smile started to grow on her face. "It was a guess, and I'm right."

"I hate you."

"Love you too, best friend."

"Fine, I met a guy named Ashton Walker an—"

"Wait," Flora cried. "I think I've heard of him. Does he play soccer?"

I narrowed my eyes suspiciously. "I think so."

"And he likes you?" Her eyes grew with excitement.

"More like I'm his new challenge," I said with a snort.

"You never know, maybe he really likes you." I swear she sounded serious.

"He's not even an option. He's hopeless, anyway." I began to wonder how I could change the subject, but unfortunately nothing came to mind.

"Hopelessly good-looking, you mean." She smirked, and I almost reached my hand up to wipe it off her face. In the friendliest way, of course.

"Thanks. Maybe we can switch places," I grumbled.

"You need him for your project, don't you?" she observed as she pulled her phone out of her pocket.

Technically, she wasn't right. "Not necessarily."

She crossed her arms skeptically. "Is there anyone else you think is better?"

I wasn't going to let her win. "Maybe." A pointed look etched itself on her face. Just kidding: she was going to win. "Okay. No."

"Yeah, so get to know him. You know. This project doesn't require you to hook up with him. You just need to get to know him and hopefully it changes your perspective a little."

And for a second, I thought it was going to be a sentimental friend moment, but that was all washed away when she grabbed a handful of popcorn and shoved it in her face.

"It's harder than it sounds."

"Have a little fun with it. Maybe even flirt with him a bit. You might just be surprised. He's got to be that way for a reason." Obviously she'd choose that time to be the wise one.

"I will not flirt with him." I shouldn't have complained, since it was my project to complete, but with Flora it was just so easy.

"Then just be friends. Don't judge him so quick. Who knows? Maybe you'll end up liking him a lot. Maybe even love." She nudged my arm with her shoulder.

"If I fall in love with him, you have permission to make me do your homework for a year." That was how confident I was that I wouldn't even dream of loving him.

She smiled. Scratch that; she was beaming. "I will remember that. But I don't understand why you're so pessimistic about love when your parents are happily married. Where do you even get these ideas of yours?" Sometimes I wondered if Flora belonged to my parents instead of me. She had this idea that love would find her, and she was just going to have to take it.

"I don't have anything against it. It's just so useless." I shrugged.

"Okay, we're done with this conversation. You're bumming me out."

"No objections."

"But seriously, you might just fall in love with him. I'm not saying it will happen, but it's a possibility. Then maybe you can finally experience the entire spectrum of human emotion."

"Ha ha, you're so funny. Whatever. Now help me study for my bio test tomorrow."

"Do you really need to study? Didn't you take bio in middle school?" She stared at me with a knowing look.

I put my hands up in surrender. "I was just kidding."

"Same old Ariel." She had that right.

"Oh, shut up. Can we watch a movie? I think it's time for our famous movie marathons. Or just one movie since it's a school night. Either way, I need a break."

"Your offer sounds quite appealing," she joked. "But it depends. What movie do you have in mind?"

"Something with action. Romance isn't exactly the direction I want to head in tonight. The thought's making me cringe."

"Ditto."

Amazing Spiderman?" I said with a grin.

Flora shook her head. "Nah, lets watch *Iron Man*. Robert Downey Jr. is the bomb."

"Come on, Andrew Garfield is where it's at. And Emma Stone is literally life!"

"Come on, Robert Downey Jr. surpasses everything. And Gwyneth Paltrow is like perfection!" Flora mocked me. My face was impassive.

Fine, Flora, be that way.

I stared at her, and she stared right back at me. My eyes began to burn, and before I knew it, I blinked.

Damn you, Flora, for being so good at staring contests. I blamed the contacts. She got up and shook her ass in my face victoriously. I sighed and pushed her away.

"I win, you lose, ha, ha, ha! *Iron Man* it is!" Flora sang in the most off-key voice I had ever heard. Then her smile dropped, and she sat back down facing me. "Now who's gonna order the pizza? We gotta get extra, because I'm assuming Stella's eating with us."

"Flip a coin?" I tried.

"Deal."

Chapter 5

When I drove to school the next morning, I had less of an urge to go in the opposite direction.

Okay, just be friends with the guy. In all seriousness, I should've prepared what I'd say to him, but I had nothing. It wasn't like an essay where I'd just zoom through it.

I ended up sitting at my desk for an hour with only one word written. And what was this amazing, moving word that I'd use to persuade Ashton to be friends? "Hi." And the rest, I'd just have to wing it, which wasn't a great idea, considering that the last time I had winged something was in seventh grade. I had had to memorize a five-sentence oral, but I could only remember the last four sentences. I ended up just saying *bonjour* and *je m'appelle Ariel* about seven times because in that moment, it felt like it was working.

It wasn't.

Maybe Ashton will be different. Maybe he was just sick, and now he's so nice and wants to be friends. Maybe

Elliot was hallucinating, and today, he won't remember me. Ha! And maybe if I tap my heels together three times, I'll be transported back to Easton.

When I arrived at school, I took my time taking my backpack out of the backseat. Flora had chosen my outfit, and I thought she was doing me a favor until I saw what she had picked out. It was that damn frilly pink top and circulation-cutting skinny jeans. Another reason I despised that stupid top was how low-cut it was in the front. My only conclusion was that my boobs would be a lot colder than yesterday.

And because she wanted to watch me suffer, Flora told me to fish-tail my hair, which was the one thing I was sure I'd never need. Yeah, I knew how to do a classic braid, but at twelve years old when I heard about a fishtail, the only thing I could picture was a fish flopping around on my head. After that, fishtails were out of the picture, at least until now.

I had to go on YouTube for two hours to master the stupid hairdo.

I walked into precalculus twenty minutes before class started, half-expecting no one to be there, but immediately my eyes locked onto those blue eyes I wasn't prepared to face just yet. He stared back at me as though he was at a loss for words, which was very unusual. His hands clenched around the corners of the desk, and his signature smirk disappeared for a split second. He whispered something to a guy who was talking to him, and the guy went to his seat.

As I got closer to him, I noticed that his eyes never left mine except occasionally trailing downward, presumably around my lips. *Okay Ashton, that doesn't make me self-conscious at all. You can continue staring at me like I'm covered in chocolate.* I took a deep breath and imitated his face. Yesterday, I had spent half an hour in front of the mirror learning how to "smirk." I'd thought I had it.

"Take a picture, it lasts longer, pretty boy," I said with confidence that I really didn't have. *That's not the plan, Ariel. You were just supposed to say hi.* But for a millisecond, I saw the beginnings of a blush on his cheek, and for some reason that made me smile.

#Winning

And yes, I just hash-tagged myself, and I'm not proud.

"Well, don't you look stunning? Change your mind about going out with me yet? Or we could skip the going out and hang out at my place."

Nope, he wasn't sick. I made a sound that was a cross between an uncomfortable laugh and the squeal of a guinea pig. *That was really hot, Ariel.* In one quick motion, Ashton got up out of his chair and threaded his arm around my waist so my chest bumped with his. I held in a yelp at the back of my throat. Couldn't he have been a little more sensitive to the fact that I had boobs, and he had a rock-hard chest?

Once I pulled up my top, I tilted my head back to look at him. *Big mistake.* There had to be only a few inches separating us, and if he just leaned down a little, our lips would've met, and my first kiss would've been taken. It wasn't that I cared who my first kiss was; it was more that I just didn't have an urge to kiss anyone. A kiss wouldn't get me into Columbia.

His consistently startling blue eyes flickered back and forth between my lips and my eyes. My breath hitched. *Too close for comfort.* I considered my options. His arms were locked around my waist, so I couldn't move. My hands were still by my sides so I couldn't subtly push him away. *This does not look like a budding friendship to me.*

"You look too good for your own well-being." He began to lean in, and I leaned back as slowly as I could so he didn't notice the increasing distance between us.

Then again, I could only lean back so far and before I knew it, my back couldn't arch any more. I cursed myself for not taking up yoga. Jesus must've heard my prayers because the sound of footsteps suddenly grew louder and louder. Ashton's grip loosened, and I seized the opportunity and spun away from him. For a second, I could feel my heart pounding out of my chest so hard that I thought I'd go into cardiac arrest. Of course, that wasn't logical.

Avoiding his gaze, I turned toward the door where Mr. Blair was just coming in. He looked back and forth skeptically between me and Ashton.

"Good morning, Ariel, Ashton." Mr. Blair lifted his coffee mug to his mouth and took a sip.

"Good morning, Mr. Blair. How are you?" I said way too quickly.

"I'm good. And you?"

"I'm wonderful, thank you," I said in a rush. I sat down in my seat, still avoiding Ashton.

Mr. Blair didn't reply, but thank the Lord a group of girls walked into the room with their beady eyes on Ashton. I craned my neck slightly to sneak a peek at Ashton, but it was an awful idea because in that short moment, Ashton's eyes were looking straight into mine.

One of the girls strutted toward Ashton, flipping her hair, which was unnecessary, considering there was so much hairspray on it that it'd stay put for days. "Hey,

Ashton, so my parents are out of town for the week. You wanna come over later?"

"Sorry, Adina. I got soccer today."

Adina. A name that meant lean and subtle. Her parents must've anticipated something else because she was as skinny as a stick and not the least bit subtle about what she wanted from Ashton.

Adina's face dropped noticeably. "How about after practice?" Now she was starting to sound desperate which was never a good quality.

"Sorry, babe, but I'll be exhausted after practice, so I'll probably just crash." He was lying. I could tell because when I sneaked a glance at his face, I saw the look of annoyance under his smooth talk.

"Okay, maybe some other time, then?" Adina added, taking an obvious step toward Ashton. It was amusing that she hadn't noticed me yet.

"Course."

I had fully spun around in my chair by now. It had left my mind that only a couple of minutes before, I was avoiding eye contact with Ashton, and now he was looking right at me without an ounce of annoyance. That was probably not a good thing.

"So gorgeou—"

"You're Ariel, right?" Adina cut in, which made me want to laugh. She plastered on a smile as fake as Kourtney Kardashian's breasts.

"Yeah, and you're Adina?" I tried to hide the fact that I had witnessed her being rejected.

"Yeah."

I had to make some friends, right? Because yesterday hadn't been a good start. "I love your hair, by the way."

She seemed flattered, which seemed like a good sign.

"Thanks, I just love that top. One day we have to go shopping." And she acted as though Ashton didn't exist anymore.

"I'd love that." I drew out the "love" part, silently praying that the bell would ring. I must've been sympathy-worthy because, after a minute, the bell dinged in my ears.

"See you later." Adina grinned and hobbled to her seat in the front of the room.

"Looks like you've made a friend, gorgeous. Just so you know, Adina and I were in the past, so you've got me all to yourself."

If I had "accidently" pushed him down a mountain, would I have gone to jail?

"Thanks?"

"And if you want, you can come over to casa de Ashton today. I'm pretty sure I won't be *that* tired."

Asshole.

"I'll keep that in mind, but I'm not sure that'll be the best for our friendship." Was I friend-zoning him? Either way, it was making me feel a little better.

But Ashton's smug face didn't disappear. If anything, it was stronger than ever. "Sorry, gorgeous, but I don't think we can be just friends. You're too pretty for that. Plus, the sexual tension will kill me."

Suck up. "Well, you're just gonna have to deal with it." With that, I turned my attention to Mr. Blair, and for some reason, I felt pretty damn good.

That is, until Mr. Blair started speaking. Class was as boring as I thought it would be. Why couldn't I have retaken another class?

Every minute felt like an hour and I found myself counting as each second went by. It was ridiculous.

I stealthily pulled my European history packet out of my backpack and started annotating some of the documents. Surprisingly, no one, not even Ashton, noticed. After a terribly long class, I was ready to jump up and dance when it was time for second period. I had read five documents and nearly finished an essay. If the class hadn't ended there, I might've started banging my head against the desk. I calmly walked out the door, pacing myself so I was constantly in front of Ashton. I strutted down the hallways, making sure he couldn't catch up.

The next few classes were the same as the first. I'd do one of my homework packets while Ashton shook my chair with his feet. I'd shift my chair and then he'd shake it even harder.

When it was time for lunch, my mouth was watering for my turkey sandwich. I didn't realize that lunch meant another uncomfortable confrontation with Elliot. Ashton had gotten distracted by one of the other guys on the soccer team and went somewhere else. I found Erika and was about to take a seat next to her when I felt a tap on my shoulder.

"You want to go outside and eat today? We can get to know each other a bit more," Elliot's voice whispered into my ear.

That's creepy as hell. I spun around so fast that I felt dizzy. My mouth was making shapes, but nothing was coming out. How was one supposed to respond to something that a serial killer would say? In the corner of my eyes, Ashton was staring at Elliot, blatantly annoyed, and I suddenly felt bad for anyone, even Elliot, who was under Ashton's stare.

The only thing I could think to compare him to was

Leo from *The Vow* staring at Paige as she swooned at Jeremy, and, for the record, Flora had forced it upon me when I made her watch *The Avengers* again when she wanted to watch a rom com. Of course, this was nothing like that. Ashton and I weren't married, and I wasn't nearly as stunning as Rachel McAdams. Plus, Ashton didn't look a thing like Channing Tatum, nor did he have the same intentions.

I hooked my arm through Elliot's, and he pulled me along. *Oh my God! We're touching. Keep calm, Ariel.*

Elliot led me outside to the bench where we had talked the day before. I wasn't the warmest I had ever been, but at least the sun was out. He didn't say anything for a minute or so.

"Listen, I probably came off as a creep yesterday. Before I start, let me say that I'm not a stalker. I promise. For some reason, I think I just thought you'd tell me who you are right away. I know it can't be easy opening up to some random guy who approached you like he knows exactly who you are." Elliot babbled as he ran his right hand through his hair.

I don't know why, but that made me smile. He seemed more like a real person, and I instantly felt a little bad for thinking he was an inconsiderate jerk.

"Thank you, I guess."

"I'm just guessing, but I assume you want me to tell you why I know all this about you?" The edge of Elliot's mouth tugged upward slowly.

I nodded. "That would be helpful."

He held out his hand, and my face scrunched as I took his hand and shook it. "I'm Elliot Calder."

Calder, Calder, Calder. Where have I heard that na—oh, Principal Calder.

"Oh God, I am actually stupid. I can't believe I didn't see that coming. And you know, you could have started with that instead of sounding like a complete creep," I grumbled. I wasn't mad that he was the principal's son; it was the fact that I had completely let that fact slip by.

"And that's just one of many flaws I have. We should start again because, from what I've heard, you sound like a pretty awesome person to be friends with." Elliot smiled and it sounded like he genuinely wanted to be my friend. "But something tells me you're not really being yourself now, are you?"

Something was definitely strange. I really wanted to be Elliot's friend, and I didn't know why. Maybe it was because he was the only one who knew my secrets. Maybe I liked how he admitted he was flawed.

"You're right about that."

"So what do you say, friends?" He nudged my shoulder with his.

"I guess so. Just as long as you aren't like your airhead of a best friend."

"Ashton's actually really awesome. So," he said, taking a bite of the pear that he had grabbed from his lunchbox. "You're a nerd?"

I let out a throaty laugh. "I guess you could put it that way."

"You don't seem that shy."

"Well, we're friends aren't we?"

"Guess so." His laugh was low and loud. "So are you going to tell me the full story of why you're here, or am I gonna have to hint at it until you get the memo?"

I stuck my tongue out at him. "There's not much to tell, but okay. I'm from Easton High—you know, the private school? Wait, you already know that. Sorry, um, so I already have all my high school credits so my teacher created this just oh-so-marvelous idea for this social project."

"That's so cool." Elliot sounded like a seven-year-old playing with a remote control car.

"Not so much. And because I'm the socially awkward nerd, they wanted me to be popular. And now I have to find someone or some people and get to know them and learn something that I haven't quite figured out yet. You know, I don't think Columbia cares how popular or social someone is." I took a gulp of my water. "I'll be here until May, which in my opinion is way too long, but I don't get a say in this. So now, I'm just going to try to make friends and hope that someone opens up to me, and I learn something."

"So you're gonna be acting?"

I thought a little. "You could put it that way."

"Why?"

Three little letters put together to form one of the most common words used on earth. But I couldn't understand the reasoning behind him using them. Why was I acting? I would've never gotten anywhere if I was myself. I'd turn back into that girl whom no one acknowledged, and I'd have no project. I didn't know a single person outside of my family and Flora who had stuck around because of who I really was.

"Because no one would want to be friends with me if I wasn't acting." I said it in a "duh" tone.

"But I want to be friends with you," he protested. I noticed a small strand of hair bouncing as he spoke.

"You're one of few, then."

He huffed. "You know what I think? I think you never let people get to know you because you don't expect them to stick around. You're actually really cool and I barely know you yet."

"Thank you." It felt more like a question.

"Anytime, friend."

"Do you mind if I take a picture of with you? You know, to put in my presentation?" I grabbed my camera out of my pocket and showed it to him. I liked that no one questioned the bulge in my pocket because they just assumed it was my phone.

"Sure." Elliot seemed completely cool with it. I took a selfie of the two of us.

Holy cow. He was one photogenic boy.

"Just one more question. Whose schedule did you get? Sorry, my mom refused to tell me."

Hesitantly, I said, "It's Ashton." At that, his face lit up. "I mean, I don't have any intention of manipulating your best friend or anything."

"The universe has heard my prayers. Ashton doesn't know what he's in for." Elliot's hands shot up in the air as he shouted a little too loudly.

"Wha ... what?"

"I will tell you this. Ashton's going to be an idiot for a while, but you're different from the girls he bangs, and he's going to see that pretty soon." He looked like he was planning something I did not want to be part of.

"Wait," I said in a rush. "I'm not looking for a relationship with him. I'm not looking for a relationship with anyone—especially Ashton."

"We're just going to let fate play out." Elliot mimicked a villain stroking his cat.

"Are you a fortune-teller or something?"

"No," He let his arms drop by his sides. "But just

stick with him because there's a lot that you don't know that'll make it worth it."

"For the project? You're creeping me out." Could I have been more oblivious? Nope.

"Not necessarily," he said, disregarding the last part.

"Then what?"

He needed to give me a step-by-step guide to what he was saying, because I couldn't understand a single thing.

"I'm just saying that your opinion of him might change over the next six months."

I blew out an exasperated sigh. "You sound like my best friend."

He grinned. "I don't know her, but I already like her."

"Not surprised."

"But seriously, please don't give up on him. Something tells me that you may just change him. He's my best friend, and I know when someone could be the one to make him wake the hell up."

"Dude, this isn't a romance novel. Besides, I'm acting. I'm not the same person when I talk to you and Ashton." The last thing I needed was a romance that wouldn't last.

"Sounds to me like you need a little spark in your life, too."

My eyebrows drew together. "I'm doing just fine. Not everyone needs to be in a relationship. Just so you know, I don't plan on dating someone for a long time."

"Just try to be yourself with him. You're cooler than you think."

"Why should I?"

"Because, he'll be worth it."

Chapter 6

Elliot wasn't wrong when he said Ashton was going to be an asshole for a while.

I found myself trying to talk to Erika more and more, even though all she talked about was her latest hookup. When she asked me who I had hooked up with, I'm pretty sure I did this weird mumbling thing, and she just gave up. But it really did amaze me how she was able to keep a conversation on the subject of her for hours. My life story was shorter than her weekend. Still, she wasn't a bad person, and I didn't mind her as long as she didn't try to dig up my past.

The guys weren't too bad, and, to be honest, I may have preferred talking to them instead of the other girls. Their conversations were quite entertaining when they weren't talking about how hot some girl was.

Elliot was the best by a long shot. He let me ramble on about how easy these academic classes were until I noticed that he was bored out of his mind. In return, I let him go on about his love for baseball, but, other than a home run, I was lost out of my mind.

The best part? He didn't think of girls as prizes to be won. Or maybe he did, but he never said anything because he knew I would punch him in the jaw. *The perks of seeing the real Ariel, I suppose.*

Those tae kwon do classes I took when I was seven were really paying off.

Ashton? Elliot had to be talking about another Ashton, because the one I witnessed didn't even seem the least bit like the one he talked about. Ashton must've experienced something traumatic, because even I knew that no one, not even Ashton, could be so heartless. I had learned that from the movies.

Or perhaps it was embedded in his brain that no girl could ever resist his "charm." Either option had to have a story behind it. The thing that startled me was that I felt a tiny bit compelled to understand Ashton and that should've been my red light. I should've stopped right there and tried to be friends with someone else. But I didn't.

And I couldn't stop questioning it when I got to school the next day.

"Hey there, gorgeous. Are you thinking about me?" Ashton smirked as soon as Mr. Blair let us go to do some worksheets.

"Pretty boy, don't think too highly of yourself. I don't appreciate it, buddy."

I shouldn't have made a habit of calling him pretty boy, either.

"I think you do."

And that's how it went for the first two to three weeks. Ashton would say some cheesy pickup line, and

I would smile as though it had actually worked. He must have been pretty damn proud of himself. I wasn't sure if I was even doing it right. I was supposed to be nice, but he was infuriating, and yet I couldn't bring myself not to reply to him.

I'd be lying if I said that I didn't miss Easton. Everything about this school made me want to hurl. Well, it was mainly just Ashton. He did well in school, though. Every single test a teacher handed back would have his name and an A with a big circle around it. He was actually really smart, and I was in no place to judge him when I spent at least twenty minutes a day on an outfit, hair, and makeup. I was becoming the girl I had never ever wanted to be.

As I walked through the halls of Lincoln Bay, I could easily spot the ones who couldn't care less about what they were wearing. I envied them. That used to be my life. With their crinkled clothes, I could tell they didn't have a care in the world, which was exactly where I wanted to be. Their only priority was to get through high school, and at this point, that was my priority, too.

When Saturday came around, I almost screamed hallelujah. Not feeling extremely joyous at the thought of schoolwork, I decided to go on a run. It was too late to join track at Lincoln Bay, but that didn't mean I was going to let myself get out of shape. I pulled on a thick jacket and two layers of pants so I wouldn't get hypothermia. Early January wasn't the best time of year to run, but it'd have to do.

I plugged in my headphones and took an extralong route away from the world. The best part about running was that I'd eventually reach the point where all my anger would subside, and I would feel completely calm.

I had run most in the summer from sophomore to junior year. Between the summer courses that I took to try to get even more ahead in school and all the stress from thinking about college, I would've broken down if I hadn't run. Or had my camera, a.k.a. my best friend. Other than Flora, of course.

Now, I wasn't as stressed about college. It was the thought of not being able to fulfill the requirements for the damn project. One month in, I hadn't learned a thing, apart from how funny the guys were and how much people really hooked up, and I was positive that wasn't what Mr. Kinsey wanted to hear.

Once Aunt Stella's cute little buggy was in view and I had completed seven miles, I was breathing hard and I couldn't feel my toes. But I felt a little better.

I spent the rest of the day with Aunt Stella, half-watching the Kardashians and half-watching some rom com that she insisted upon. It wasn't my ideal day, but with Aunt Stella, it was always fun. The weekend flew by, and I barely comprehended the fact that I was supposed to be paying close attention until biology began on Monday.

"Today, you all will begin a new project. I will be partnering you guys up into pairs. Accompanied by your partner, you will write an essay, after much research has been done, about a marine species of your choice. The rubric will explain everything you will need to include," Mr. Karowitz explained.

Mr. Kinsey's words flew into my mind. I wouldn't have to do it, right?

The class groaned.

I always hated partner projects. There was just something off in teachers' minds when they thought that working with someone else was easier. It wasn't easier when I'd be trying to talk to someone who barely acknowledged my existence. It was just a bonus that I had already done this project about a special species of jelly fish a while ago.

Eventually it would be me doing the project and my partner slapping their name on it. I never complained, though. Whatever limited my social contact with people was okay with me. But everything wouldn't be that easy at Lincoln Bay. Everyone knew who I was, and it was awful.

Mr. Karowitz grabbed a sheet from his desk and walked to the front of the room. Mr. Karowitz was a fairly nice man. He had never been particularly rude to me, but I assumed that was only because I made sure I never interrupted his lectures. He would give me an okay partner, right? I scanned the room lazily, which was useless because there wasn't one person I really wanted to work with. My brain screamed "Ashton" because this was a golden chance to get to know him, but my stomach grumbled in a way that yelled no.

"Now for your pairings. Dax and Kate, Carson and Maya, Erika and Tom, Max and Sierra, Ariella and Ashton—" I froze. *Called it.* I turned to Ashton, but instantly regretted it when I saw the corner of his lips tug upward, amused.

I zoned out after that. But it was only for ten minutes, because Mr. Karowitz generously gave us the rest of the period to plan our essay.

Ashton was rambling off times when we could research together. He really could've just asked to hang out, and it would have felt like the same thing. I don't know what happened, but I eventually snapped.

"Listen, Ashton. I know you don't want to do this project, so I'll make a deal with you. I'll do this project on my own, and when I finish, you can write your name on it. Then we both get good grades, and we don't have to go through any trouble." My eyes widened as soon as the words left my mouth. *Did I just say that? Yep. Oh, God.*

Ashton didn't seem as confused as I expected. He almost looked ... entertained. "And why would I do that, gorgeous? Don't you want to spend time with me? And how do I know we'll get good grades? Besides, I'm liking this feisty you. It's hot,"

"I don't know why I said that, to be honest. Shit. Sometimes I just don't shut up when I need to. I mean, if you want, I'll just do this, and I promise to get an A—"

"No can do, gorgeous. We are doing this project together, and besides, we can get to know each other. Who knows? You may even fall in love with me."

Incompetent jerk.

"Fine, whatever. And can you call me Ariella? Or Ariel? Anything like that works. I guess it'll be like friendship building."

"Why? Does it bother you?" he asked. I nodded. "Well, I'm sorry to inform you that no, I will not stop calling you gorgeous. I quite like it, actually. It's got a nice ring to it. And I really think you need to stop believing that we can be friends. By the way, *gorgeous*, you can catch a ride with me to my house after school. We can start our project. Now don't look so glum about it. This will be fun."

"No, thank you. And I have a car," I muttered.

"Aw, gorgeous, don't look so sad. So many girls would kill to be in your position now." Ashton lifted my chin to look him in the eye.

"Lucky me."

"We can walk together after eighth period."

"Not if I run away before you can get there."

"Then it's settled, gorgeous." And as to what happened at the end of school … I tried to run when the bell rang but Ashton had caught up to me with ease. I debated driving off, since he had a car as well, but of course, he just had to call me every minute to make sure I was following his lead.

Of course. Stupid, stupid, stupid.

Ashton's parents were rich.

I knew how rich some people in Cercis were, but I had never actually step foot in any of the mansions I had passed while driving to school every day. Ashton lived in one. And I was in awe.

Once we reached his skyscraper of a home, I asked to go to the bathroom. I didn't necessarily need to pee, but I did need a deep breath before I could start the essay.

With him.

All alone.

After accidently opening the door to a closet, the stairs to the basement, and a long cabinet with towels, I finally found the bathroom. And it was spotless. The countertop was made of granite, and the sink was a shiny, sterling silver. I had trouble comprehending that I was in a room where Ashton peed. I splashed some water on my face, but, idiotically, I had forgotten that I had a full face of makeup on.

The second I looked in the mirror, I almost jumped back a little. My eyeliner had found a nice spot right under my eye to settle, and I felt like a raccoon. With rabies. I spent the next five minutes furiously scrubbing off the eye makeup that wasn't near my eye with toilet paper. When there weren't any dark spots left, another problem emerged. I was bare-faced, and it wasn't my prettiest phase. Ashton was probably wondering what the hell I was doing in his bathroom for this long.

No matter what, I had to face him, so I puffed my chest out and marched out of the bathroom, retracing my steps. But instead of seeing Ashton there on his phone, a woman was staring straight at me.

"You must be Ariel," the woman said with a smile. "I'm Roseanne, the housekeeper."

She seemed like a very sweet woman, if I had to say something about her. She was a bit shorter than I was, and if I guessed right, I'd say she was 5'2" and in her midforties.

"Hi," I said, tracing small circles with my left foot. "I'm Ariel. Wait, sorry you already knew that."

Her brown eyes crinkled when she smiled. "You are too cute. Ashton's upstairs in his room. He took your backpack up there, just so you know. It's the second door on your left."

Up in his room. His room. Alone.

"Thank you," I said and started up the long staircase. Once I was on the top step, I turned left and counted the doors. Ashton's door was open. I glanced inside before he could see me.

He had a queen-sized bed layered with silk sheets pressed against the right side of the room. Above the head of the bed was a large, rectangular window. On the left side of the room was a plain black dresser as tall as me. Okay, it wasn't very tall, but what caught my eye was the rows of snapbacks on the dresser.

I had seen him wear one to school once. Once.

Maybe it was just a collection.

Of hats.

There was a tall, beige lamp in every corner of the room except for the corner that was occupied by his bed. It wasn't a magnificently decorated room, but it was big.

Papers were sprawled out on the plush carpet, most likely for the project. His back was facing me as he typed something into his phone.

With a single knuckle, I tapped on the door. Ashton's body flipped around immediately, and I felt like a painting in a museum under his gaze.

"I thought we should work in here," Ashton gestured to the floor. "Roseanne's going to be all over us if we're down there."

Right, it was because of Roseanne.

I started to walk toward him, but my feet decided that they didn't want to work. My left foot caught on my right, and I went face-first into the plush carpet. My face scrunched up when I heard Ashton's bellowing laugh. Of course this had to be the first time I tripped after coming to Lincoln Bay.

"You all right?" he asked between his laughs. I could see how hard he was trying to compose himself, but the corner of his lips kept pulling upward.

And it was the first time I had really seen him laugh. Before, he was all smug smiles, but now there was a twinkle in his eyes and I could really see his dimples just popping. I kind of liked it.

No, you don't.

"Wonderful." I pursed my lips, but eventually I ended up giggling with him.

"Okay," he said, breathing in and out. "Down to business."

I grabbed the rubric off the floor and skimmed through it. "So how about we do the project on Hawksbill sea turtles? They're really pretty," I finally said. When Ashton didn't reply, I made the mistake of looking up. He was staring at me with those clear blue eyes. The fact that my favorite color was his eye color didn't help at all. I waved a hand in front of his face and he blinked a little. "If you don't like that, we can do something like vampire squids. Just so you know, they're not nearly as cute."

"You look pretty without makeup."

That was the first time I could remember ever blushing. I wasn't one to get embarrassed over a compliment, but it was like I couldn't control it.

"Uh, thanks," I shrugged my shoulders. "So, Hawksbill sea turtles, then?"

"Sure, but let's put aside this homework for a sec."

"Wha-why? You just said to get down to business," I stuttered. Homework was good. Homework was safe.

He looked at me with an innocent smile. "Don't you want to get to know each other, friiiiiiieeeeeeeennnnnnnnnnd? Let's play a game."

"Uh, okay, I guess." I refused to sound like an uptight homework freak. "So what do you have in mind? Like Monopoly or—"

"Not a board game." He rushed. "How about something like asking each other questions and instead of taking shots, we just answer?"

I didn't know where this was heading, but all I saw was flashing green lights for the project. *Here's your chance to "learn" something. Don't blow it.*

"Okay," I said for the billionth time today.

"Ladies first." He twirled a piece of my hair around his finger. I was pretty sure this was some sort of violation.

God, what to ask what to ask what to ask uhhhh.

"So do you play soccer?" *Idiot. Of course you ask the question you already know the answer to.*

His laugh came out hearty, and I wanted to bang my head against a wall.

"Yeah," he breathed. "Gotta love playing for Lincoln Bay."

"Isn't the season over?"

"That's private schools, gorgeous. Soccer season starts in spring."

"Then what do you do when you say that you've got soccer after school?" If he wasn't playing, where was he going when he told Adina he had soccer?

"Off-season training."

I could see that he genuinely loved it, and I got this strange urge to see him play.

"That's cool."

"Are you planning on going to go see us play?"

Was this an invitation?

"I'm not sure." *Hah, more like no one would want to go with me.*

"I'll be there. Don't you want to be there to support yours truly?"

"Change my mind. I'm not going," I teased.

"I'm quite offended, if I can be honest with you. You ever been to a school soccer game?"

"No."

Was there even a point in saying yes and have him start talking about the sport, and I'd have no idea what he was saying?

"Then this will be a memorable year."

"Looking forward to it." I gave him a shy smile. "It's your turn."

"Oh yeah, so you play any sports?"

I could've lied and said something cool like lacrosse, but it felt a bit wrong to lie to him. We were supposed to be friends, right? "If you count track as a sport, then yes."

"So I take it you're one of those fit girls, then?" He smirked, but I saw the tease in his eyes.

"Um, I believe it's my turn." I cleared my throat.

The thing was, I should've thought it through, because he was waiting, and I didn't know what I was going to ask.

"So are you going to ask?" Ashton tapped his fingers on his carpet.

I could've asked anything. "Yep, um, cats or dogs?"

The edge of his mouth twitched. "Cats. Blue or pink?"

"Blue, definitely blue," I nodded my head. "Summer or winter?"

"Summer, duh. Prime time for soccer." He fired back. "Favorite joke?"

"Um I'm not—oh wait I got one. Knock, knock." I could feel my lips twitching.

"Who's there?"

"Interrupting cow."

He paused. Then he gave me this strange look. "Interrupting cow w—"

"Moooooooooooooooooooo!"

He rolled his eyes, but the smile on his face told me that I was obviously the funniest person in the world. Duh.

"That was so incredibly stupid."

"You're incredibly stupid."

He chuckled. "Fair enough. All right, next question."

"Cheesiest pickup line?"

"Oh that's easy…" He trailed off and then faked a sneeze. "Sorry, I sneezed because God blessed me with you."

At first I snorted and then I couldn't hold in my laughter. "Okay, that was pretty good."

"I know. I'll be here all night." He got up and bowed.

"How many girls have you used that precious gem on?"

"Just you. It's a new one I was working on."

"Well, if you want my opinion, that's the best pick-up line I've ever heard."

"Clearly. Here, feel my shirt."

I paused for a second. "Why?"

"Trust me."

I lifted a finger and touched his sleeve. "What about it?"

"Nice, right?"

"I guess."

"It's boyfriend material."

I rolled my eyes. "My brain can't even process that right now."

He grinned cheekily. "I'm feeling extra nice today so I decided to give you the privilege of hearing another one. So … partying or staying at home."

"Staying at home," I said without thinking. My eyes grew. *Oh God, he's going to think I'm the biggest nerd, and he won't want to be friends and—*

"Surprisingly, I'm glad you said that." Ashton's fingers brushed mine, and I shivered.

Then my cheeks felt warm again. "How about you?"

I waited for an immediate "party" as a response.

"You know what, I'm not too sure at the moment."

My lips formed a perfect O.

"Uh, your go." I stared at the palm of my hands.

He chuckled. "So where did you come from?"

Shit, he knows he knows, he knows.

"Florida," I mumbled, my eyes trained on the case of soccer trophies next to his bed.

"That's pretty cool." His fingertips touched mine, and this time it didn't feel accidental. It occurred to me once again that I was alone with this boy.

"Yep."

The moment we shared had been ruined. And it was all my fault.

"Why'd you leave?"

"It's my turn." I said defensively.

"Fair enough. Okay, shoot."

"Do you have any siblings?" I quickly directed the topic away from anything that involved me.

He froze. It was as if he couldn't look at me, and I knew I had struck a nerve. It was a horrible talent I had.

Why couldn't I have been blessed with something like singing? Instead, I had the ability to calculate the exact number of words that would be inappropriate in a situation. And then blurt them out. In other words, I didn't know when to shut up.

But when he finally looked at me, I felt bricks of guilt piling up on top of me.

He almost seemed … hurt.

But he couldn't be. Ashton Walker was a player, bad boy, and heartbreaker. He couldn't possibly be broken.

"No," he mumbled. I let it go. "So, um, what's your favorite book?" he coughed out.

"Can't pick."

"Of course." He rolled his eyes.

There was a possibility that I shouldn't have been

showing so much of myself, considering that he was probably going to think I was nerdy and boring, but I felt a strange pang in my gut any time I tried to lie. Plus, it seemed like Ashton didn't hate me yet.

"I'm still a girl."

"Nerd," he coughed.

"You think you've got me all figured out, don't you?" I teased.

"Almost. True or false?" He narrowed his eyes at me. "Better to have loved and lost than to have never loved at all."

"False," I said way too quickly. He raised an eyebrow. "What? I've never been in love and I feel fine. Great, actually."

"How have you managed to surprise me so many times? And it's a good kind of surprise, just so you know."

"Oh, shut up." I said grinning. "So, are your parents at work or something?"

The one thing I had noticed about this huge house was how empty it was.

"Business trip."

"Do you miss them?"

He didn't look like he did. "I'm used to it. And besides, Roseanne is awesome to hang around with."

"Your turn." I ended it at that. We didn't need to dwell on how his parents didn't seem like they were being great parents.

"Favorite type of car?"

"Anything with an engine and four wheels," I replied with a wink. "Favorite movie?"

"*Amazing Spiderman*," he said.

I couldn't stop the smile from crossing my face. I was really starting to like this guy.

"I love your taste. You know, Ashton, when you're not surrounded by those jerks and fake girls, you're pretty cool." Why couldn't I keep my mouth shut around him? "Sorry, that was uncalled—"

"Well, *Ariel,* you're not too bad yourself. I'll be honest. I expected you to be a quick hookup, but I was so wrong. And I sort of like that."

"Good, because that's never going to happen. Besides, Andrew Garfield occupies my heart at the moment."

He was grinning from ear to ear. "See, this project isn't so bad, right, Ariel?"

"You mean asking questions while avoiding actually doing the essay?"

"Exactly. But are you having fun?"

"Nope. You're a terrible person, Ash, and I hate you," I teased.

He put a hand over his heart and faked hurt. I turned around to move but he grabbed my waist and pinned me down on the bed.

I felt a sensation on my stomach, and I realized that he was tickling me.

"Asht-Ashton, s-stop it," I forced out, trying to pry his hands off my waist. He just shook his head as a response.

"Take that back."

"No," I squealed. "I'm warning you to let me go right now."

The sensation in my stomach was growing.

"And what if I don't?" he challenged.

Well, he asked for it. When I couldn't take it anymore, I lifted a fist and punched him square in the stomach. His arms wrapped around his stomach as he fell back onto the bed. He pouted, but the twinkle didn't leave his eyes.

"For a girl, you really pack a punch, gorgeous," he said with a chuckle.

I just sneered. "I will take that as a compliment."

Then Ashton was straddling me again. He leaned forward, and I thought he was really going to kiss me. But surprisingly, I didn't panic. His mouth was right next to my ear.

"You called me Ash." I could feel his breath prickling my ear.

"Sorr—"

"I like the ring to that. You know, you really are prettier without makeup."

Just like that, he flopped back down on his back, leaving me flustered to no end. My eyes fluttered shut so I could gain some composure. If Flora saw what just happened, she wouldn't have recognized me. I hadn't pulled away. I hadn't tried to keep my distance. I didn't know why I had done what I had done, and it irritated me to know I couldn't figure it out.

"We should get to those turtles," I said softly. I sat up and reached to pull my laptop out of my bag, also creating a bit of space between us. Personal space was good. The more personal space not invaded, the better.

"You are too cute." Ashton tapped my nose with his finger and scooted closer to me. Our thighs were touching. And he didn't move his leg away.

"Uh, thank you."

How many times was I going to blush today?

A lot of times, that's for sure.

Ashton just chuckled and draped an arm over my shoulder, pulling me into him.

Well, there goes all that personal space.

Chapter 7

I distinctly remember a day during sophomore year when I accidentally overheard a girl talking to her friend about how she recently lost her virginity. At the time, I only thought two things.

One was, how on earth the girl had lost her virginity when I hadn't even come close to having my first kiss.

And two was why she was so casually describing her "special milestone" while walking through the crowded hallways. It was alarming how unconcerned she was that I could have spread this gossip to the whole school.

I didn't, but still, I could've.

At the time, I couldn't have cared less. I had much better things to be dealing with than spreading all those R-rated things to the entire school. If I had to feel something toward the girl that day, I felt slightly bad for her. It might've been exciting for a while, and it might've occupied a lot of her time, but eventually she was going to regret what she had done. She might not have dealt with any of the consequences, but it was going to come back one day and screw her over.

And I wasn't going to feel bad for her when she experienced heartbreak or regret. Maybe I was being a bit too opinionated, but it never occurred to me why a girl would ever feel compelled to have to lean on a guy. In a world like this, the truest person I could've ever imagined me leaning on was me. Then there'd be no heartbreak, no regret, and everything that'd happen I'd be able to see coming. It was quite simple, really. Life was quite simple when crushes and fairytales were shut out.

It was so much easier to focus on school once I didn't let myself drift off into dream land. And I didn't have a single regret.

The next day, something was different. I felt different. As hard as it was to admit, I may have had a slight desire to see Ashton again. I just wanted to crack a joke with him, make him laugh, something. I just wanted that really bad and, as much as I tried, I couldn't figure out a logical reason why.

I had only spent a real couple hours with him, and I was looking forward to his presence as much as I did when Flora would said she'd come over. But the circumstances were so different ... He was a boy. She was a girl. Flora and I had been best friends since sixth grade. Ashton and I barely knew each other.

All I knew was that I needed this feeling to leave right away before it turned into something I definitely didn't want. For example, a crush.

God, the last thing I needed was a crush.

Even middle school me knew that.

It was in middle school that I started to avoid people, realizing that socializing only caused more drama. Okay, "avoid" was a bit of a strong word. I talked to people. It wasn't like I couldn't carry a conversation. I was fully capable of doing that. It was more like I just didn't put in much of an effort to have everyone know who I was.

Most of my socializing came in when other people would come and ask me to tutor them. Honestly, I was a shit tutor, and I admit it. Learning was not at all the same thing as teaching, and it felt like the hardest thing to explain what was so easy to me to someone else. Not long after, people stopped asking me for help.

That was also when I met Flora. There were times when I'd pass her in the hallways, but I never had a real conversation with her until one night she and her parents appeared at my doorstep for dinner. Turns out, her dad and my dad were buddies. I didn't remember the exact moment we became friends. It just happened, and she was too awesome of a person not to let our friendship flourish.

The next day, I got to class twenty minutes early—like always. It was one of the many habits I couldn't shake when I came to Lincoln Bay. What surprised me was when I stepped into the room and came face-to-face with Ashton … again.

When Ashton saw me, he smiled. And it was a real smile. Not those arrogant smirks he always had on his face. It was real. It made my stomach gurgle, and I couldn't tell whether it meant something good or bad.

"Good morning,"

"It is now, gorgeous," he said.

"Wow, a totally predictable line that you've most likely used on every girl in this school."

"Actually, you're wrong but I'll let that accusation slide."

I made my way toward where he was sitting, but he held up a hand.

"Try not to trip, okay?" He tried his best to keep a straight face, but I could see the corner of his mouth twitching.

My confusion turned into embarrassment, and, just like that, I felt my cheeks heating up. I took slower steps toward him, even though I knew there was more teasing to come. "Jackass."

"You mean, hilarious guy that you adore?"

I giggled. "Something like tha—"

"Oh, there you are, Ashton. You weren't with Elliot, so I thought you weren't here today," a voice chimed in.

Dakota. She was one of the girls who weren't bad to be with, but her obvious crush on Ashton irritated the crap out of me. She displayed what I saw as the biggest turnoff anyone could ever reveal. Desperation.

But other than that, she was nice. Nicer than I expected. I couldn't understand why Ashton wouldn't just date her already. She was nice. And pretty. No, scratch that. She was striking. Dakota had pin-straight, auburn hair that reached the middle of her back. She was tall and skinny—model material—but she was still shorter than Ashton. She was perfect, even if she'd just be a fling.

I scrunched my eyebrows as she bounced over and sat right on his desk. *Last time I checked, desks weren't for sitting.* I felt bad for the other people in different periods that sat at his desk.

"Hey there, Ashton," She giggled much higher than her real voice was. "Oh, and hi, Ariel."

"Hey, Dakota."

This was probably not the best time to start

conversation, so I just lifted my face in a strange smile. When I turned to Ashton, he was grinning at her. I watched as he looked her up and down. I chewed on my lip.

Big whoop, he likes her. The guy's allowed to like a girl.

"So there's that new film that just came out. You want to go see it this weekend?" She batted her eyelashes.

Well, she's got a date in the bag. He'll say yes in three … two … one … "Sorry, Dakota, Ariel and I have that bio project, and we need to get it done. Some other time, okay?"

Huh?

I almost wanted to scream a big "What?" in his face. One, the project, a.k.a. the essay, was pretty much done. I didn't know why Mr. Karowitz gave us so much time. Two, she was practically showing how much she wanted him. She was an easy catch, so why wasn't I witnessing the Ashton that all the girls and guys had been talking about?

Dakota was without a doubt disappointed. I prayed that she wouldn't be mad at me. "Okay." Then she glanced at the clock. "Well, I better get to class, or I'll be late."

That was a lie. We still had ten minutes.

"See you at lunch, then." Ashton saluted.

Dakota walked out dragging her feet ever so slightly that Ashton hadn't even detected it.

When she was gone, I turned back to Ashton. "You just basically scored a date or a bang, whatever you call it, and you say no?"

He shrugged. "Just not interested."

"You? Not interested?" I watched him skeptically.

His eyebrows furrowed, and his lips were set in a thin line. "Okay, quit thinking that I'm always up for a hookup. I'm a person, you know. And I wasn't interested. I'm interested in someone else at the moment."

Oh.

"Sorry." I bowed my head, ashamed. God, why couldn't I keep my mouth shut around him?

"Don't worry about it." His voice softened.

"So who do you like? I could help you, maybe."

This was good. He has his sights on someone else. A new target. That gave us a chance to be friends. Nothing more. And I'd still be able to do the project without humiliating myself any more, I hoped.

He chuckled. "That's for me to know and you not to worry about."

Friends. Friends. Friends. It was embedded in my brain, but the tingly feeling in my fingertips wouldn't leave.

Luckily, that was when Mr. Blair decided to come back from whatever errand he was running, and I was glad there was a distraction. More and more people filed in as the warning bell rang.

I pulled out a random Easton packet and a pencil. When Mr. Blair started talking, I read through the notes and scribbled answers down.

Second period passed, then third, then fourth, and it was time for lunch. Ashton opened his mouth to say something, but he was swept away by one of his friends.

I scampered out of the classroom, making my way toward Erika and Tara when someone tapped me on the shoulder.

"Are you deaf? Because I swear everyone heard me call your name but you!" Elliot said, his breath ragged.

I flushed. "Oh, uh, sorry."

"It's cool, but maybe you need to get those ears checked out." Elliot paced himself so we were in a synchronized walk. *"Ariel, can you hear this?"* he blasted in my ear.

I frowned and poked him in the shoulder. "Okay, we don't need to keep making fun of me."

"Sorry, I'm done." He laughed. Elliot stopped right in front of the media center. "Hey, you mind coming with for a couple minutes? I need to find a book for something."

"Why should I? So you can make fun of me more?" I asked.

He rolled his eyes, and I grinned. "Don't be a smart-ass, and come on." He opened the door, motioning for me to go in.

I snickered. "I'll take that as a compliment."

"Whatever helps you sleep at night." Elliot took the lead and headed straight for the fiction section. "Oh, and how was spending some quality time with Ashton last night?"

That pushed me off my train of thought. No, more like it threw my train of thought on the ground and squished it. "Uh, okay. We just did the bio essay thing."

"That's not what he said." Elliot slowed down and scanned one of the bookshelves.

"What did he say?" I asked tentatively. "Just wondering, by the way."

He wiggled his eyebrows. "You like him, don't you?"

I got defensive all of a sudden.

"No, you need to understand that we will not ever be in a relationship. One, Ashton doesn't do relationships. Two, I don't want to get in a relationship for a long time. Three, he has an interest in someone else."

"You're oblivious," was the only thing he said.

I shook my head. When was he going to get that I wouldn't let that happen?

"And you have false hope. Why do you want us to be together more than I do?"

He crossed his arms. "I have my reasons. Why don't you want a relationship?"

"They're pointless. I don't like having to depend on someone," I said as if it were the most logical thing on the planet.

"Ah, the independent one."

I blew an annoying piece of hair off my face. "You know what, let's just go find your damn book already."

Chapter 8

On Saturday, the rain was pouring like there was no tomorrow, so logically, Flora wanted to go shopping. She wanted to step outside and get moderately soaked, just to buy a new jacket.

Yep, logic.

If I took a guess, I would say she didn't really want that new jacket as much as she wanted to meet Elliot. Somewhere between my whining and storytelling, she had developed an interest in him.

If there really had to be a relationship coming out of this project, Elliot and Flora were the best match I could think of. I approved—not that I had any influence.

"You know, if you really want to meet Elliot, we can go somewhere else. I hate malls," I said way louder than I should have.

Flora's cheeks grew pinker by the second. "I don't understand why you're pushing that when you think high school relationships have a one percent chance of lasting. Besides, I already told you that Gabe dyed my favorite jacket vomit green."

Gabe was her fourteen-year-old brother, who was currently in his practical jokes phase. I found it hilarious. Flora, not so much.

A weird sound escaped from the back of my throat as I tried not to laugh. It was a cross between an elephant and a cat when a little kid grabs her tail. Which basically meant that it wasn't the prettiest sound I had ever made.

"It was more of a forest green," I said, trying to sooth her.

"It was a vomit green, and you know it." She wiggled a finger in my face.

"Just get him back."

She slapped a hand against her forehead. "You know he's better at pranks than me."

"Spray paint his room pink—"

"Whose room are we spray painting pink? If it's Ashton, I'm all for it. I still need to get him back for painting my bedroom door purple." Elliot's deep voice interrupted.

By the looks of it, Flora forgot all about what Gabe had done in an instant. Her jaw dropped slightly, and I swore she didn't blink for a minute.

"He painted your bedroom door purple?" I snorted.

Elliot just shook his head in shame. "And he painted little daisies on it. Explaining that to the parents was a nightmare." His eyes were on Flora as he spoke. "God, I'm being an ass. I'm Elliot."

Flora sheepishly lifted her hand to shake Elliot's. "Uh, I'm, um—"

"Flora," I whispered to her.

She shot me daggers. "Sorry, I'm Flora."

"That's a cool name. It's good to meet you. Ariel didn't tell me how pretty you are."

Her cheeks turned bright pink as I pretended to gag. "Thanks."

"So whose room do you want to spray paint pink?" he pressed.

"Uh, my brother, Gabe. He dyed one of my jackets green."

She didn't look that mad anymore. Huh, what a coincidence.

"I'll be right back. I'm going to go grab a smoothie," I announced. Flora bobbed her head.

I took a step away, already sick of how cheesy they were. Another minute, and I would've been the third wheel. I stood in line waiting to get the banana smoothie that'd keep me going as Flora shopped.

And for some reason, Ashton's face popped into my mind. What was he doing and why was I thinking about him?

Friends.

Columbia.

Happily-ever-afters don't exist.

When Ashton was successfully booted out of my brain, and I had gotten my cup of joy, I strolled back to where Elliot and Flora were standing. She was laughing at something Elliot had said. I had never seen her so giggly before.

"Guys, it's been twenty minutes, and you already look like a couple."

As I expected, they were embarrassed out of their minds.

"Come on, l-let's g-go shop," Flora stuttered. She

hung her head and pulled me two steps in front of Elliot and whispered. "He's actually perfect."

"Keep that in mind the next time we buy pizza, and one of us has to pay."

She slowed her pace so she was back in sync with Elliot. "That's manipulation."

"I've got a feeling you don't really mind."

Two hours and five shopping bags later, Elliot and I were exhausted, but Flora looked like she was in her own personal heaven.

"As much as I love watching you two flirt and shop—" *my two favorite things* "—could we take a break?"

The look on Flora's face made me think she was a sadist. Without waiting for a reply, I plopped onto a bench and exhaled exaggeratedly.

"I don't understand you, Ari." Flora slowly sat down, as did Elliot. "You can run seven miles easy but two hours of shopping, and you look like I've sucked the life out of you."

I stuck my tongue out as Elliot's laughter rang in my ears. "Don't judge me, Miss I-don't-run-voluntarily."

Flora arched an eyebrow, but I could see the twitch on the corner of her lips. "You do enough running for the both of us."

"I'm going to have to side with Flora. Running is like death," Elliot chirped.

"You play baseball! You run like every day!" I complained.

A crease formed between his eyebrows. "Oh, yeah, um, but I still don't run seven miles."

I pouted like a little girl. "I didn't know this was make-fun-of-Ariel day."

"Oh, shut up. You're having a fun day. Just admit it."

97

"Okay, I'm having fun," I smirked. "That smoothie really made my day."

Flora narrowed her eyes as I cracked up. But in honesty, this was probably the most fun I'd ever had shopping.

I had spoken too soon.

Elliot was silent. A little too silent. I turned my head toward him to see his eyes zeroed in on something behind me. His lips were set in a straight line, and I craned my neck to try to see what kind of catastrophic disaster he had witnessed, but my inflexibility was not very lenient.

"What are you staring at?" I asked, making a funny face. He didn't laugh. He didn't roll his eyes. He didn't even move.

I turned to Flora, and she was as confused as I was.

"Oh, n-nothing," Elliot stammered. He broke his gaze and smiled nervously.

I narrowed my eyes and decided that this had to be worth seeing. I tested the flexibility in my neck once again, but he stopped me.

"Ariel, don't."

"It's not like the world is end—" My hands fell into my lap, and my mouth parted. Gravity felt really strong.

There, right in front of American Eagle, which was a couple of yards away, stood a boy and a girl obnoxiously making out. The boy was Ashton. His hands traveled up and down her waist as she tugged on the tips of his hair.

It shouldn't have bothered me, but it did. My stomach sank.

It's not like he's cheating. It's not a big deal. So why did it feel like I'd ran twenty miles with a fever? And gotten hit by a bus halfway through? And stomped on by an elephant?

For a while it was quiet except for the other people at the mall who didn't know what on earth was going on. My brain wanted me to turn to Elliot or Flora to see what they were thinking, but my eyes continued to bore holes into Ashton's face, which was connected with some girl. She didn't even look familiar. Either she was from a different school, or she had been invisible since December.

It had to be the girl he was after. The girl he didn't even give Dakota a chance for. He had rejected a fling for another fling.

I closed my eyes for five seconds. When I opened, they were still pressed up against each other. Weren't they ashamed of how much PDA they were showing?

I hadn't even noticed the slight tremor in my right leg until I finally tore my eyes away from them. But just like that, my eyes were back on them. It was such a rude thing to do, stare at two people making out. But it was like I had been shot with a freeze ray.

When Ashton most likely ran out of air from shoving his tongue down her throat so many times, he pulled away. I didn't know why, but he spun his head around almost as if he had felt me watching.

He didn't see me at first. It was my chance. I could've gotten the hell out of there and pretended this had never happened because it shouldn't have affected me so much, but my feet felt superglued to the floor.

Those azure eyes met mine, and the color drained from his face. He acted like I had caught him red-handed, and I probably had.

The worst part was that he didn't say or do a thing.

He was a deer caught in the headlights. A terrible, stupid deer.

It felt like his eyes were trying to say something, but I was so far gone I didn't even bother to understand. My frozen muscles melted, and I fidgeted with my hands. One step at a time, I backed away.

That turned into a jog. Then I was running from the faint sound of someone calling my name. I weaved my way through all the people watching me like I was crazy.

But they were right.

I *was* crazy. I was overreacting to something that never should've struck a nerve.

I needed fresh air. Thank the Lord it wasn't still pouring because either way, I wasn't going to stay inside. The universe was just being nice by not having me get soaked.

I dropped onto a bench, not even caring that I was going to be getting some hard-to-explain wet spots on my butt. I buried my head in my hands.

I was stupid. Stupid even to let myself feel hurt. Stupid for even letting Ashton affect me in the first place. Stupid that I had been a coward back there. I shouldn't have ran. It was pathetic, really. *Extremely, mortifyingly pathetic.*

"Ari?" a tentative voice said. Then there were footsteps and the squishing sound of someone sitting down next to me.

"You're going to get your ass wet, Flora." I still didn't look at her.

"It'll dry, and besides, I wouldn't want you to be embarrassed by yourself. What kind of friend would I be?"

The worst part was that it didn't even make me smile. Not even a little bit.

I finally tilted my head up. *Big mistake.* She looked like my cat had just got run over by a car. And I hated it. Absolutely despised it.

"Sorry about running. I don't even know why I did that. I think I might've eaten something weird because something's wrong with me."

Flora slung her arm around my neck. "Nah, I just think you're finally experiencing some real emotion that wasn't programmed into your genius robot personality. If you want, I can go punch Ashton for you."

Ashton. Elliot. Elliot was there. God, I'm going to get a shit ton of "you like him" comments soon.

"It's fine. And I don't like him, if that's what you're getting at. Where's Elliot?"

She cocked an eyebrow skeptically. "He's talking to Ashton. He looked pissed."

"Why?"

"Ari, just because you say you don't feel a thing doesn't mean Elliot isn't mad at his best friend."

"Flora," I sighed. "That's who Ashton is. He hooks up with a different girl every week. It's in his blood. I'm just a friend. And it's so much better that way."

"Have you seen him with any other girls since you went to Lincoln Bay?"

"Uh, no. But I've heard from all the girls who've hooked up with him. Even Elliot admitted it."

"Ariella Winters, you got a full score on your SATs, and you took them a year early, yet right now, you are this stupid?"

"Thanks, friend," I jeered.

"Ever think that he likes you?"

"Flora," I said, but it felt like I was talking to myself. "This project isn't for me to get into a relationship. It's to learn something about myself or someone else that changes my point of view on things. What happened then is something that I pray you never speak of again. What's at stake right now is my completion of this project."

"Ari, what'll you do if you start to really like this guy? I'm not taking his side, but you honestly don't look fine."

"Well, believe it. And that won't happen. I won't let that happen. Relationships are a big no-no for high school. I've said it a million times."

"But what if—"

"There's no 'what if.' Right now, I'm clearly not learning anything, and that's a problem. Obviously Ashton doesn't really want to open up to Ariella Winters, so being me is out of question."

"Wha-huh?"

I was about to answer, but I heard the sound of footsteps growing louder. If it was Ashton, I wasn't going to run. *You can't be a coward again. That's weak.* It was Elliot.

"Uh, hey, so how are you?" Elliot rubbed the back of his neck and then began running a hand through his hair over and over again.

"I'm fine. I just realized that your idea of my just being me with Ashton isn't working. I'm not learning anything, and I want to get this project done."

"You know—"

I held up my hand to stop him. "I'm not done. I'm going to go back to acting, because, as you can see, I've got nothing. Maybe he'll want to open up to that person."

If Ashton wouldn't trust the real Ariella, then he just had to trust the fake girl I had always planned on being.

Confident. Mean. Obnoxious. And nowhere near real.

Sure, it was a stretch. But the pros outweighed the cons. If I was fake, I wouldn't have to worry about all those weird feelings with him. I admit I had been skidding off track a little. What Ashton did actually helped me get back on track.

"But—"

"You know what?" I slid my hands over my knees and pushed myself up. "I'm so tired. I think I'm going to go home and crash. Maybe the night will clear up so I can get some good photos. See you Monday, Elliot."

I started to leave but stopped when I realized Flora was still there.

"Sorry, Flora. Do you still want a ride?" I turned around lazily.

"Uh, I can take her home," Elliot suggested.

Flora flushed, and it was the sweetest thing ever. "Um, okay."

"Cool, I'll talk to you guys later." I dragged my feet all the way until I reached my car and slid in. I spent the rest of the night watching the Kardashians with Stella and pretending nothing had happened.

Chapter 9

On Sunday, I went for a fifteen-mile run to clear my head. When that didn't work, I grabbed my camera and tried to get some nature shots. That eventually backfired on me when I just ended up cold and disappointed by the photographs I was getting.

Then I did some of my Easton High packets.

Then I did an ab-circuit, which only caused me undesirable pain.

Then I helped Stella cook dinner.

Ultimately, I just gave up and went to sleep.

On Monday morning, I considered locking myself in my closet so I wouldn't have to go to school. I made the necessary preparations to channel my already amazing acting skills, which included me splashing myself in the face with some water.

If there was going to be one day I'd look back on this project and cringe, today was the day. If I was going to try to be a different person, I had to go all out. *Do it for the A, do it for the A,* I chanted as I grabbed a crop top that was way too small and some denims that cut right under my belly button.

The jeans were ripped in certain places, and I cursed Flora for making me buy these, which had cost more than jeans that hadn't been ripped. *I can make my own holes, thank you very much.*

Going through my usual routine, I trotted down the stairs to grab an apple. Stella was already in the kitchen making coffee.

"Morning, wow, look at you, all edgy," Aunt Stella greeted me with a yawn.

I suddenly regretted even the idea that I could've pulled it off. "I should go change. This doesn't look nice—"

"Nonsense, but I am going to have to do some parenting because I know for a fact that your mom would say this." Stella poured the coffee into a cup. "Go put on a jacket. It's still winter, you know."

"Yes, ma'am." I saluted. I picked up an apple and slipped into the living room and grabbed the jacket I had left on the couch yesterday. "See you later, Stella."

"Have a good day at school," Stella shouted back.

By the time I got to school, I had already had a heated debate with myself on whether I should've turned right around and changed my outfit. It was a ridiculous idea anyway. I didn't know why I ever thought I could've really pulled off acting.

But alas, if I turned around, I would've been late, and no matter how much I dreaded this school, I refused to get the only tardy I had ever had in high school. I hadn't known exactly how I'd be with Ashton, but it definitely wasn't going to be good. I hoped more than ever that I would not fall on my butt.

I didn't get to school twenty minutes early as usual. The thought of seeing Ashton without other people around was too much to handle. The idea of being with any guy alone was too much to handle.

Once I reached 101B, most of the students were already there. Ashton and his friends from the soccer team were fooling around in the back, and I really didn't want to get in the middle of that. I ran a hand through my hair, even though I had already brushed every single tangle out.

Then I stepped into the classroom like it was just a normal day at school. And from any other person's point of view, it was.

Maybe if I just stepped really softly, Ashton wouldn't see me. Then I'd have at least a couple of seconds to go over what I'd say to him.

But like most of my plans when it came to Ashton, it failed.

I hadn't even taken a full two steps before Ashton cut off what he was saying to his friend midsentence and watched me.

Well, that didn't work. At all.

Refusing to look like a fool and run away, I puffed out my chest and kept going. I wasn't going to him; I was going to my seat.

Like there's a difference.

I dropped my backpack right next to my feet and tried my hardest not to catch his eye. *You know that feeling you get when someone is clearly staring at you? Magnify that by one hundred and that's how I feel.*

Was I supposed to be satisfied by all the attention? If anything, I was angry.

For some reason, I had the urge to knee him in the

balls so hard he would never be able to have babies. I assume those anger management classes from third grade were working because I kept my cool.

Calm.

Composed.

Confident.

"Damn, Ariel. You look hot today." Dawson, one of Ashton's friends, whistled.

In the corner of my eye, Ashton's hands clenched.

"You don't look too bad yourself," I apparently responded.

"There's a new action movie coming out this weekend. You interested?" Dawson pushed himself off the desk he was sitting on and stepped close.

No, no, no, no, no, NO. "I'll check my schedule."

"Course, ba—"

"The bell's about to ring, you should go sit down," Ashton butted in. His face was blank.

Dawson held his palms up in surrender. "What's got your panties in a bunch today, Walker?"

"Nothing. Just don't want you to get marked tardy, Epstein."

Dawson just smirked. "Thanks, bud. And Ariel, don't forget about my offer."

"I won't."

With that, he walked to his desk two seats away from mine. I finally took the risk and faced Ashton eye-to-eye.

He didn't look like his normal I-know-you-want-me self. His shoulders slouched, and his right leg was bouncing up and down so fast I was getting dizzy just looking at it.

"So you like Dawson?" he asked through clenched teeth.

"Not really."

"Oh."

Pretty sure this is torture.

"Yup." I looked up at the lights. They were really bright …

"So about Saturday—"

"Huh?" I tried my best to act confused. "I don't know what you're talking about."

"I want to explain—"

"There's nothing you need to explain. We're as cool as ice."

As ice? Really? Is that the best you can come up with, Ariel?

"I'm sorry, but what's going on with you? You look different. Good different but—" He pursed his lips.

I cocked an eyebrow. "I'm just the same old, pretty boy. The only one who seems different is you."

"Uh—"

"So you play soccer competitively, right? How long have you been playing?"

Is this interrupt-Ashton-every-chance-you-get day?

His face displayed a mix of emotions that I wouldn't let myself try to pick apart. "Since I was five."

"Wow, that's more than ten years." *Great observation, dipshit.*

"Yeah."

"Morning, class. You all look so very excited for precalc, so let's dig in." Mr. Blair clapped his hands together.

The rest of the class groaned, but I silently cheered as I angled my body to face the board. This was beginning to come back and bite me. What had I even learned? That Ashton played soccer for a long time? That he liked running back and forth on a field with a ball? I declared to myself that I wouldn't try to spark conversation for the rest of the day because I was already beyond mortified.

Ten minutes into the glorious subject of precalculus, Ashton's eyes were still laser beams on my cheek. Or my nose. Or my mouth. Or whatever he was looking at.

After three class periods, he was still looking at me, and I hated it. He didn't try to say anything; he just watched me with those eyes I loved.

No, I didn't love those eyes.

I only loved the color.

When the lunch bell finally rang, I didn't even wait for Erika before I practically sprinted out of the room. I swear there was a significantly lesser amount of oxygen in that classroom.

I didn't get very far before I stupidly wasn't watching where I was going and slammed into a very hard chest. I lifted my head fully prepared to let out a string of apologies but froze when I saw that Elliot was smiling down at me.

"Whoa, girl, is there free pizza or something or do you always sprint this fast?"

"Sorry about leaving so quick on Saturday." I planted my feet firmly on the ground to avoid being shoved by the people walking through. "By the way, I think I grew another head, because Ashton's been staring at me for the past three hours."

"It's totally fine. And I can see why Ashton hasn't been able to keep his eyes off you. But my best friend was a moron last week. I think we should get some revenge."

The creepy smile on his face worried me. "Um, no thanks. I think I'm done speaking to Ashton for the rest of the day."

109

"Darling," Elliot said in a villainous way. "Don't you want to finish this project?"

"I still have almost five months. I'm okay today." No, I wasn't okay. I wasn't okay with still having this not finished. These months were going to pass in an instant.

"Liar."

"Okay, a little less than five months. What do you want me to do?" I moaned. "I'm not getting the epiphany that I'm apparently supposed to have, and I don't know what I'm supposed to do. How do I make Ashton tell me something that makes me see the world a different way?"

"Ariella, my friend, you're going about this all wrong." He shook his head.

"Your face is going about this all wrong." I murmured.

"It's a process, and I can tell you that over the month and a half that I've known you, what Ashton's not telling you yet will change how you see him."

I frowned. "Why are you even helping me? Aren't you scared I'll exploit all your best friend's secrets?"

"I think Ashton might actually like you."

"My ass."

"Do you want to hear my idea or not?" He folded his arms across his chest.

"Not really, but you're obviously going to tell me anyway so go ahead."

"Flirt with—"

I plugged my ears. "No, no, and no. La la la la la la, I'm not listening."

He pulled my fingers out of my ears. "Let me finish. I talked to Flora about this, and she thinks this is an amazing idea."

"You pulled my best friend to the dark side?" I whined.

"Yup. Now pay attention."

"Your face can pay attention."

"Okay, that's it. I'm not even giving you an option. You're going through with the plan if it's the last thing I do."

"Care to elaborate on the 'plan' first?"

"I've been trying to for the past five minutes. Go flirt with Xander. I promise he'll flirt back. Go in for a kiss because I know Xander will go through with it—"

"No, I don't want to kiss him." I huffed.

"You won't have to."

"Then what's the point of trying to get a kiss from Mr. I Know Everything? That doesn't even include Ashton in any way."

"It does if you let me finish. Ashton will stop him."

I stroked my imaginary beard. "Let me think ... No, no, and oh look, another no."

"Ashton will go nuts," he sang.

"That's not what I'm going for," I said mockingly.

He pointed to the watch he didn't have on his wrist. "Oh look, I'm not giving you a choice. And look, it's time. You wanted to show your brilliant acting skills, right? Here's your chance."

He was mocking me.

I tried to step around him. He stepped with me. I backed up. He grabbed my shoulder. I swatted his hand away, but because I had no upper body strength, it looked like I was poking his hand.

I exhaled. "You promise there will be no DNA swapping."

He laughed so hard that his belly shook. "Swear on my baseball bat." I didn't answer. "I'll take that as an A-okay. Let's go."

He pulled me along. *If I just tilted my shoulder slightly, I'd be able to run ...*

"You can try to run, but I will find you."

Damn you, Elliot Calder!

"We should do this tomorrow. I haven't let this sink in." I rushed in a last effort to stop this.

"Nah, it's simple. Just wing it."

"Please don't touch me."

"Stop stalling."

The walk to the other guys was way too short, in my opinion.

Ashton was talking to Xander. *How convenient.*

"Are you just going to stand there like a statue or are you going to go?" Elliot whispered.

I glared at him. "Don't rush me."

Be flirty ... how do I be flirty?

"You can start by doing that little girly skip over to Xander."

"Shut up, Elliot."

I tried my best to make sure I wouldn't remember this and then I "girly-skipped" over to Xander and plopped down right next to him. Our shoulders were touching, and I was already freaked out.

"Hey there, cutie." I flashed a teeth-filled smile at Xander.

I didn't even want to see Ashton's face. But Xander looked happily surprised.

"Hey, yourself. What can I do for you, darling?" Xander asked, flinging an arm around my neck. My cheek hit his chest with a thud.

"Well, you could give me a kiss."

Good job, Ariel. How subtle.

I waited for the rejection. That didn't happen.

"This must be my lucky day." Xander winked at Ashton.

I puckered up my lips and kept one eye on Elliot as Xander began to lean in. I was close to sticking a middle finger at Elliot when he began to count down from three.

Someone cleared his throat, and in my brain, I jumped up and cheered. Xander opened his eyes, obviously annoyed.

"Sorry, Xander, but I have to speak with Ariel for a moment," Ashton fumed.

"What the fuck, Ashton?"

"Don't push it, Xander."

Ashton stood up and grabbed my wrist, pulling me up, and I began to wonder if this was the better way for the scenario to have ended. Ashton glared at Xander so intensely I thought Xander would disintegrate.

"Hey, Walker, your mommy called. She wants her tampon back." Xander called out right before his face was out of view.

I'd be lying if I said I didn't think that was funny.

We kept walking, and he kept pulling me, until we reached an empty hallway. He dropped his death grip on my wrist and paced back and forth. I rocked forward and backward on the balls of my feet.

"What the hell was that, Ariel? So you like Xander now?" Ashton scowled at me.

"No."

"Then why the hell would you go around asking him for a kiss? What's next? Free blowjobs because you're in a good mood?" He demanded.

"Quit being such an asshole."

"I know what you're doing."

"Care to enlighten me, wise guy?"

"This is your revenge, isn't it? For what I did?"

Uh, yes. Well, technically, it's Elliot's revenge.

"News flash, Ashton, not everything has to revolve around you."

He sighed. "Look, I'm sorry. The whole blowjob comment was uncalled for and rude."

"I know."

"Can you come over to finish the essay today?"

But I finished the essay. Say no. Politely decline and say—

"Sure."

"Good." He linked his hand with mine and hauled me back to Elliot and the others.

God, I hadn't even wiped my hands on my jeans. They were probably clammy and gross. I waited for him to drop my hand and make a comment about how disgusting I was, but it never happened.

In fact, he didn't let go of my hand.

When we got back, Elliot had sat down right next to Xander. Ashton took the open spot right next to Elliot and pulled me down right next to them.

The furthest away from Xander.

Elliot smirked as Ashton pulled out a pear from his lunch box. I narrowed my eyes at him, but I couldn't help but notice that Ashton was doing everything with one hand. Because the other one was firmly holding mine.

And those tingly feelings I had had the last time I was at Ashton's house were back and so much stronger.

I slowly pulled my hand out of his and ran it up and down my thigh. Niagara Falls was currently flowing out of my hand at the speed of light.

I couldn't help but notice Ashton's hand twitch slightly. And also the fact that those strange prickly feelings from my palm had relocated into my stomach.

Chapter 10

Very few situations tend to make me actually hope I embarrass myself just to break an icy layer of awkwardness.

This was one of those times.

I had actually counted the number of words Ashton had said to me from the last bell to the present time, in his room.

Three words.

Three words in the span of three hours, one being "Sorry," when he accidently bumped into me and the others being "Come on," when I was walking sluggishly slow. I don't even know how I spent three hours silent, but a laptop certainly helped.

It wasn't like he had suddenly caught a sore throat, because he had said "bye" to his friends and laughed at a joke they made.

It was me.

Every time he looked at me, his smile went away.

I felt like that pair of underwear every kid gets

on Christmas, and while they can't say that they absolutely hate it, they certainly don't love it. I was the lame underwear in the sea of remote-control cars and Legos.

"Could you, uh, not stare at me like you want me to burn in a fire?" I faked a cough.

He didn't say anything in response.

Figures.

Ashton simply turned his head and turned those freakishly blue eyes on the trees outside. If I hadn't been watching him with equal intensity, I wouldn't have noticed the slight coral tint on his cheeks.

Just the sun.

Then we were back to the awful silence we had before. Even Roseanne was out. When I followed Ashton into the kitchen, I got a slight peek at the note taped on the refrigerator. Something about her son being sick.

Marvelous.

"So are you planning to go on that date with Dawson?"

Fourteen words.

"I don't know." I traced little circles on the carpet with my finger. "Probably not." *Probably never.*

"That's nice," he said out of politeness.

I'm not quite sure why I decided to say something so intrusive next. I blame it on my desperation to pull myself out of this nightmare.

"So are you and that girl dating?"

That must've sparked something in Ashton because he perked right up. "What? Oh, um, no."

"Okay."

What a constructive conversation this is.

All I knew was that I wanted to go home to the

comfort of all my textbooks and the food Stella would be so kindly cooking.

"Ashton," I breathed, completely sick of how sad this was. "The essay's done. Is there really a reason you brought me here because it doesn't seem like I'm very welcome. I should really go—"

"There's this winter carnival like ten minutes away. Do you want to go?"

I lost count of how many words.

"When?"

"Now," he said, twirling the strings of his hoodie.

"Right now, right now?"

"Is there another right now?"

"There could be." I bit my lip.

The edges of his mouth drew upward, and I couldn't believe what was happening. He was smiling. It was a smile that I hadn't seen all day. Well, technically, I had seen it, but it just hadn't been directed toward me.

"Then I'm talking about the right, right now."

"A carnival," I said to myself, but apparently I wasn't very quiet.

"Well, yeah, only if you want."

Keep sitting here in this pool of discomfort, or go out somewhere where there'll at least be people?

"That sounds lovely."

"Great," he said, placing his palms on the carpet and pushing himself up. "So I wasn't exactly planning to go out for the rest of the day. Right before lunch, I kind of slipped and got this stain on my pants."

Indeed, right on the left knee of his navy-blue jeans was a dark stain that roughly covered his whole kneecap area.

"I'll go outside," I declared and hauled myself up in a nanosecond.

"You can go in, uh," he began before pausing. "You can go into the room r-right across from me. I'll come get you in a minute."

He didn't need to tell me twice. I shut the door to his room and went into the room he'd told me to go into. I flicked on the light, fully prepared to see a guest bedroom, but that didn't happen.

The room looked like it belonged to someone. The walls were painted periwinkle but were just as tall and wide as the walls in Ashton's room. In a straight, horizontal line, a row of photographs hung on the four walls. It was kind of like a choker necklace. For the bedroom.

Hesitantly, I stepped further into the room and looked closely at one of the photographs. The photo had to have been taken years back. There was a smaller version of Ashton on his tippy toes, doing his best to put his arm around a girl's shoulders.

I couldn't take my eyes off the girl. If there had been a female version of Ashton, she was it. They had the same chiseled nose and pink, plump lips. Her wavy, brown hair flowed down a couple of inches beneath her shoulders. The significant height difference showed that she had to be a couple of years older.

She had the same dimples that Ashton had, the right being a little deeper than the left. Her eyes were blue, but they were borderline gray. The mysterious girl and Ashton were in what seemed to be a park. In the right corner was a giant pile of red, orange, and yellow leaves.

I arrived at the conclusion that she was downright beautiful. And that was being conservative.

They looked too much alike to be cousins, but I was sure Ashton didn't have a sister. I mean, he said he didn't have any siblings.

I vaguely studied the other photos, the feeling growing that I was a disturbance here. Most of the pictures on the wall were of her and Ashton. Rarely, I'd see the two of them with an older couple I assumed to be their parents.

The photo I ogled most at had to be the one where elementary-school-age Ashton was in a black and white tux. He was showing that same precious beam I had seen the other day when he looked happy—genuinely happy. Standing next to him, I could only assume, was the same girl from all the other shots. There just had to be—

There was a small knock on the door. He cracked the door open and, through the crack, I could see him rubbing his hands on his new pair of jeans.

"You good?" I asked softly as though he'd change his mind and ask me to go home.

"Yeah, you better g-grab your coat. It's cold outside."

Sheepishly, I made my way back into his room with a whole new set of questions. I wasn't planning to ask, of course, but I wasn't going to deny how confused I was.

My center of balance must've felt the need to take a break because as I bent down to grab my hat and jacket on the floor, I flopped back on my ass. And it was the opposite of graceful.

It didn't go unnoticed. A strange sound escaped the back of Ashton's throat right before ringing laughter emerged from his mouth.

I muttered a series of obscene words. "How does that even happen to someone?" I closed my eyes and maybe if I shut them hard enough, I'd disappear.

"You know," Ashton choked out through his endless fit of laughter because it was oh-so-funny, "closing your eyes doesn't make you invisible."

119

Then I opened my eyes. I was still there.

"I don't understand how I always manage to hurt myself when I'm near you," I huffed.

"It's probably because I knock you off your feet."

Only he found this joke funny.

"Okay, I walked right into that one."

"Here," he said, giving me his hand.

He tugged me up, and I slipped on my knit beanie. One-handed. Because, God help me, Ashton was still holding on to the other hand. He pulled me down the stairs as I wondered why I had this stupid grin on my face.

He eventually broke our touch when he grabbed his car keys and stepped into his sneakers.

"I can drive," I offered, though I somehow knew he wouldn't let me.

"Nah, I can do it. How do I know you're not a maniac who may risk my life?" He looped his finger through the keychain.

"I can drive perfectly fine, I'll have you know."

"I guess we'll never find out."

Once I had my jacket and Uggs on, Ashton intertwined our fingers yet again. Now why didn't I have the courage to pull away? I turned my face so he wouldn't be able to see my red face.

"I know that you're blushing. You don't have to look away. Besides, you're cute when you blush."

I wasn't prepared for how cold it was when Ashton opened the door. It had only been a couple of seconds, and I could already tell that my nose was turning red. I stuffed my free hand into my pocket and, peculiarly, the hand that Ashton held was warmer than the one in my pocket.

That is, until Ashton's hand left mine so he could get into the car. A sudden wave of chilly air replaced the warmth, and I found myself actually wanting to hold his hand again. I grasped the car handle and yanked the door open. I lowered myself in the passenger's seat and watched Ashton take his place in the driver's seat. The engine roared as he turned the key. A sudden burst of heat blasted in my face, and I relaxed a bit.

Whoever had invented heaters was my idol.

The ride there was faster than I expected. Before I could find something to say, because apparently now I couldn't think of anything, we were already there. But of all things, those ten minutes were comfortable, and I sort of really liked how Ashton didn't feel the need to fill a silence with useless conversation.

I leaned forward to get a better view of the carnival just as Ashton shut off the car, and I certainly wasn't disappointed. There may not have been real snow at the moment, but the giant white snowflakes made up for it. I didn't think I had ever seen so many sparkles in my life. White Christmas lights were wrapped around every pole, every sign, every booth.

I hadn't realized how long I was gawking out the window until I felt a gentle tap on my shoulder. I twisted my neck to see Ashton pointing toward the door. *Great, be the colossal idiot who zones out at the worst time.*

Nervously, I stepped out of the car and waited for Ashton to come out. After a few seconds, he was by my side. And I was that girl who stared wide-eyed at him as he laced our fingers together and strode toward the entrance.

He stopped at the ticket booth, and it wasn't until after he pulled out his wallet that I realized I had forgotten to bring mine. What kind of person thought the carnival was free? They obviously had to make money other than selling funnel cakes and cotton candy, which actually sounded pretty delicious.

"I promise I'll pay you back. I'm really sorry." I dug my heel into the gravel just as Ashton handed the woman a ten-dollar bill.

"No."

"Really, I promise. When we get back, I'll take it out of my wallet. I don't know how I forgot it. Sometimes even I can't believe how stupid I am—"

"I'm paying for you today. Besides, I took you here, didn't I? It's only right for me to pay." Ashton squeezed my hand, which was yet another reminder that we were touching.

I didn't complain after that. I'd probably end up sneaking a five-dollar bill on his pillow when we'd go back to his house. For now, I observed just about every inch of the carnival, getting drawn into this winter wonderland. My eyes jumped from the teacups ride, to the bottle tosses, then to the humongous Ferris wheel in the middle of all the madness. I ended up wondering why I hadn't wanted to come when I was younger, because this was fantastic. I breathed in the fattening yet savory scent of corn dogs lingering in the air as Ashton and I walked around the huge landscape of the carnival.

The drool was about to slip out of my mouth just as I noticed that we weren't moving anymore. We were facing a plate-breaking booth, and even though I hadn't ever played one before, I knew it was rigged. Those plates had to be secretly cemented.

"You will never win that, Ash."

He slapped two dollars on the table. "Wanna bet?"

"You're setting yourself up to lose."

"You have to give me a kiss if I win."

What?

"S-sure," I croaked.

He won't win. It's one in a thousand.

And I guess he was that one in a thousand because one plate broke, then the next. He didn't even have to throw the third ball.

"What were you saying?"

"You're shitting me right now."

"Ariella Winters, I shit you not."

"H-how did you do that?"

"It's a secret." He brought his finger up to his lips, and it was the first time I found myself staring at his lips. They were a fleshy pink, and I just—

No.

Ash's back was facing me as he claimed his prize, so I couldn't see what he was getting. He made his way over to me with a stuffed Spiderman in his hands. Of all the bunnies and teddy bears, he had chosen a plush Spiderman ... and I loved it.

"I don't understand."

He won. He really won a game that I couldn't win if I tried fifty times.

Ashton just grinned delightedly. "Now, my end of the bet, Miss Winters."

I panicked. Without any notice, Ashton brought his face right up to mine and pecked my cheek. Can't say I wasn't surprised that he hadn't gone for the lips.

"Um ..." Of all the words in the English dictionary, I picked one of the stupidest ones.

"What? Did you expect me to plant one on you right

on the lips?" He feigned hurt. "That's preposterous. We're not married. Yet."

For a second I was speechless. Then my lips were set in a thin line. "Hardy-har-har. You're so funny."

"I know."

It was then that I got this weird sense that someone was watching me. I snapped my head to the left just as two girls scowled at me as they walked away—the two girls being Tara and a girl I didn't recognize. At least I thought it was them. It certainly looked like them from the few seconds I saw them. I guess the plate-breaking booth at the fair was the place to be.

Then curiosity got the best of me. "Hey, Ash?"

"I'm not telling you how I did that."

"Do you and Tara have a thing going on?"

Ariella Winters: Master of Subtlety.

His smile washed out, and his face paled.

"Why do you ask?"

"Uh, just wondering. Sorry, I don't know why I can't learn to just shut my mouth. I don't normally have this problem. To be honest, I'm normally never this wordy. I think it's genetics just starting to show a little late."

"I like how much you talk," he said a little sadly.

"Thanks."

His eyes were even bluer at night. "Regarding Tara, can you just promise me one thing first?"

"Sure?"

He honestly looked concerned. "Promise we won't be awkward again."

"So you felt it too?" I asked.

"More than you know."

"Same."

Cool story, bro.

"So, you promise?"

"Uh, yeah, I promise."

My brain flooded with all the possibilities. What if they were secretly married? What if they were a couple, and they adopted a dog, then they broke up, and she wanted to tell him that the dog missed him? Or what if they were secret agents, and she was pretending to be obsessed with him?

"We hooked up once or twice in sophomore year."

Well, that was a letdown.

"Oh."

"She was just a fling. She means nothing to me now. Come to think of it, I never really liked her." he added frantically.

"You don't have to explain yourself to me." It was his business, which in no way included me.

"I actually really like someone right—uh, I just … never mind."

I actually really like someone right now, was what he meant to say.

"So you're finally giving up your whorish ways?" I joked.

He really likes someone.

"Hey," he protested. "I am not a whore. I just—I don't. I have no idea how to explain myself in a way that sounds good."

He likes someone. She probably looks like a model. Hell, she probably is a model.

"Cough, I'm right, cough."

Big whoop, it wasn't like we'd ever be together anyway. Columbia, Columbia, remember Columbia.

"No uncomfortable silences, right?" He brushed away a strand of hair that was poking me in the eye.

"Right," I tore my hand away from his and shoved it in my pocket. If he really liked a girl, it was one more reason we shouldn't be holding hands. "Let's walk around."

I began walking even though I didn't have a clue where I was going. For all I knew, if I had kept leading the way, we'd end up walking in circles. I heard a sigh and then footsteps, and Ashton was right next to me, making sure, I hoped, that I wasn't taking us to our deaths.

There wasn't much to say after that. It definitely wasn't that I was angry with him; it was just that I had nothing to say, and I may've been eating too many apples since coming to Lincoln Bay because this tingly feeling wasn't normal. Maybe he thought it was anger.

Ashton reached for my limp left hand, but my brain yelled abort, and before he could successfully touch my hand, I stuffed it in my pocket.

How's the weather? — no, that's the worst starter ever. So, you come here a lot? Nope, definitely not that one.

Then it dawned on me. I had never truly been speechless before, yet here I stood, completely unsure what to do. In other instances, I'd find something to say, but here, I could open and close my mouth a dozen times, and nothing would come out.

I didn't know what to say.

I didn't know what to do, and it sucked.

So naturally, I didn't say a word.

Something about Ashton was just really bothering me. Why was he even being this open with me? I hadn't done a single thing to make him trust me. It was a good thing. He was opening up, and I was really getting to know him. It just felt like there was one thing left that put everything together, and I hadn't figured out that one thing yet.

The guy I was hanging out with certainly wasn't the guy I had known for the first month of school. The guy I met in the beginning of December was the egotistical soccer star, even though I had yet to see him in action. He was the guy every girl wanted to change.

I liked to think I was the exception. A: I had no interest in changing him. All I wanted to do was learn whatever I was going to learn from this inconsistent boy and go back to sweet Easton High. B: He already liked a girl, which made us nothing more than friends. That was a good thing. Yep, a good thing.

I had thought an awful lot about whether I really did regret coming to Lincoln Bay. I certainly didn't like learning my schoolwork from a thick packet, but deep down, I was having a little fun.

At the same time, I was glad that I'd met Ashton. I couldn't explain exactly why I was glad to have met this boy, but I was. I liked having him around—when his cockiness was shattered with a wrecking ball, that is. Or several wrecking balls. After all, his ego was the size of the Appalachian Mountains, perhaps even bigger.

"You know," he said, breaking our word drought. "You're not doing a good job of keeping your promise. I feel mighty uncomfortable."

"Sorry."

"Is it because of Tara? Is she bothering you?" *Like he'll do anything if I say yes.*

"Not really. If I'm honest with you, I'm not surprised you two have hooked up. She talks about it enough. Besides, a man whore's reputation can't all be a lie." It was supposed to be a joke, but maybe it wasn't all that funny, because he didn't laugh. "I'm kidding."

"I'm starting to wonder if the only reason you hang out with me is because you want to make fun of me."

I shook my head. "Nope, it's because some idiot told me that he'd call me every two minutes if I didn't agree to come over."

"You'll have to forgive me for wanting an A."

"Is that all you wanted?" I pressed.

"It may also have had something to do with my wanting to hang out with a pretty girl."

These were the kinds of things that were going to make staying on track hard. "Flattery won't get you anywhere."

He wiggled his eyebrows at me. "How about cotton candy?"

I tried my best not to drool. "That, my friend, will get you mighty far."

Chapter 11

I wasn't born an early bird.

It took three different alarms clocks blasting in my ear every morning to wake me up. And on special occasions when I'd sleep through the bird caws, beeping, and extreme drum solos, Stella would have the privilege of yanking me from my bed.

But her presence usually meant that I'd have five minutes to get ready and out of the house which is exactly why I panicked when someone shook me out of my deep slumber.

"Wake up already. Ariella Winters, you sleep just like your mother! I swear there could be a whole marching band playing in your ear, and you wouldn't hear a thing."

For the first ten seconds, I hadn't let what Stella said sink in, so I just let out whatever sound wanted to escape my mouth first. Then I shot up when I realized that I had slept through my carefully timed alarms.

"Oh my God, did I miss those alarms? Stella, I

knew those bird calls weren't working for me anymore. I should've changed it. What time is it?" I wheezed.

She just watched me as I raided my closet. Then she smiled. And that turned into a chuckle.

"Ariel, sometimes you're just so sweet."

"I'm going to be late, oh my God. Why is that cute?"

It didn't matter what time it was. All that mattered was that I needed to get a pair of jeans on as fast as I could.

"It's Martin Luther King Day. You don't have school."

I let my jeans drop onto the floor and collapsed back into bed. "Oh,"

"Now, don't get too comfy. I'm only waking you up because a cute boy name Ashton just came over to drop your backpack off. He's downstairs."

That marked time number two today that I gave myself a headache by jumping up too fast. "Ashton? He's here?"

She raised an eyebrow at me. "Why not? I think that he's being extremely amazing. Does my little Ariel have a crush?"

"What? No!"

She didn't believe me. "I know I should be that person that says be careful if you get into a relationship, but I'm pretty sure you know all about consequences and things like that."

"Stella, I'm not getting into a relationship anytime soon."

"Whatever you say." She pulled the plug from my phone and tossed it to me. "Now, don't keep the boy waiting. Go get dressed. I have to go in five minutes."

I went to pick up my jeans as Stella left the room.

It hadn't fully sunk in that Ashton Walker was at my house. Being way too lazy to be constricted by denims, I eventually chucked the idea and put on some penguin-covered pajama shorts. I shimmied into a navy-blue hoodie, washed my face, and brushed my teeth in the span of three minutes, and I was fairly proud of that.

Ashton most likely wasn't going to stay, so I didn't bother with the makeup. We were friends. It shouldn't've mattered if I didn't wear makeup.

I slipped on my glasses and zipped down the stairs just in time to stop Stella from pestering him.

"So, Ashton, do you have an interest in Ariel? She's only my niece, but I've had careful instructions from her mother to—"

"Good morning," I chirped a little too loudly.

"That's my cue to go. It's wonderful to meet you, Ashton, and I hope to see you more often." Stella stood up and winked.

"It's great to meet you, ma'am."

She pulled him into one of her tight squeezes. "Call me Stella."

With that, she fast-walked out the door. I heard the faint sound of her buggy starting up and then she was gone.

"Hey." I apparently felt like this was the only way to start a conversation.

"Hey, you." Ashton got up from the cream couches.

Man, how did the guy manage to rock navy sweatpants and a white T-shirt when I looked like a seven-year-old in my penguin shorts?

"You, uh, left your backpack at my place on Friday, so I wanted to bring it to you."

"Thanks, but why not Saturday?"

"Oh, right. I had soccer all weekend, and I may've wanted use this as my excuse to talk to you for more than five minutes."

When I imagined him saying things like this, I imagined this smooth guy who made it seem like he said it on a daily basis.

My imagination was wrong.

He had his hands shoved in his pockets, and our eye contact didn't last for more than five seconds at a time. For some reason, that made me smile.

"So, um, do you want to stay and watch a movie or something? I mean I haven't eaten breakfast so I need to make that, so I have to do that first, but you don't have to stay if you don't want to." *Oh, Lord, Ariel, just shut up.*

"I'll stay if you'll have me." Ashton smiled, and I found it really sexy how ruffled his hair was. He had clearly woken up not too long ago, and he managed to look even better than he did when he actually tried to dress nicely. *Did I just say "sexy"? Yes, apparently I did.*

"Cool, but fair warning—I'm not that great of a cook so …"

"I can help," he offered. "Roseanne taught me a while ago, so don't be surprised if I'm a master chef."

"Come on, then." I motioned toward the kitchen, and he followed. The house certainly wasn't as big as Ashton's, but he didn't seem to mind.

We ended up making pancakes. Correction: *he* ended up making pancakes. All I really did was get out all the pans and give him flour and eggs.

"And voilà." Ashton kissed his fingertips as he set down two plates stacked high with pancakes. "By the way, where are your parents? Do they not live with you?"

Please sit down so I can eat. "Oh, right. My grandma

lives in Tampa, and she's not doing well right now, so they went to stay with her for the rest of the school year." I said completely forgetting that it didn't make sense. In his mind, I had moved here in December. Thankfully, he didn't dwell on the logistics of what I was saying.

"Don't you miss them?"

"Sure, but I've got Aunt Stella, and she's just as awesome, despite the fact that she's in a reality show craze right now."

I breathed in the aroma of perfection that Ashton had created and powered through the temptation to stuff my face.

"That's really cool."

He sat down—code for me being allowed to shove a large amount of pancake into my mouth.

"This is suh goob. No wonber e'ery gir lufs ou!" I exclaimed, but it was muffled by all the joy that was filling my taste buds.

"Actually, believe it or not, I have never cooked for a girl before," he admitted, but the cheesy moment we could've shared exploded as I inhaled my pancakes.

"How about this one?" Ashton asked, holding up paranormal activity.

Movie time wasn't sounding as awesome as it once did.

It wasn't even my movie. It was Flora's. She once brought it over in hopes of persuading me to watch it, but I didn't give in. She must've forgotten to take it home, and I had a feeling that my getting scarred for life was going to be the price to pay.

"We can't." I fidgeted with the strings of the hoodie.

His dark-brown eyebrows drew together. "Why?"

Perhaps I should've prepared what I was going to say after he asked why. "I just, I can't, I don't do scary movies."

"Oh don't worry, gorgeous. I'll protect you." Ash smirked while putting the disc into the DVD player.

"When my nails dig into your arm, don't complain."

"I won't," Ashton sang as he hopped back onto the couch.

Half an hour into the movie, and I was sure of the nightmares I was going to have. *It's not real. It's not real. It's not real. You won't die today.* My palms covered my face as one eye peeked out. I felt a sudden strong grip on my waist, and Ashton pulled me into him. Being too petrified to think straight, I buried my face in his shoulder. I gripped a piece of his shirt so securely that my knuckles were turning white. Ashton rubbed small circles on my back, and if I hadn't thought I was going to die, I would've yelled at him for picking the one scary movie out of thirty different choices. For the millisecond I looked up at him, he was grinning like an idiot.

Stupid idiot making me watch scary movies and scarring me for life.

But the fact that my forearm was touching his stomach made distracting myself a little easier. I could feel the subtle indents in his stomach, and I had no doubt in my mind that he had abs.

Since when do you care about if guys have abs?

I shut my eyes so tight so that I couldn't even detect the lighting changes in the movie. The vulgar sounds of I-don't-even-know-what filled my ears and kept me from falling asleep.

After what felt like a year, the music from the credits started to play. I exhaled loudly and let go of the part of Ashton's shirt that I had held on to for most of the movie. I cringed as I tried to flatten out the now crinkled bit of his shirt.

"You might want to iron that," I told him, pointing to the wrinkled bit.

He simply beamed, his arm never leaving my waist. I could've stared at his smile all day, in a noncreepy way, of course.

"Now that wasn't so bad, right, Ariel? You're not dead."

"Not bad? That was torture. Now you have to sit here with me for the next few hours to make sure I'm not murdered and ..." I trailed off when something caught my eye out the window.

The lower three-fourths of the sun was being covered by pearly, white clouds making the rims of the clouds look like they were glowing. The sky itself looked like someone had melted a sky blue crayon and painted it in clean-cut strokes. I didn't normally photograph a lot when the sun was out, but I felt compelled to do it today.

"What's wrong? Is someone out there? Is it a murderer?"

He was mocking me now. I saw how it was. But I didn't have time to come up with a comeback.

"Do you want to come upstairs for a second? I want to do something," I blurted out, tearing my eyes away from how beautiful it was outside.

I hadn't noticed how wrong that sounded until a smirk slowly crossed Ashton's face. "What exactly do you have in mind?"

"No, wait, not *that*. I mean the sky looks really

amazing right now and I want to get a shot of it." I could feel my face heating up.

"We'd better go then."

I practically sprinted up the steps to my room and pulled out my Canon EOS and slung it around my neck just as Ashton came in. Lord, he was in my bedroom. His eyes wandered to every photo as his breathing slowed.

"Damn, did you take these?" Ashton took another step further into the place where I spent most of my time.

"Yeah."

"What's this?" He pointed to one of the photographs.

"Ursa Major, a.k.a. the Great Bear. I took it last spring. If you look closely you can see the bear." I traced it with my finger. "That's the tail and the legs and body."

"Whoa."

"It's cool, isn't it?"

He looked at me with those blue eyes, and my legs felt like jelly. "It's really cool. Do you want to be a photographer when you grow up?"

"No, not really. It's more of a hobby. I just really like catching these constellations on camera. They're really cool to look at."

Ashton observed the photograph of Cassiopeia, then another photograph where, though there wasn't a constellation, the stars shone just as marvelously.

"Where do you take these?" he asked after a long time.

"You're about to see."

No one had ever been out on my spot except for me. Flora had a massive fear of heights, so she was never able to force herself to come out there. It had only been me, and I liked that. But having Ashton be out there too made me feel all tingly, for reasons I couldn't explain.

Then I realized that if I didn't put pants on, I'd get hypothermia. "Wait one sec."

I grabbed a random pair of gray sweatpants and hopped until the waistband was up and over my shorts.

"I look at these pictures and then see you doing that, and I wonder if you've Googled photos and stuck them to your wall."

I scowled. "I will take that as a compliment. Besides, I'd like to see you finding a more attractive way to put on sweatpants." I pushed my windowsill up so there was enough space to crawl out. "I'm going to go first. Follow me, and be careful."

I slowly swung one leg over, then the other one, and then I inched to the middle of the platform. I didn't care how many times I had done it; I wasn't about to die from slipping off my own roof.

"Is this safe?" Ashton poked his head out the window like a little kid coming to his parents' room.

I almost took a photo of that right there. "If it's not safe, then I've just gotten lucky at least one hundred times."

Ashton did exactly as I did until he made his way right next to me. I leaned back until my head was pressed against the roof. I had always loved the angle it was constructed at because it was the perfect angle for most of my shots. Ashton followed me and when our knees clanked together, the sparks shooting in my arms transferred to my knees.

"I can see why you like this. Once you get past the I-might-fall-and-break-my-face stage, it's really pretty."

"You should see this at night."

"I hope that's an offer because I have every intention of taking you up on it." Ashton's eyes were closed, and

I took him in. The sunlight reflected off his face so perfectly that I almost wanted to bend over and kiss him. Scratch that. I didn't almost want to kiss him. I kind of really wanted to kiss him, even though I had never kissed a guy before.

It was then that I realized that I might have been developing a tiny crush on the boy next to me.

I brought my Canon up to my eye and changed the settings to adjust to the time of day. Once I was content with how things looked, I started to take shot after shot with my hands as steady as I could. Forty photos later, I took the camera away from my eye and rested it on my chest.

"What are you staring at?" I said once I noticed Ashton's heavy gaze.

"The most gorgeous person I've ever seen."

That sealed the deal. I was officially falling for Ashton Walker, and it was catastrophic—with a pinch of electrifying.

Chapter 12

I never really understood crushes, considering that the last time I had a crush was in third grade.

And that was debatable, since the only reason the crush developed in the first place was because a boy, whose name I couldn't remember, lent me a marker, and I thought he was the sweetest person on the planet. All I really remembered about that time was that I could've sworn I was in love. Of course, at the time, I was also picturing how we would get married on a boat and then adopt some dolphins so I could fulfill my everlasting dream of becoming a dolphin trainer.

But this time was different. For one, I didn't imagine Ashton and me getting married on a boat, since I knew all too well that that would never happen. And I no longer felt the urge to become a dolphin trainer, which was probably for the best.

But most of all, I didn't remember feeling my stomach churn whenever the boy from third grade gave me a high five (possibly because back then, I was still processing the fact that cooties were indeed, not real).

All I really knew was that crushes were always a bad idea. Even when I developed a crush on Ashton Walker, I still knew it was a bad idea. Nothing would happen. He liked someone else. And I refused to allow myself to ruin what I had spent years of my life maintaining—a steady trail to Columbia.

But I couldn't control it. And that's what freaked me out. Not being able to control what I was feeling felt kind of like a scam. It was my body, my brain, my heart, yet I didn't have the power to dictate whether I liked someone or not. Call me a control freak, fine, but I liked to have control over my feelings.

School was great because whatever happened was my own doing. If I didn't get a full score on a test, I hadn't studied enough. I managed my own time in and out of school. When I controlled what happened and what I did and didn't do, nothing bad would happen.

And now, something bad was sure to happen, and I couldn't stop it.

Plus, there were thousands of questions I couldn't just crack open a textbook and find the answer to.

What surprised me even more was how much I liked the feeling of spontaneity whenever I was with Ashton. And I wasn't a spontaneous person at all. I was the type of person who avoids any kind of thrill if it means I can decrease the possibility of danger.

I couldn't even fully explain to myself why I was attracted to Ashton. I just liked him, and that was about it. I liked how I felt when I was with him. I liked it a bit too much.

It was so overwhelming that it felt like I was lying to

Flora when, in fact, I hadn't even spoken to her yet. But the feeling of guilt wouldn't go away until I told her, so I rang her up and told her that I was coming over. It was Sunday anyway. I doubt she had any plans.

Instead of driving, I decided to walk to her house. It was a decision on impulse. One that I didn't make often. One that I'd probably regret on the way home.

It was just so nice outside. The sun was out, and, even though it wasn't a summer day, the streams of warmth gave me a fuzzy feeling under my beanie. I strolled past the same cemetery that had been smack dab right in the middle of the route between our houses. I had to have gone past that cemetery thousands of times. One would think I'd know more about it, but I had never really paid attention to it.

I sped up a little and power-walked the rest of the way.

It gave me time to think that maybe this wasn't a crush, and it was just some weird hormonal thing. Maybe this was all a hallucination, and I was just feeling a little bit lonely.

That's how "normal" teenagers were supposed to feel, right?

By the time I arrived, I was out of breath. I jogged up the driveway and Flora yanked the door open before I even had the chance to knock.

"Ariel! Oh look, you're wearing clothes that are actually your size."

I scowled. "It's good to see you, too."

"Come on in. Gabe's playing video games in the basement, so we can take the living room."

I flicked my shoes off and followed her, though I probably could've drawn a detailed blueprint of her entire home right then and there. We walked through the kitchen, where I was stopped by the delicious scent of cookies floating in the air.

Mrs. Reynolds was pulling a batch out of the oven. "Hey there, Ariel. How are you today?"

"I'm great, and you?"

"Wonderful. I just baked some chocolate chip cookies, so when they cool, the two of you are welcome to take some. I've got to head out for a few errands, so I'll be back in an hour."

"Thanks, Mom," Flora chirped.

"Oh, and Flora," She gave her daughter a pointed look. "Spare some of these for Gabe, all right?"

"Got it, Mom. Now come on, Ari."

I think I was having separation issues from the cookies because for a few seconds, I didn't budge, but then I finally followed Flora out of the kitchen. I plopped down on the corner part of the couch and sank into the plushy cushions.

"What's up?" Flora sat down, propping her legs on the coffee table.

"I think I might be developing the tiniest crush—"

"Holy shit! You have a crush. Little Ariel has a real crush? On a boy? The girl who said she wouldn't date until she's twenty-eight has a crush?"

I cringed. "Could you not tell everyone within a 10k radius? And I said 'might.'"

"Don't be stupid. You like someone. Is it Ashton?"

I hesitated.

"You like Ashton. I knew it. This project has more perks than I thought."

"No, it's horrible. I can't like him. I bet I just haven't run enough for track, and now I can't think straight."

"That's the worst, bullshit explanation I've ever heard,"

"You're my best friend. You're supposed to agree with me on this."

"Well, I don't agree. And as you can see, I'm not in jail. So clearly, I don't have to agree with you."

"This sucks. By the way, I'm also pretty sure Ashton has a sister he's not telling me about."

"Everybody has secrets." She paused. "Sorry, I heard that in a movie."

"Not helping," I cried.

"Sorry. Wait, what's your problem again?"

I scowled. "I need to stop liking him."

"Sorry, Ari, but that's not gonna happen. I bet he likes you and that's why you're panicking. You're afraid to date the guy."

"Unfortunately, you're theories are flawed. And he doesn't do relationships, remember?"

Flora tossed a Skittle into her mouth. "Maybe he'll change." I glared at her. She tossed her hands up in surrender. "Hey, if you're going to be the pessimist in the room, then I might as well play the optimist role." She crossed her arms over her chest.

In my book, there wasn't anything wrong with being a pessimist.

"Oh, shut up."

She gave me a sly smile. And what she screamed next made me want to lock her in a box and then stomp on it.

"How can I help it? This is really exciting for me. My little Ariel is finally growing up," she began. "Ariel and Ashton sitting in a tree. K I S S I N G. First comes love, and then comes marriage, and then comes the baby in the baby carria—"

"I despise you with a burning passion."

"I'm so right. Gosh, I definitely win the bet with Elliot ... uh ... I mean, there's no bet." Her eyes grew big, and, just like that, the topic was off me.

I wiggled my eyebrows suggestively. "So, is there something going on with you and Elliot?"

1-0 Ariel. Boo yah.

"Oh, of course not. Um, I have no idea how you would think that."

"Liar."

"Why would you accuse me of lying?"

"Because you are."

"I may have gone on one date with Elliot," Flora admitted sheepishly.

"And when did said date occur?"

"The night you went to the carnival. I didn't really want to tell you because you were so busy." She shrank back, almost as if she were preparing for my scolding. I grinned.

"Because you're my best friend," I began. "Flora loves Ellioty Poo. Ellioty Poo loves Flora. Flora and Ellioty Poo sitting a tree. K I S S I N G. First comes love, and then comes marriage, and then comes the baby in the baby carriage."

"Okay, I deserved that," Flora admitted, perching her elbows on her knees.

Our conversation carried on for hours. Flora and I talked about everything. Everything that had happened in these last few months was pretty much life-changing. Never would I have imagined that I would ever get involved with the popular crew or hang out with the jocks or be alone with Ashton.

Flora and I just kept talking. She constantly directed

the topic to Ashton, and when that occurred, I would direct the conversation toward Elliot just to see her cheeks turn light-pink. I could tell how smitten she was with him.

How cute.

I guess he really was able to get to her. That lucky bastard.

However, everything great had to come to an end. I glanced at the clock and saw that it was half past five. When I had arrived, it was eleven a.m. I sighed. I had missed these times with Flora where we could both just let everything out.

No stress.

No pressure.

No Ashton.

But that didn't stop him from popping in my head. *Stop it, Ariel. No.*

"Well, it was fun talking to you and stuffing myself with cookies, but I got to get home. Stella's waiting."

"Do you want a ride?" Flora asked politely. "I know you're regretting not driving here. I don't blame you. You're an idiot to want to walk two miles here."

"No, I'm fine," I said out of pride.

"Last time you can take my offer," she sang.

"I'm good."

"Going once, going twice."

"Thanks, but I actually like walking, unlike someone else." I wouldn't admit it, but the walk home felt so long. *So, so, so far away.*

"Okay, fine. Talk to you soon."

I left her house and began the journey home. Once I reached the one-mile mark, the cemetery was in my view once again, but this time I stopped when something caught my eye. There was a familiar figure hovering over one of the gravestones.

Ashton.

He was on his knees, his back facing me.

I couldn't say I had a right to be there. Gosh, this was a cemetery. I was pretty sure I could get arrested for intruding on him like this. I'd be in the same facility as all the psychopaths and drug dealers.

All it took was a couple of steps and I would've past him and given him his privacy. But no, my legs decided to make a sharp left and then I was standing in the middle of a cemetery.

"Hey, Amelia. I hope you are doing well. Me? I'm coping. I miss you. And, I met a girl, and for once, I really like her. I know you're probably tossing and turning at what I've been doing, but this time she's the real thing. At least, I think. She kind of reminds me of you. I really miss you. When I met her, well, really met her, not just tried to hit on her, I almost swore it was you inside her. She's the sweetest thing ever. Sometimes it feels like you never left, Leah. I know you'd like her."

Ashton dropped onto his hands after he set a bouquet of flowers on the ground. This was a whole new Ashton I was seeing. His voice was uneven and weak, and I almost walked right up and hugged him.

But I was glad he had found someone new. I didn't know who Amelia was, but she had to have been someone important. I couldn't lie. I didn't love the feeling of Ashton falling for another girl, but, seeing him here, I'd have given anything just to get rid of all that hurt.

I needed to get the hell out of there. This was wrong.

I slowly backed up, but leaving wasn't as simple as coming in.

Snap.

Fucking shit. Why do twigs exist again?

He jumped at the sound and flipped around. His eyed bulged out a little, and I wanted to hurl. "Wh-what are you doing here, Ariel?" His words were forced out, laced with embarrassment.

I didn't know what I expected out of it all. Did I want him to see me? Explain himself? He had nothing to explain. I was the one who needed to explain. *See, this is why you can't be impulsive.*

"I'm really sorry. I can't believe I came here. I'm being so rude. Please believe me when I said it's not normally like me to be this awful. I'm sorry. I don't know why I did that. If I did, I would tell you, but it seems that even I can't understand my brain right now, which I totally should be able to, but—" I closed my mouth. God, I was rambling, too. "I should get going now. I apologize again for being so rude. So I will see you in school, yeah? And I'm really sorry." Without hearing his response, I ran.

I ran as fast as I could, but before I could get to the exit, someone caught my wrist and yanked me back.

Oh my gosh, I'm getting kidnapped. I deserve it, too, for what I just did.

I looked up at Ashton, and his eyes were the saddest eyes I had ever seen.

"It's not your fault." Ashton hesitated.

"What?"

Of course it was my fault. My stupid feet walked in on his conversation.

"Amelia."

I wasn't going to ask. No, I had done enough damage already. I also resisted the urge to hug him as hard as

I could because it wasn't appropriate. Me being there wasn't appropriate.

"And I know you probably want to know who Amelia is, so I might as well start from the beginning."

"You don't have to tell me," I interrupted. I just needed to get out of there.

"No, I want to. I really should have told you a while ago, but I liked that you didn't pity me. I'm surprised no one told you."

If he wanted to let it all out, hell, I was going to listen to him. If he wanted to punch me in the face, I'd probably let him, too.

"Are you sure? Just know you really don't have to do this."

When we finally made eye contact, I nearly rumbled. The eyes that were bright and shining just a few days ago, were now filled with pain and tears threatening to spill.

The one thing I noticed was that, through everything he said, he never let the droplets fall. And I really admired his strength in not breaking down.

"Yes."

Ash latched his hand with mine, and a surge of electricity went through me. He pulled me over to the nearest bench and took a seat.

Deep breaths, Ariel. He's only holding your hand. Ashton Walker is holding your freaking hand even though you practically barged in on him.

Slowly, I sat down as well. His hand never left mine, and I didn't pull away.

"We should sit. It's a long story, and if I'm going to say it, I might as well say it all."

"Okay," I replied meekly.

"Amelia's my sister. I mean *was* my sister. Sorry, I don't know when I'll get that right."

With that, I knew that what I was about to listen to was what would change me.

"It happened on my fourteenth birthday. The thing is, before that, I was a completely different person. When I was thirteen, I was the typical eighth-grade boy. I played soccer with my buddies and had a few minor crushes. I wasn't really popular, but I had a good group of friends. Out of all of them, Elliot was by far my best friend. I was a decent guy. I wasn't a heartless asshole back then because there was always an individual who kept me in line. Hard to imagine, right?" He chuckled drily. "Me not being a man whore? I know, I can tell that you probably think I'm a jerk now, but I wasn't always like that. Well, believe it or not, that is one hundred percent true."

"I don't think you're a jerk now," I confessed, and he really seemed surprised. And like the awkward girl I was, I felt my cheeks warm up.

"That's good to know. The person who kept me in line was my sister, Amelia. She was eighteen at the time, about to go to college soon. She was headed to Princeton. Leah was a nerd, but she was also the sweetest person I knew. She was always very shy with most people, unlike me. I didn't think she had one bad bone in her body. Nobody did. Everyone loved her, too. She could never find it in her to hate anyone. She was crazy smart, too. Leah tutored me a lot. My parents were always on business trips together, which left me and Amelia alone except for Roseanne. She was my best friend. I could talk to her about anything, even things I couldn't bear to tell Elliot."

I'm pretty sure he wasn't talking to me anymore. It was more like he was speaking to himself. Like he was reliving the memory. A horrible, sad memory.

"Then came the day of my fourteenth birthday. As always, my parents were a no-show, so it was just me and Amelia for the night. I never argued, because Amelia was the best. And even if I did argue, it's not like they were coming home anyway. And when my parents were around, we would barely talk. It was like I was invisible unless something was happening with soccer. I guess they had more important things to deal with than me.

"I was kind of happy they didn't come 'cause it would've been really awkward. Since I couldn't drive, Amelia had to go pick up the cake for me. I offered to go with her, but she insisted that I finish decorating the house. I did as she said and stayed behind. When she left, I was probably in one of the cheeriest moods ever.

"But she never came back. It was a fifteen-minute drive to the bakery, and I ended up waiting for an hour. I began to get more and more panicky. Then a phone call came." Ashton hesitated. I squeezed his hand to comfort him, but my small gesture didn't do much. He was in his own world.

"It was a call from the police. They asked for my parents, and when I said they weren't there at the moment, they told me that Amelia had been in an accident. There was a dumb-ass driver who was drugged out of his mind driving ninety miles per hour. He ran a red light just as Leah was driving across the street. He hit her by surprise and sent her car spinning out of control. The car ended up flipping a couple times.

"When the police arrived, it was already too late, or at least that's what they told me. Said she was killed on impact. All because some nut job was high and wasn't being careful. He's in jail, if you're wondering. I think he still has five more years. He had to pay, but what did it matter? We didn't want money to say that he was sorry he killed my sister. I wanted my sister. I still want my sister."

If I had guessed, I would have said he was going to break down right then and there, but he held it in. He was using everything he had to be strong.

"I ran to the scene right away. It only took five minutes, and I don't think I've ever run that fast. I'll never forget it. There was a long, cream cloth covering her body, but I could see little droplets of red bleeding through. I almost ripped it off, but one of the officers stopped me. He gave me a hug and said it was going to be all right. I don't think I've ever cried more than I did that night.

"For so long, I felt like it was my fault. I should've gone with her to pick up my birthday cake, but I didn't. I constantly think about how things would've gone differently if I had been there. Perhaps I could have spotted the drunken driver, and she would be alive today. Everything was miserable. It still is. I'll never forget the last thing she told me before the accident. 'Don't be so sad that I'm making you stay, Ash. It's not like I'm going anywhere. Those decorations better be perfected by the time I come back. Love you!'" Ashton choked out.

I didn't even realize tears were flowing down my cheeks until one dripped onto my hand. It hadn't even happened to me and I was crying as though it had. All I could picture was a fourteen-year-old Ashton being torn apart.

"Roseanne had been picking up the pizza. When she came home, I was already gone. The police had called again, and Roseanne was next to me in an instant. She called my parents.

"They flew home immediately, and the burial was a week later. They seemed to be in a better emotional state than I was. My mom was crying into my dad's shoulder. I think Amelia's death made my parents even more distant. Still, out of everyone, I think I took it the worst. I barely ate for weeks. I never recovered. It was like I was stuck in a depression with no way out. When it was my turn to talk about her during the funeral, I couldn't get a single word out. She was gone, and it was entirely my fault."

"It was not your fault. No one knew that would happen." I threw my arms around him in a tight hug.

Eh, screw it. It's just a hug.

Slowly, his arms wrapped around my waist, and he wedged his face into my neck. It was more of a comforting hug than anything else, but when his breath hit my neck, my stomach churned. After a few minutes of silence, he pulled away, collecting himself.

"Elliot was the only one there for me. He was my only real friend left. I kind of pushed all the other guys away. I even tried to push Elliot away, but he wouldn't let me. The annoying bastard was glued to my side every day. When I went to high school, so many girls seemed to be fascinated by Elliot and me for some reason. I still don't know the reason, but just like that, we were sucked into the world of popularity."

It all made sense. And it was heartbreaking.

I tried my best not to pity him. The last thing he needed was more pity.

"And I never realized how pitiful my life still was until you came along."

My ears had to be cheating me. "W-what? Me?" I crinkled my nose.

"Yep, I know you heard me talking to Amelia back there. I just think you're too oblivious to know that you're the girl I was talking about."

"Me?"

"Uh-huh."

"Why?"

I was the girl he liked.

"There's a bunch of reasons, but I think I'll keep those to myself for now. And I want to apologize for that day at the mall. I wasn't thinking. I was starting to really like you and that scared me, so I tried to get rid of it. Of course, it didn't work because I felt like a complete douche bag for it."

"You were." I said to myself but apparently I had a problem with keeping my thoughts to myself.

"I know, and I'm sorry."

He liked me.

"It's okay," I mumbled.

"You are way too forgiving for your own good." Ashton's finger lightly grazed my cheek. "And I may just be falling for you."

I held my breath. "What?"

I had heard him fine. That was when my pact to not get in a relationship got shredded and burned up.

He rubbed the back of his neck awkwardly. "Oh God, I didn't mean to say that, and I don't want to scare you off but yeah, I kind of really like you."

Before I had the chance to say anything back, his face was centimeters from mine. My breath hitched.

Our lips touched.

And it was completely and utterly intentional.

In other words, Ashton Walker was kissing me. Voluntarily. While being one hundred percent sane. And it would've been a lie if I said I didn't like it. Because I did. I really, really did.

I stood there stiff as tree for a while and then all at once, I threw my arms around his neck and did my best in copying how his lips moved against mine. First kisses were supposed to be awkward and strange. But this didn't feel awkward. Everything just felt ... *right*. And the fact that we were in a cemetery faded away. My fingers weaved their way into his hair as he pulled me closer to him.

I hadn't realized it yet, but that kiss shattered everything I had spent my whole life believing and, because Ashton was there with me, I let it all change.

I couldn't hold back the smile on my face as we kissed. He ran his tongue along the bottom of my lip and my lips parted slightly. My brain couldn't even comprehend what was happening. It was like when his lips were on mine, my brain shut down, which wasn't necessarily a bad thing. Unfortunately, I needed air to survive, and when I had none left, I tore away from him.

"You didn't give me a chance to respond."

"You're gonna have to deal with it because I'm not sorry. Not at all." He flashed me a grin.

"And before you cut me off again, I just wanted to tell you that I kind of really like you, too."

His eyes were unbelievably hypnotizing.

"I knew you would fall for my charms, gorgeous."

I rolled my eyes and scooted back so there was some

space between us. If I hadn't done that, I might've just kissed him again. "Arrogant idiot," I mumbled.

Ashton laughed as he brought me into a tight hug. Then I was right back into him, and I loved it.

"But that's also the best news I've heard all day," he admitted, and the butterflies in my stomach went crazy.

Chapter 13

I never considered myself an exciting person.

Sure, I took college courses, and sure, I liked to run and take photos at night but nothing really made me that way. I had never been traumatized by an accident. I had never been damaged by the death of a loved one. I had never won a lottery for a million dollars. Nothing tragic had ever happened to scar me for life. At the same time, nothing overly wonderful had ever happened to the extent that I could easily recall it as my favorite memory.

Instead, every memory, good or bad, had been sort of blended together in this giant mosh pit of memories. It was all a bit fuzzy.

But as bad as it might sound, I kind of wanted something to remember. Of course, I would never wish death upon anyone in my family, but I just wanted something that made my life a little less ... plain.

Since these thoughts were always minor, I had shoved them to the back of my brain. But when Ashton Walker spilled out his past to me, I realized how different our lives really were. I thought about Columbia. He thought about getting by without his sister. I thought about when constellations would be out. He thought about how his parents barely came home.

So I didn't really know the best way to react when he told me about Amelia. I'd like to assume it was the shock of one person having to experience what sounded like a living hell, all alone.

I felt really lucky that he didn't hate me.

On Monday morning, I woke up three minutes before my alarms started ringing. The last time I had done that was the night before I took my SATs. I had barely slept that night, and it wasn't because I went to bed late. I was under the covers by nine o'clock, but for a good four hours, I tossed and turned. It was to be expected. If I hadn't done well on that test, my future could've been extremely different from what I wanted it to be.

I woke up feeling ready for school, without an ounce of sleepiness. When I left Ashton the night before, my brain was all over the place. I had enough energy to sprint all the way home. And I did exactly that. Stella was waiting for me, and that night we crashed on the couch watching reruns of *The Bachelor*. I can't say I wasn't getting any enjoyment out of her reality TV obsession.

I swiped my iPhone and flipped through Instagram. I had let Flora post all my pictures so it didn't look like I scrambled an account at the last minute. I swiped through my feed but stopped at a photo Ashton had posted the previous night.

It was a picture of the full moon. *It's been a good day.*

I blushed, and he wasn't even intentionally trying to make me all flustered. I was almost positive he was talking about what had happened to us. If he wasn't, then I'd feel extremely awkward. I liked the picture and chucked my phone back on my bed.

I dragged my feet all the way to my closet and grabbed a black sweater and floral-patterned pants and began to get ready. When I checked myself in the mirror and was satisfied with how I looked, I hopped down the stairs.

Aunt Stella was there making her coffee, as always.

"Well, look at you waking up, and I didn't even get to hear the ear-shattering sounds of your alarms." Stella was always in a good mood in the morning. I couldn't understand how, but she was.

"Good morning to you, too." I took an apple from the fridge and rinsed it in the sink.

"What's the occasion?"

"No occasion," I said and began humming.

She looked skeptical. "Yeah, right."

"See you later, Stella." I hugged her and then headed for the door. I grabbed my keys and slung my backpack on my shoulder.

"Bye, Ariel."

In the car, I blasted the radio. No one could hear me singing, and I took the opportunity to sing as loud as I could. I knew singing wasn't my strong suit. I liked to embrace it when Flora was annoying.

I arrived at Lincoln Bay twenty-five minutes early, as always. I never broke the habit of coming to school early. There was never traffic when I tried to park, and I didn't really have to face anyone in the halls because barely anyone was there.

The one strange thing I never questioned was how Ashton was always there when I got to precalculus.

When I asked Elliot, he said he didn't know, either. Apparently Ashton didn't start coming early until I arrived at Lincoln Bay. I guess we both changed.

I hoped I hadn't completely imagined what had happened the night before. That would be a real day-wrecker. In some weird way, thinking about Ashton made me oblivious to my surroundings, and what happened next was just one more thing that proved it.

My face came in contact with the wall. I checked to make sure no one had seen what happened. That was another perk to coming early. I turned left, as I had originally intended to, and stopped at 101B.

He was there.

I wasn't shocked, but a shiver went down my spine.

"Hey you," he said, smiling lazily at me.

"Morning," I crooned.

He got up from his seat and came toward me. He stopped about a foot away.

"You look really pretty today," he said, his minty breath hitting my face.

"Thank you. Uh, where's Mr. Blair?"

A cheeky grin was pulling at his face. "Getting some papers. Which gives me time to …"

He cut himself off and eliminated the space between us. I noticed how he'd pause for the slightest millisecond before he kissed me. And every time, I would stop breathing.

There we were in the middle of an empty classroom tangled with each other. No one ever told me how kissing someone could be like a drug. How once I got a taste, I'd only want more. And the more I got, the more addicted I'd be. How even though I was clearly running out of oxygen, I couldn't force myself to stop kissing him.

And I felt like one of those clichéd high school couples that showed slightly too much PDA. But what was alarming was that I didn't care. I understood why people dated in high school. Just seeing Ashton made my day.

Even though whether we'd be together after I left was undetermined, I couldn't stop myself from wanting to spend every second with him.

"Sorry, I just had to do that," he murmured as he tucked a strand of my hair behind my ear.

I felt the blood rushing to my cheeks. "It's okay with me."

"Good. Because I intend to do that more often."

"O-okay—"

"You're so pretty. I could look at you all day."

Jesus, take the wheel.

"Thanks. Uh, you too." Glad to know I hadn't turned cool in the last five minutes. "I mean, um, I don't know what I mean."

He chuckled. It could've been worse. He could have stopped liking me right there due to my inability to speak proper English.

"Thanks. So how do you feel about us getting milk shakes after school?"

Date. He's asking you on a date. Or it could be a friendly thing, right?

"Milk shakes?"

"Or we can do something else. Ice cream? Burgers?"

"Milk shakes sound great."

He flashed me the smile I couldn't get enough of.

"It's a date, then."

That certainly didn't help the electricity surging through my arms.

"Cool." *What?* "I mean, um, great." *Wait, I already said that.* "Gosh, I don't know what's wrong with me right now. I promise all I've eaten is an apple. I think Stella may be injecting caffeine in my apples—"

"Do you always talk this much?" He cut me off and I was sort of glad, because I didn't know when I'd stop.

"Do you always interrupt people this much?" I stuck my tongue out.

I expected him to say something like I sucked at comebacks, but I was wrong.

"Just you, gorgeous."

"We should, uh, sit down." I ducked under his arm to get to my desk

Then my foot decided to hook itself around one of the legs of the desk.

I braced myself for the face-plant that was to come.

It didn't happen.

And for a fraction of a second, I thought I had developed supernatural powers that let my body lean at a forty-five-degree angle without falling.

Then reality struck, reminding me that supernatural powers didn't exist, and it was Ashton who was holding on to my backpack.

"I can't believe I like a girl who's a klutz," Ashton said, shaking his head.

"Your face is a klutz."

I am just the queen of comebacks today... Not.

"You're so original." He looked at me blankly.

"But you like me, so the joke's on you."

He got ahold of my backpack again and yanked me back into him. "You can say that, but I feel pretty damn good right now."

"'Sup man? Oh, my eyes are burning with the PDA right now."

"Get in there, Walker!"

"Shit. I do owe Flora twenty bucks."

I jumped back so there was a good three feet between me and Ashton and looked toward the door to see Dawson, Elliot, and a boy named Jaxon looking way too smug.

"Calder, did you bet on us with your girlfriend?" Ashton blinked.

"Maybe." Elliot threw his arms in front of him in defense. "Don't hurt me. Ariel, you'll protect me, won't you?"

"What's she going to do, Elliot? Take a picture of me beating you up?" A sly smile spread across Ashton's face.

"Don't be a smart-ass."

"Elliot ..." Mr. Blair walked in with a cup of coffee in one hand and a stack of papers in the other. "I don't have you until third period, right?"

"Yeah, Mr. B." Elliot grinned cheekily at Ashton.

"Therefore you can scatter until then."

"Later."

And Elliot was gone.

Then, at last, I sat down at my desk. Dawson came over and bent down until he was right next to my ear.

"I don't really have anything to say, but this'll piss Ashton off, and, as you know, it is my duty to annoy him," Dawson whispered.

Ashton's eyebrows drew together as Dawson passed him.

"What did he say?"

"He was telling me about how devastated he was

that he didn't win your heart over." I slapped my hand over my heart.

Dawson was cracking up.

"Seriously."

"Dude, she's right. Truth is that I'm in love with you. Ariel was just a decoy," Dawson cried out. Jaxon was just laughing his ass off next to him.

"What did he say?" Ashton whined. I noticed how Mr. Blair had the smallest smile on his face.

"That he wants to win your heart."

"Ashton, we're going to the mall. You coming?" Tara asked right when school ended.

Oh look, another thing Tara had planned that I wasn't invited to.

She hadn't even noticed me, and I was right beside him. Or possibly she had and just didn't want to acknowledge me.

It hadn't really snapped in my brain that a lot of prettier girls, skinnier girls liked Ashton and stopped at nothing to have him. If he had gone with Tara, I wouldn't have been flabbergasted.

She was prettier than me, and I was here for a project and would be gone in three months. But there was a slight churning in my stomach at the thought of him going with Tara.

"Sorry, but I've got plans." Ashton rejected her as though it were the normal thing to do.

"With who?" She watched him suspiciously.

I liked that I was one foot away, and she still hadn't even looked at me.

"Ariel." He glanced at me, flashing a smile.

Then she looked at me. And I regretted complaining about her not seeing me. If an I-want-to-scratch-your-eyes-out look was what she was going for, she was succeeding.

"Hey, Ariel."

Her greeting shouldn't have sounded scary. It was two words. But she made them sound like I had truly done something so bad that I deserved to pay.

"Hi," I chirped. "You're going to the mall?"

"Yep. So, Ashton, another time, then?"

Wow, what meaningful conversations we have, Tara.

"Sure." Ashton didn't seem to see how much Tara wanted me to disintegrate.

"See ya, Ashton." She fluttered her fingers and turned to leave. At the last minute, she stopped herself and turned back around. "Oh right, bye, Ariel."

"Praise Jesus that we have plans. If I told her that I have off-season training again, she might just show up at the gym waiting for me."

Ashton wrapped an arm around the middle of my back and squeezed way too hard.

"You're welcome," I wheezed. "You can repay me by letting me breathe."

He let go, and I let the oxygen fill my lungs.

"If you want to go, you can." I was giving him the ability to walk away now.

He looked at me like he was horrified. "I'd rather make mud pies with you than do anything with Tara."

"You hooked up with her for a reason," I muttered.

"It was a long time ago. And I was deluded by how much I missed Amelia." His eyes drooped a little, but then he shook his head and there was a smile on his face. "Come on. Let's go get those milk shakes."

"Gosh, you weren't meant to hear that ... sorry. Okay, let's go get those milk shakes. Where are we going, anyway?"

"Golden Diner."

"What's that?"

Man, I needed to get out more.

"Only the place with the best milk shakes in town." He began to walk toward the exit, and I followed.

"So do you want me to drive behind you?"

It was times like these that having two cars got awkward.

"Nah, let's go in mine. I'll drop you back here when we're done."

And Ashton always knew how to make it not awkward.

We got to his silver Acura TLX—the only reason I knew the name was that it was engraved on the back—and I opened the car door and got in.

The ride there wasn't very wordy. I didn't know what to say, and Ashton didn't feel the need to fill our silence.

He pulled into Cercis Village where I had bought groceries so many times. Then it snapped. I had driven past the Golden Diner so many times I couldn't count. I was never a big fan of experimenting with restaurants, because, if I didn't like it, then it would've been money wasted.

But, according to Ashton, that was a mistake.

Ashton pulled up into a spot right in front of the diner, and I took a good look at it. The name perfectly represented what it looked like.

Gold.

It was fairly small, one story, and just a bit run-down. It epitomized what a diner in the 1980s would look like. Bright. Flashy.

Other than the strip of blue at the top and the red *Golden Diner* sign painted in bold letters, everything was coated in different shades of gold. Some shades were leaning toward yellow, while others were a shimmery gold.

I unbuckled my seat belt and pushed open the passenger door.

"So what do you think, before we go in?" Ashton's head popped out over the hood of the Acura as he got up.

"Am I supposed to be giving a review?"

"Maybe."

"It's very ..." *How do I put this without making it sound like I'm judging?* "Gold."

I expected for him to roll his blue eyes at me, but instead I heard the roar of his laughter.

"You could say that." He started up the sidewalk, and I hurried after him.

The inside of the diner was exactly what I had imagined a diner would look like. In the back, there was a bracket-shaped bar with red stools. The black and white checkered floors went surprisingly well with the gold booths.

Ashton strode up to a woman standing behind a podium. She was possibly in her midsixties, but the way her grin reached her eyes when she spotted Ashton showed that she was still flourishing with life. She was in a lemon-colored dress that if I had put on, I would have looked like a walking bottle of mustard.

"My Lord, Ashton, I thought you'd never come back." She tucked a strand of her gray hair behind her ear.

"I came in here last month," he said with a chuckle.

"Which isn't often enough." She put her hands on her hips.

I didn't consider myself tall, but I was a couple of inches taller than Adela, which is what was printed on her white name tag. She had to be stretching to reach five feet, so I found it pretty funny that she wasn't the least bit intimidated by Ashton, who was a good foot taller than her.

"You know I can't get that fat for off-season."

"Soccer is turning you into one of those health freaks you see these days. Next time you come, you better not be raving about those kale juices. Things like celery are never meant to be juiced," she scolded.

"I agree with you 100 percent. They're disgusting. Don't worry. We'll get extra whipped cream on our milk shakes today," Ashton replied with a smile.

Then her gaze landed on me. She didn't smile at first, and I felt like I was being tested. She scanned my face and finally broke out in a grin.

"Is this your girlfriend, Ashton?" she asked, raising an eyebrow at him.

Even she made me blush. Come on.

"Uh, no. I'm Ariel. We're … friends," I cut in.

She didn't quite believe me, but she held out a hand for me to shake. "It's wonderful to meet you, Ariel. I'm Adela. I have a feeling Ashton over here is quite enamored with you, because you're the first girl he's brought here."

"Adela!" Ashton protested. "You can't say that."

"I can say whatever I want, darlin'. We're in America."

I was starting to like her more and more every second.

"Of course. Is the booth open?" He shook his head.

"You're very lucky. The couple sitting there left fifteen minutes ago. You can go seat yourselves. I'll be there in a second."

Ashton worked his way through the rather small walkway to a booth in the very back of the diner. He sat right down, and I took the spot right across from him.

"You come here often?" I asked, not realizing that it sounded like a cheesy pickup line.

"When I was younger."

Adela came over with two menus.

"We don't need menus. We'll both get a Chocolate Paradise with extra whipped cream."

She jotted down the order on a small pad. "Coming right up."

"How you do you know I'm not allergic to whipped cream?" I asked curiously once Adela had left.

His face paled. "You're allergic to whipped cream? Crap! Sorry, I'll tell—"

"I'm not allergic. I was just wondering."

He frowned. "I guess it just didn't occur to me."

"So you've never brought another girl here?"

Fun fact: I made myself blush.

"Uh, Adela meant ... well ... nope." It sounded like Adela had exposed his most embarrassing secret.

"Why?" *I need to learn how to close my mouth.*

He shuffled in his seat. "I—"

"Two milk shakes are coming your way," Adela chanted. She placed two tall glasses in front of us.

"Thanks," Ashton said, grabbing his glass.

"Enjoy."

Ashton wasted no time before digging in. It wasn't until he had held the straw in his mouth for a while that I realized that he was avoiding the question. I decided to try the milk shake for myself.

I took a sip, and when I did, my eyes bulged. Damn, it was good. So good. More than good. This was life.

"Good, huh?"

I didn't even look at him. "Amazing."

"Told you," he sang.

"So why haven't you brought any girls here?"

Shut up already, Ariel.

He went to take another gulp, but I grabbed his glass and pulled it toward me. He raked a hand through his perfect combination of messy-and-nicely-done hair.

"Eh … hooking up with someone doesn't necessarily include a date. And uh, Amelia and I used to come here a lot." He blurted out so fast that if I had let my mind trail off in the slightest, I wouldn't've heard him.

Right, because he doesn't do relationships.

"But it's different now." Then he grabbed his milk shake and drank more.

Did he not get brain freezes? Three fourths of the glass was already gone. Then again, I had a little less than half a glass left, so I couldn't talk.

"It is?"

"Yeah."

Soon, there was one last drip of milk shake that I couldn't slurp up no matter what angle I put the straw at. Knowing I had to look really stupid if I kept it going, I gave up.

"What's your plan for the rest of the day?" Ashton sat back on the chair, pushing his empty glass away with a finger.

"Nothing, really. Except for the math homework, but that isn't much." But technically I wasn't required to do that, so I had no plans.

"Can I take you somewhere?"

"You know," I scrunched up my nose. "You should

elaborate, because that sounded a bit too creepy for my liking."

"I want it to be a surprise, but I can assure you that I won't kill you."

"That sounds like something a murderer would say, but okay." I sent a quick text to Stella saying that I wouldn't be home for a bit. "How long is this going to take?"

"I was hoping we could come back here for dinner."

If dinner was half as good as the milk shakes, I'd be gaining five pounds by the end of the month.

"Okay."

There was this ounce of spontaneity that made me say yes to him but not to anyone else. He gave a thumbs-up to Adela and, after a minute, she strolled up with the check.

I patted my pocket and was relieved to find that I had my wallet. "I've got my wallet," I declared as if this were an accomplishment.

Congrats, Ariel, you remembered to bring money. You want a cookie?

"Great. Sucks that I'm not letting you use it today."

My jaw dropped. "Huh?"

"I'm not letting you pay for this." Just as Adela came back over, he threw my twenty back at me, slipped his credit card into the little pocket, and handed it to Adela. She took it with a smile.

"You know, I can pay for my own stuff," I protested.

"I know that you are capable of paying. I'm just not letting you today."

"I'll find a way to pay you back," I grumbled.

"Have fun with that, gorgeous. Now, let's get going."

He placed two hands on the table and pushed himself up, bumping straight into Adela.

"I better see you here more often," she said, handing him his credit card. Ashton put it back in his wallet. "And bring Ariel. I like her."

"We're coming for dinner, actually," Ashton said proudly.

"I'm expecting you, then. And Ariel, it's great to see that Ashton is back. I don't know what you're doing, but keep doing it."

"Adela, I'm standing right here."

"Hush up, and get out of here. I'll see you at dinner." She waved her hand at Ashton.

"Bye, Adela," I called as Ashton pulled me toward the door.

"Bye, dear."

"You know, Ash, I quite like her."

"Not surprised," he mumbled as he searched his pockets for his car keys.

"So, where are we going?" I asked as I pulled the seat belt across my chest.

"Not telling."

"Can I guess?"

"Sure," he replied as he pulled out of the parking lot.

"If I get it, will you tell me?"

"Nope."

He was smirking.

"Are we going to the … zoo?"

His face went blank. "Why would we go to the zoo?"

"Just wondering,"

"Isn't it closed?"

"I thought they're open all year round."

The corner of his mouth twitched. "This is why I like you."

Then my cheeks got warm. *Shocker.* "So, are we going to the movie theater?"

"I don't know."

Okay, he was going to be that person.

"Ice skating?"

"Don't know."

"Park?"

"Not sure."

"Grocery store?" I asked exasperatedly.

"I can happily tell you no on that one."

I kept an eye out the window as we passed all the different places we could go.

"I give up," I said, sighing dramatically.

"Good, because we're here." Ashton turned right into a run-down bowling alley.

"*Martin's Bowling Alley and Arcade*?" I read out loud.

"Yup," Ashton said as he shut off the engine.

"We're bowling?"

"No, we're going to the arcade." He released his seat belt.

"Why?" *Of all the places, why an arcade?*

He raised an eyebrow. "Why not?"

God, that sounded really rude. "No I don't mean it in a bad way, I'm completely open to going into an arcade. I was just wondering why this one?"

"I know, and I'm not really sure why I brought you here, either. I haven't come in ages. Since Amelia's accident, actually."

Then I got it. He was taking me on a little tour of

his past. He was opening himself up to me. And I felt honored to be the one who got to see all this.

My hand hovered right above his. He flipped his hand and linked our fingers together.

"Then we better get in there, shouldn't we? I don't know about you, but I'm ready to smoke your ass at ski ball."

Chapter 14

There were a couple of reasons why I chose to join track, one of which was the fact that I didn't really need any athletic skill or strategy to pick it up. I just had to run.

Plus, running was what every person learned to do since we could walk. All I had to tell myself during track was to move my legs really fast and just keep going.

And it was individual. It wasn't like I had to run with someone. If I wanted, I could just plug my headphones in and drown out the rest of the world.

Which is exactly what I did.

It was also a bonus that it helped my application for Columbia.

I never had to worry about waking up and just not being able to run as fast. That is, unless I broke my leg.

It wasn't like soccer, where a player really had to spend a lot of time with people working on endurance, teamwork, and so much more I could never see myself even attempting. I had a lot of respect for people who spent so much of their time on a sport and never gave up.

Sure, I didn't spend my time watching all these professionals play the sport they loved. In fact, I didn't take much interest in a lot of sports, but that didn't mean I didn't respect them for what they did.

Perhaps that was one reason why I began to like Ashton. When I first met him, he was the cockiest guy I had ever spoken to, but when he talked about soccer, something changed. I could see in his eyes how much the guy loved it. I didn't know how good he really was at it, but I could tell he always gave 110 percent, even though I had never seen him play.

He never boasted about how good he was—not to me, at least. He never gave himself props. He only talked about soccer when I asked him about it, and I saw a real athlete in him. One that didn't need to talk to everyone about his sport twenty-four seven. But if someone were to ask, he'd show nothing but love for what he did.

This was one reason why when soccer season started I wanted to go to one of the games. Another being my sheer curiosity about whether Ashton was really good or not.

We were on the couch at my house "studying" for the precalculus test I wouldn't be taking. He didn't know that. *He should by now*, my conscience echoed. It was the first time of many that my conscience would tell me to come clean.

I didn't listen.

Ashton typed something into his phone and then set it down. "So, gorgeous, the first soccer game is tomorrow, and Elliot wanted us to go out to dinner with him and his girlfriend after. That is, if you go to the game, which

I really want you to, but you don't have to," Ashton said as he put aside the binder he had on his lap.

"Flora?" I wondered, way too excitedly.

"I think that's her name. Yeah, she goes to that private school, Easton High."

I had mixed emotions. First, I was excited because I liked the idea of seeing Ashton play soccer. Then I was a bit angry that I hadn't really spoken to Flora about how she was doing. But, given what Ashton had said, I'd assume that she and Elliot were doing just fine.

He should've known that she was my best friend. But the horrible part of me didn't let me tell him.

"I'd love to. What time's the game?" I remembered Erika saying something about it, but I never seemed truly to catch on to what she said.

"Five. So it'll end at like six thirtyish. We can grab a bite with them after."

"Kay." Seeing Flora and Elliot did sound pretty awesome.

"One more thing." He tugged on the string of his hoodie. "Will you wear my jersey tomorrow?"

"Huh?"

"Will you wear my jersey at school tomorrow?"

"Don't you need it for the game?" I was pretty sure he didn't need my sweat in his jersey right before a game.

"You can just give it to me after school. I have to stay after, but I'll see you at five."

"Um, okay." I felt a jolt of electricity in my bones.

He unzipped his backpack to reveal his jersey scrunched in a ball.

I shook it to reveal a number seventeen. It had to be a coincidence that seventeen was my lucky number. It had to be.

"It's clean," Ashton reassured me.

"Did you carry this around all day?"

"Maybe," he said, his cheeks turning a faint rosy color.

The next day, I slipped on his jersey, and to say it was slightly big would have been an understatement. When I put on dark skinny jeans, it looked like I was wearing a dress with leggings.

At school, everyone stared. By everyone I meant most of the girls, especially Tara. Most of them held in their anger and had a fake smile, but she didn't hold back at all.

"So are you and Ashton a thing?" she spat out at lunch.

"I'm not quite sure."

After that, Erika came over, and I had never been so grateful for her existence. Ashton went to practice, and I drove home and texted Flora that I'd meet her there at five.

And after a six-mile run, I had a good amount of time to get ready. How was I even supposed to prepare for a soccer game? Did I wear cleats? *No, that's stupid.*

Eventually, I settled on some jeans and a random top. I was wearing a jacket and anyway, it was cold as hell, which gave me even more respect for the guys who were being forced to wear shorts. I prayed that they wouldn't get hypothermia.

Okay, maybe I was being a little over-the-top.

But that didn't stop me from turning on the heaters on the ride there.

To say it was hectic wouldn't fully capture how crazy the soccer game was. Originally, I only thought football games got this chaotic. But man, there were more students here than the entirety of Easton High.

I was just staring in awe at the crowd when my phone vibrated in my pocket.

Flora: *I see you.*

Me: *That's not disturbing at all.*

Flora: *Look to your left. We're in the middle.*

I did as she said and indeed, in the massive sea of students, Flora was waving her arms in the air frantically. I jogged up the steps and tried my best to take up as little space as possible when I passed people. But unfortunately, I didn't have the power to shrink myself so instead, I looked like a moron who was hunched over.

"Ariel," Flora cooed. "I heard you wore Ashton's jersey today. Something you're not telling me?"

"Is that what you're starting with? No hello? No I miss you at school?" I think I really needed to see a doctor because never had I blushed so much in such a small amount of time.

"I said your name."

"You know what? I don't want to answer your question." I turned toward Elliot. "Elliot, I'm sorry you have to deal with her full-time now."

"I know, right. She's such a pain." He made his voice grow ten octaves higher.

"You guys both suck," Flora shrieked but because the stadium was so noisy, it sounded like we were all having a civilized conversation.

"Sorry, Flora, that was my alter ego, Ellie. You can't blame her for being jealous."

"Glad to know you're a happy couple," I snickered.

Flora pursed her lips. "I could say so many things about Ashton right now, but I choose to be the better friend."

"So Elliot, who do you think will win?"

He looked at me as if I was crazy. "Lincoln Bay ... duh."

"Just wondering," I mumbled. It was a reasonable question.

"It's obvious. We've got Ashton."

I glanced at Flora. "What about him?"

"He didn't tell you?"

"Tell me what?" Was there some huge secret I was missing?

"Ariel, he's the best striker in the county. Top five in the state. He's scored 101 goals with two seasons left. As long as he keeps on an upward trend, he'll be the best in the state."

"Oh."

That answered my question about whether or not he was good at soccer.

"All the freshman soccer guys have him on a pedestal, but it's the one thing he's never arrogant about."

"Damn! I knew about it and it still sounds so crazy." Flora whistled.

"Just watch. You'll see. It also helps that the school we're against is shit."

I could hear the smirk behind his voice. Ashton was amazingly humble about it. I'd constantly be rubbing it in Flora's face if I was top five in the state of Maryland.

Elliot was right. The opposing team *was* shit. Even a girl like me who knew absolutely nothing about soccer saw how bad they were. I couldn't really see Ashton's face, since he was so far away, but my eyes were trained on number seventeen.

I thought I could run fast, but I couldn't even compare to how quick Ashton was. And he had a soccer ball.

Any time he had the ball, he was a good five yards in front of the guy chasing him.

The one time I had accidently flipped to the soccer channel, I remember the guys being so close together and battling for a ball. This seemed like a breeze for Ashton.

The atmosphere was crazier than the actual game. Everyone was yelling and screaming. The school spirit was ten times better than at Easton.

We won. Eight to one. And Ashton scored six of the goals.

How? I couldn't even try to explain it. I blinked and then the crowd would go wild. I'd poke Flora, and she'd tell me that he had scored.

All I could really say was that I'd hate to be chased by Ashton.

I watched as all his teammates piled onto him. When they got up, I could see the sheer happiness on Ashton's face. And I was so far away.

"Let's go find Ashton and get some food. I'm starving." Flora placed a hand on her forehead dramatically.

"And he thinks I love food too much," I grumbled.

"I'm just saying what you're thinking, Ariel."

We trotted down the steps, Elliot leading the way.

"Elliot, you want to tell us where we're going?" I called out.

The three of us walked out of the stadium toward the parking lot.

"Meeting Ashton."

"Where?"

He pointed to the figure coming toward us.

He was right. There was Ashton. He had changed

into regular clothes, but his hair was slightly damp. He had a bag in his right hand, and even an idiot like me knew that it held his uniform.

Ashton was beaming. Not just smiling, but beaming.

"You see that, gorgeous?" He brought me into a tight squeeze, and I knew that if I opened my eyes, Flora would be smirking.

"That was awesome."

"It was okay," Elliot interrupted.

"Of all the people in the world, I think you boost my ego the most, Calder." Ashton patted his heart. "And you must be the famous Flora. You know, Elliot never stops talking about you. Oh, Ashton, she's so pretty and funny and wow, that smile—"

"Shove it, Walker." Elliot pushed Ashton lightly. "I don't think you want me to talk about all the things you've said about little Ariel over here—"

"Who's hungry? I'm starving," Ashton declared. "We'll meet you at the pizzeria."

Elliot nodded, and he and Flora went to the opposite side of the parking lot.

"Who's driving?" I chirped.

"I'll drive. I want you in the same vehicle as me today."

There were the tingles again.

"Fine by me." But he was already leading me to his silver Acura. "You never told me you were the best in the state," I said once we were both buckled in.

"I'm not."

"Okay, best in the county."

He shrugged. "I just didn't feel like I needed to."

I decided to leave it at that. "So, pizza, huh? How classy."

Truth is, I really was craving some pizza.

"Only the best for you."

It took ten minutes to get to the pizzeria, but it only took ten seconds of thinking about pizza to make me drool.

Once Ashton parked, I practically jumped out of the car, but a hand pulled me back down.

"Oomph, what? Why did you—"

Our lips collided and, for a moment, I completely forgot about the pizza. His kisses were better than pizza and coming from me, that was a huge shock. Our lips moved together, his cold hands traveling under my layers of clothing to rest on my waist. I probably should've been uncomfortable—one, because his hands were actually freezing and two, he was touching my bare waist, but I found myself being perfectly content with it all. Damn, and we weren't even officially a couple.

"I've wanted to do that since school ended." He pressed a feathered kiss to my jawline.

"You can do that again if you want." I heard myself say right before I went beet red.

"You are the cutest." He pecked my lips. "But as much as I want to sit here and kiss you all night, they're waiting."

Fifty-five degrees suddenly felt like one hundred and ten degrees.

"Let's go," I said, my desire for pizza growing again.

"If you'll let me, I promise that isn't our last kiss."

I didn't respond. If I had, there would have been a whole lot of stuttering. Ashton met me at the front of his car and dropped an arm around my neck.

I guess restaurants really liked sticking to a couple of colors. First the diner was gold, and now the pizzeria was a faded red. There were little bits of white and black, but the dominant color was red. Even the waitresses and waiters were in red-collared shirts.

Elliot and Flora had already occupied a booth, so we went straight to them. We slid in, Ashton to my right, while Flora sat across from me. I resisted the urge to kick her under the table because she kept wiggling her perfect eyebrows at us.

"We left at the same time. How did we beat you in here by five minutes?" Elliot tapped the table.

"I don't know. Maybe because I was being a good citizen and driving the speed limit." Ashton picked up a menu.

"Yeah, right. Something tells me you were occupied by someone, not the speed limit."

"Shove—"

"How may I help you?" A high-pitched voice squealed and interrupted the secret stare-down Flora and I were having.

I looked up from the menu and cringed at the girl in front of me. She was clearly in her midtwenties, but that wasn't stopping her from eyeing the two seventeen-year-old boys, who were clearly taken. *Pretty sure that's illegal.*

She had fiery red hair, which matched the generous amount of lipstick she treated herself to. I never knew that outfits like the one she was wearing could be slutty, but she made it possible. The shirt had to be a size smaller than she actually was, and the buttons in the front were undone so that there was a small V. On her left breast, she wore a name tag that read Britt.

Britt … Brit … Brat … Britt. Yep. Name suits her well.

I heard Flora humph as the guys reeled off their order. Once the boys were done, they turned to Flora and me.

"You guys good with this? Allergic to anything? Vegetarian? Vegan?" Elliot asked.

Flora snorted when Elliot said "vegetarian."

"Nope, we're good."

She wouldn't last a week as a vegetarian. To think of it, she wouldn't even last a day as a vegetarian, so being vegan was clearly out of the picture.

When Britt's beady eyes landed on us, her fake smile was replaced with a dirty glare. And it wasn't a subtle glare, either. It was more of a I-hate-you-and-that-boy-will-be-mine stare.

Weren't waitresses supposed to be nice? She was acting like it was our fault that we were with the guys and not her.

Maybe if you weren't wasting the best years of your life serving people at a pizzeria, you'd have a chance. And if you were like six years younger, so it wouldn't be so ... illegal.

I waited for her to walk away and put in our order but she didn't leave. Instead she giggled and twirled her hair at Ashton.

Excuse me? I'm hungry, and we want our pizza.

It was one thing to flirt with someone else's date, but it was another thing to do that while she was hungry. I felt someone squeeze my hand and turned to Ashton. I faked a tight smile, my teeth clenching. I was never a great actress.

"How's it going, sweet thing? If there's anything you need, I'm right here," she squeaked out.

"Sorry, but I'm taken," Ash replied, not amused by the waitress's actions.

"Isn't flirting with taken customers against the rules or something?" I asked innocently. Her eyes turned to slits, and I heard Flora stifle a laugh.

She completely ignored my comment. "You don't know what you're missing. I'll be back with your drinks."

My eyes trailed down to my fingertips, and I twiddled my thumbs—just like I used to at school.

"And I thought I'd end up being the jealous one in the relationship," Ashton whispered in my ear, a playful glint in his eyes.

"I'm not jealous," I snapped.

"You are."

"Am not."

"You're jealous."

"Shut up."

"I'm going to head to the bathroom," Flora announced, breaking the silence.

I glanced up at her to see her giving me a look telling me to come as well. Stealthily, I nodded my head slightly, letting her know that I had understood her message.

Elliot watched her, concerned. She was even more fired up than I was.

After a few seconds, I spoke up. "I have to go to the restroom as well." I said quietly, letting go of Ashton's hand and standing up.

Once I entered the washroom, I found Flora fixing her hair in the mirror. Luckily, the ladies' room was empty. When Flora saw my reflection from the mirror, she spun around, an unreadable look on her face.

"What kind of sick woman flirts with guys who are clearly taken? I mean, she just completely ignored us. Not to mention how slutty she was acting. I'm pretty sure her boobs aren't proportional to her body." Flora ranted, pacing around slightly.

"She's desperate," I mumbled.

"You showed her. I like what Ashton's done to you. Now I can confirm that you're not a robot. Anyway, oh, my goodness gracious, Ari, I like that we're not bingeing on movies together." Flora's mood lightened up a bit, and she flung her arms around me.

"I know. It's so great to see you when we're not being fat asses and eating pizza on the couch."

"Instead, we're eating pizza in a restaurant."

"It's an improvement."

"And now you have a boyfriend."

"Not official." To be honest, Ashton could be with anyone. He wasn't tied down to me.

"He said he's taken."

"He was saving himself from a girl who doesn't know how to put lipstick on."

"That's not the only reason. And I forgive you for not telling me about your first kiss." It was as though her anger had been packed in a bubble and floated away.

"You don't know that I've already had my first kiss."

She crossed her arms. "If you're trying to say that you haven't had your first kiss, you can stop, because I know that's bullshit."

"You're so nice to me, I can't even comprehend it sometimes." I scowled but replaced it with a grin in a second.

"Anyway, you've got nothing to worry about. Anyone from a mile away can see how much he adores you."

"I could say the same about Elliot."

"I like to think of that as a good thing, so thanks, I guess?"

"I really wanted to take a picture of his face when you left." I stifled a laugh.

"Oh, he'll be fine. It's not like I'm mad at him."

"That's not what he thinks. I'm pretty sure he's sweating a well out there."

"What fun would it be if I don't make him sweat once in a while?"

I scoffed. "Why not take it a notch further and start a small fight just so you can have make-up sex?"

"Are you inferring that we've already had sex?"

"Oh, I'm sorry. Do you prefer the term 'make love' instead?"

She gasped. "How could you take me for that kind of girl? I thought we were best friends. For your information, your idea never crossed my mind. You know, you're so much more manipulative than when I last saw you."

"Everything I've learned is from you."

"I never said it was a bad thing."

I just shook my head. "I pity that boy."

She mocked shock and punched me right in the stomach. I winced. "Hey, bitch, you're supposed to be on my side."

"Sorry not sorry,"

"But seriously, I think I like Ashton. You've got my approval." She patted my head.

"Gee, thanks."

"This is exciting. And who knows? You might end up falling in love with this guy."

Love.

Four letters, but arguably the most meaningful on the planet.

And it scared the shit out of me, knowing that it was a possibility.

"Can you please stop saying that? Let's get back. I'm starving, and I don't like that the guys are probably eating all the food." I held the door open for Flora, motioning for her to go.

"Yeah, let's go. I bet you can't stand to be away from Ashton."

"You want to know something?" I whispered so she would lean in.

"What?"

"Sometimes I wish I could run you over with a bus."

"Aw, you wouldn't do that. Jail is a place that I could never see you associating yourself with." Flora reached up and pinched my cheeks, and I slapped her hands away.

The rest of the night went quite well. By that I mean that I got to stuff my face with pizza, and I didn't have to feel self-conscious because Flora was doing it with me. And I completely zoned out whenever Britt decided to grace us with her presence.

But before I knew it, we were saying out good-byes.

"Stay safe and use protection, kids," Flora whispered in my ear.

"I think you'll need that advice more than I do," I whispered right back, and she cracked a smile.

"See you later, Ariel." Elliot ruffled my hair.

"The two of you are too mean to me today."

I walked back to Ashton's side, and he finished saying his farewells.

"Shall we go?" he asked, taking my hand in his.

"We shall," I replied, waving one last time to Flora, who was already getting pulled away by Elliot. We got into his car, and I felt like I was having a food baby.

"You know," Ashton began, once we were on the road. "You don't have to be jealous. You're way hotter than that girl."

"I told you I wasn't jealous."

"You're a shit liar, you know that?"

"We are done with this conversation."

"Of course, Miss Winters," he chanted like a second grader replying to his teacher.

I didn't say anything as I interlocked my fingers with the hand that Ashton left limp on his right thigh. His eyes flickered to mine for a second before returning to the road in front of him.

"You are too cute."

I blushed, ripping my hand out of his, but his grip tightened, and my attempt to pull away failed. I tried to shove his arm off, but it didn't work. Eventually, I just gave up trying and relaxed in my seat.

The ride home was rather relaxing, and I didn't remember that my car was still at school until Ashton was parked in front of my house.

"Crap, my car's still at school." I slapped my forehead.

"I guess that just means I'll have to come over tomorrow," Ashton said, wiping away a pretend tear.

"Did you do that on purpose?"

"Yes," he exhaled. "I brainwashed you with pizza just so I could see you tomorrow."

"I knew it tasted weird."

"Maybe it's because you forgot to chew it."

"On that note, I should go now." I put one foot on the gravel but then my weight was yanked back, and my butt hit the seat with a soft thud.

"Aren't you forgetting something?"

My hand felt the pocket of my shorts, making sure I

had my phone and wallet. When I found that they were still there, I looked back at Ash, confused.

"No?"

"I want my good-night kiss, gorgeous." Ashton smirked in a "duh" voice.

I got hot in seconds. I quickly pecked him on the cheek so he wouldn't see my blush. I started to get out of the car, but once again I was pulled back, and Ashton slammed his lips to mine. Automatically, my arms went around his neck, tangling in his hair while his hands had a firm grip on my waist.

His eyes were closed so he couldn't see my red face.

We both pulled back, Ash's forehead leaning against mine. Our breathing was heavy but I certainly didn't mind. When I finally caught my breath, I smiled and pulled open the car door.

"That's more like it."

"Good night, Ashton," I said in a daze.

"Good night, princess."

Chapter 15

I was never a girl who thought dating at a young age was a good idea.

Relationships in high school were practically a setup for disasters because, by the end of senior year, it would be time to say good-bye. And if there wouldn't be a good-bye, there would be a complicated long-distance relationship. Rarely would they last, and I gave props to the ones that did.

For example, my parents.

But for those that didn't make it, the aftermath of the breakup would suck. So all that time in high school used for hanging out would end up worthless.

Flora never really got why I didn't believe in relationships. I didn't exactly have a single reason for it. I had never been heartbroken or exposed to someone who was ruined. I didn't have an explanation, but some things were like that.

I just never liked the idea of relying on someone. I was perfectly capable of getting on with my life without a guy. And if I really wanted the company of a guy, I'd do it once I had a successful job. A relationship wasn't essential to a happy life.

I didn't need a guy to help me do what I was perfectly capable of doing on my own.

I never considered myself a hypocrite—until I went to Lincoln Bay, that is. Then again, at Easton I had never fallen head over heels for a boy that I shouldn't have associated with in the first place.

Time flew by and, before I knew it, it was mid-March. *Two and a half months left.*

Were we in a relationship?

I don't know.

Did I want to be?

Well, uh, I don't, um … yes.

"Right hand, red." Ashton called out.

"Why the hell did I let you talk me into this?" I cried as I slowly placed my right hand on the only red circle available, which brought me right under his body.

We were in the middle of a painful game of Twister at his house. Was this a good idea? Probably not.

He smiled cheekily. "So I could do this."

Then he did the unthinkable.

He relaxed his body and collapsed over me. His chest hit my boobs, and for a second I thought they had popped. My ass hit the ground with a hard clunk, and I could already imagine the unexplainable bruise I'd get there.

Guess who isn't planning on swimming for the next month?

This girl.

"Ow! Could you at least try to be a little nicer to the well-being of my boobs?" I howled.

Suddenly, at least half the weight of him was lifted off my body. It was then that I realized he had propped himself on his forearms.

Man, he must have had a lot of muscle.

This is not what you should be thinking about right now.

"Crap! Sorry, that went a lot smoother in my head."

He didn't move.

"You think?"

And I wasn't quite sure whether I wanted him to stay right where he was or get off.

"Sorry."

"Did we really have to go through fifteen minutes of this game just so you could plop on me?" My throbbing butt completely took away from the fact that we were lying on the carpet, and he was on top of me.

"I think I won, by the way."

"What?" I frowned. "You fell on me."

"But your body hit the ground first."

"That's cheating." I pushed at his chest but my arm strength was as great as that of a twig.

And not one of those sturdy, branchlike twigs. It was the type of twig that a six-month-old baby could've broken. Asleep.

"It's called tactics, my dear. You should learn from me."

"Your tactics are going to come back and haunt you when I sneak into your room at night—"

"Why's that bad? Pretty sure that'd be a prize."

"—and dye all your clothes neon yellow," I said a whole lot less audibly.

"And I would rock it with pride."

Was it just me, or did he move so we were only centimeters apart?

193

"So what do you want then, winner?"

"Let's play another game."

"No, we are not playing that again. I'm pretty sure I have a bruise on my butt because of that—"

"Not Twister."

By the look on his face, whatever he had in mind was even worse.

"No board games."

"No. I just made it up. We each ask each other a question, but I am allowed to lie because I'm the winner."

I just looked him in the eyes flatly.

"That's the worst game I've ever heard of," I said after a minute.

I could tell he wasn't expecting that, because his jaw fell.

"You're so rude to me. And for that, we are playing it, and you can go first."

I grunted. This was my chance to ask him anything I wanted.

And I had nothing.

"So, uh, what's your favorite plant?"

It was times like these even I didn't believe that I was smart enough to take college classes.

"What kind of question is that?" Ashton chuckled. "I guess I like Venus flytraps because they're kind of like the beasts of the plant world."

"I bet you're lying."

"If I lied about my favorite plant, that would be kind of sad. What's your favorite flower?"

"Pink amaryllises."

"Why?"

"They're gorgeous." *And they represent determination.*

"You're gorgeous."

"Is that your question?"

"No," he said. "Who was your first kiss?"

"Why do you ask?"

"I want to know."

"Do I have to answer that?"

Please say no, please say no, please say no.

"Yes."

"Are we doing anything tonight?" I changed the subject.

He wasn't amused. "Answer the question."

"I don't want to," I said, my voice muffled, avoiding eye contact with him.

"You lost."

"Because you cheated."

"Answer the question."

"What question?" I looked straight at one of the ceiling lights. "Wow, that's a really bright light bulb. Where did you buy—"

"We are not talking about light bulbs. Just answer the question."

"Ashton," I whined, looking into his eyes, a pout forming on my lips.

"Ariel."

I stared into Ash's bottomless eyes, which were never anything less than captivating.

I groaned. "You," I muttered, as fast as I possibly could.

"Say that again," Ashton demanded.

I had a feeling that he had already heard me just fine.

"It was you," I repeated with no confidence.

I tried to stare at the ceiling, but it was pretty hard considering that the lights were blinding me everywhere that wasn't Ashton's face. And I couldn't help but notice that he kind of looked like Jesus with the rays of light emanating from his face.

"You're joking, right?" Ashton deadpanned.

"The ceiling's a pretty color, don't you think?" I pointed upward. Was it douche-y to want to wear sunglasses inside? Yeah, definitely douche-y.

"You have to be lying."

"Um, I'm not allowed to lie, remember?"

Ashton sure knew how to make me uncomfortable.

"You definitely didn't kiss like it was your first time. My first kiss involved bumping heads and a fist pump afterward."

"Thanks?" I could already feel the heat traveling into my cheeks.

"Were all the guys at your school blind?"

If only you knew.

"No."

"I know for a fact that all the guys here want you like crazy."

"No, they don't."

"Yes, they do, and you know it."

"It's not like they ever ask me out."

Thank God, because if they did, I wouldn't know what to do besides pretend there was a UFO in the sky and run.

"I might have something to do with that." Ashton laughed nervously.

"What?"

"I may or may not have made it clear that I liked you on the first day you arrived."

"Is that why most guys didn't even say hi?"

"Maybe," he mumbled.

"Awwww, Ashy-poo, you are so darn cute!" I cooed, pinching his cheeks.

196

He groaned. "Wait, most of the boys? Does that mean some still hit on you?"

"Just a few." I said. "For instance, Dawson."

It wasn't like I had a sign on me that said I had cooties.

"Bastards."

"Awwwwww, is Ashton jealous?"

"I was never jealous," he exclaimed sheepishly.

"Was too."

"Was not."

"You were jealous."

"No, I wasn't."

"Just admit it!"

"I was not jealous!"

"You still are jealous!"

"Was not."

"Yes you we—"

I was cut off when Ashton covered my lips with his, a smirk forming on his lips when I began to kiss back. *Stupid, irresistible, idiot.*

"I was not jealous." Ash whispered breathlessly when we pulled apart.

"Okay," I replied in a daze.

"By the way, you don't know how happy you've made me after hearing that."

"Are you ready yet?" Ashton whined.

"Just a second." I hollered back, checking in the mirror one last time.

It was eight o'clock now. I hadn't planned on doing much, but supposedly, Ashton had this big thing in mind that I couldn't even know about.

We were at my place, since I had to change.

Stella was still working, and it was times like these I felt bad for her. But she always said spreading her love of art kept her going.

Ashton was waiting at the bottom of the steps. He had put on a black and white flannel with navy-blue jeans and a pair of sneakers. The grin on his face was one of those genuine smiles that showed his dimples, and I wasn't going to lie by saying it didn't make me melt.

My arm brushed his as I passed him to grab a pair of shoes. "Where are we going again?"

Maybe he had forgotten that it was supposed to be a surprise.

"Nice try, princess. You're just going to have to wait and see."

Nope, he hadn't forgotten.

I blew on a strand of hair that was tickling my cheek and slipped on a pair on sandals. Ashton said it wasn't formal, so I settled on a pair of high-waisted, black denim shorts paired with a cream blouse.

"If you kidnap me, I will escape and sue you," I warned in the most threatening voice I could muster, which, frankly, wasn't very intimidating.

I was like a baby hamster trying to warn a snake not to eat her.

"You're going to sue me?" Ashton wondered, a smirk tugging on his lips.

"Yes."

"I'd like to see you try." He laughed.

"Oh, I would. Suing someone is on my bucket list."

"Well, sorry to burst your bubble, but I'm not kidnapping you, gorgeous. So unfortunately, you're bucket list will remain incomplete," Ashton assured me.

He sauntered in my direction, grabbing the keys to his car, and holding out his hand to me. I didn't notice that he had his hand out, so I just stared at him blankly. His blue orbs traveled from my eyes to my hand, motioning for me to take his hand. Once I noticed his hand, I took it sheepishly, face-palming for being so oblivious.

Again, Professor of subtlety over here. Bow down.

Ash chortled as he tugged me by the hand out the door. I was met by a light breeze as well as the full moon shining. The stars were scattered, each shining at a different degree. The night was there in all its natural beauty, and it was truly magnificent.

So magnificent that my hand twitched for my camera.

I fastened my seat belt, only to feel a hand place a piece of cloth over my eyes. I frowned, flinging out my arms for defense and smacking a hard surface. It was later that I realized I had hit Ash in the chest.

"Ow!"

"What the hell is going on? This is the start of a horror movie."

"I'm sorry, but I don't want any surprises until we get there."

"What's on my eyes?" I tugged on the fabric, but Ashton—at least I hoped it was Ashton—swatted my hand away.

"A bandana." He said it as though it was obvious.

"Where did you get this said bandana?"

"My pocket."

"Gee, thanks."

I heard the car engine and then we were moving. I sat back, getting comfy in my seat.

"Are we there yet?"

I had been bugging Ash for the past five minutes. I felt

like it was rather appropriate, as I was being blindfolded against my will.

"No," Ashton groaned, undoubtedly peeved.

"What about now?" I asked innocently.

"No."

"Now?"

"No."

"What about now?"

"No. Now stop asking me questions."

"I'll stop when you tell me. Are we there yet?"

"No."

"What about now?"

"We're here. Thank the Lord. You can take that Goddamn blindfold off. Remind me to never surprise you ever again," Ashton grumbled grumpily.

Indeed, we had stopped moving. I pushed my blindfold up so one eye could peek out.

A grin spread on my face when I realized we were at the same carnival Ashton had taken me to in January. The only difference was that the decorations were no longer set to be a Winter Wonderland theme but a spring theme.

The white and blue lights had been replaced with pink and green lights. The sign at the entrance was no longer painted white with black script but yellow with purple cursive letters. And it certainly wasn't as cold as it had been in January. I never knew carnivals changed their decor.

If I were to explain spring, this carnival would be the essence of it all.

"Does this place ring a bell?" Ashton asked, as if he thought I had forgotten.

Of course I hadn't forgotten. *It's almost impossible to forget.*

"Of course I remember."

I could see Ashton's leg trembling in a way that mine would if I were about to take a nerve-wracking exam. "Well, care to take a trip down memory lane? Well, the good memories, that is."

"That sounds wonderful." I stepped out of the car, breathing in the familiar scent of corn dogs and cotton candy.

Ashton walked up beside me, locking his fingers with mine. The familiar warmth from his hand surged through mine, which put me in an even better mood than before. He squeezed my hand gently before hauling me to the entrance.

This time he didn't pay, and the ticket person didn't stop him.

The familiar tune of the carnival played through speakers located all around the fair grounds. But for some reason, there weren't many people around. Most of them were volunteer staff who nodded toward Ashton as we walked by.

"Remember when we went to this booth?" He stopped right in front of that same booth he had played ages ago. "And I quote, 'You'll never win that, Ashton.'" He mocked me in a high-pitched voice.

"I don't sound like that."

"Yes, you do," Ashton insisted in a high-pitched voice.

I thought he was going to play the game again, but instead he pulled me away from the stand. We stopped in front of the Ferris wheel, which was shockingly empty. The man controlling the machine smiled when he saw Ashton.

"So this is the lucky lady, Ashton?" The man's voice came out rugged as he grinned a toothy smile.

Ashton nodded sheepishly. I could have sworn I saw a blush creeping on Ashton's cheeks that wasn't from the moonlight.

"Well, go on up and take your time." The man motioned toward one of seats.

"Thanks, Nat."

When we were all buckled into one of the seats, Ash gave Nat a thumbs-up, and he returned the gesture. With one click of a button, the Ferris wheel began to move slowly.

"You know I still remember everything from that day. I remember how I took you here after I was a complete douche, but you forgave me."

My mind flashed to him sticking his tongue down a girl's throat.

Not the best memory I've ever had.

"But you were weird, too. You almost hooked up with two of my friends." His smile dimmed a little.

"Sorry about that."

"Don't be. I was the idiot who initiated it. You just made me see that if I didn't stop being an idiot, I'd lose the girl who actually means something to me."

A tinge of guilt ran down my spine as I remembered that I still had a secret that'd he didn't know. But I still wasn't exactly sure why I didn't just tell him. I didn't lie that much, so lying couldn't be a reason he'd hate me.

Just tell him.

I can't.

You mean you won't.

"After that carnival, I couldn't get you out of my mind. You reminded me of Amelia. You still do. And before you think I'm friend-zoning you by saying you're like my sister, I mean that I'm as happy as I was when

Amelia was alive, which hasn't been that way for a long time. And I just can't stop myself from falling for you." There was a weak smile on Ashton's lips that was gradually growing.

"Glad you don't see me as your sister, because that'd be really awkward." I grinned.

"It's strange because even when I'm sad, you make me smile." He continued, "When you were talking about Spiderman, I recall you saying that Andrew Garfield is the epitome of perfection."

Vaguely, I remembered telling him that.

"I'm not perfect. Hell, I'm far from it. I'm going to screw up, I'll tell you that. I already know. I wasn't bitten by a radioactive spider, either, but if you let me, I'll give everything I have to try and be your real life Spiderman. I know, I know, too cheesy, but I can't help it around you. I guess what I'm trying to ask is Ariella, will you be mine?"

My breath hitched. My stomach did flips. I was pretty sure the smile on my face couldn't get any bigger even if I tried.

I didn't care if I was a hypocrite.

I didn't notice that I had been quiet for a minute until I noticed the growing worry on Ashton's face. I was savoring the moment, but I guess that wasn't what Ashton was doing. *Oops.*

"I—yes."

With that, I grabbed his face in my hands, and smashed my lips onto his and kissed the life out of him. I had the right to do that now. Or at least I hoped I did, because this felt pretty damn good.

Chapter 16

omecoming was never something that snagged my interest.

It was the idea of a bunch of high school students dressing up and coming to school at night to dance. That's right, dance. I never saw the point. I could dance at home. I couldn't understand why people thought it was fun or why people went. It sounded like a big waste of a night.

So even I was surprised when I was the one who brought the topic up with Ashton.

Easton High's homecoming had already happened a month ago, and to me, it was just an ordinary day. Well, as ordinary as my life could be at the time.

I could tell that Lincoln Bay's homecoming was coming soon because it was always the month when guys made the most creative posters to ask their girlfriends to the dance. I always had to admit that the amount of time they spent on perfecting it showed. I marveled at how straightly drawn or painted they were.

Ashton and I were at his place—something about studying, but I wasn't the person to study at the moment. Most of my packets were done, I had been getting A's on the monthly tests at Easton, and most of the videos had been watched.

"What'd you get for number seven?" Ashton scribbled on his precalculus worksheet.

"Thirty-five point four." I punched numbers into my calculator.

If I had to name my best subject, it was math. For some reason, I just always found it a breeze. Easton never had a math team. Otherwise, I would've been all over that.

He wrote the number down and then threw his binder a few feet in front of him. "I hate this class. I'm done," He whined. He flopped on his stomach and rolled like he was on fire.

"Is that how you express hatred for something?"

"It feels appropriate to do this now." He stopped on his back, and I couldn't help but see that his shirt had been clumped up, and a bit of his waist was showing.

Why do I even notice these things?

It felt like I was turning into the main character in a romance movie. Next, there'd be a montage of us doing stupid things together like getting ice cream or taking walks in the park. Except, getting ice cream wasn't stupid—it was actually pretty genius.

"At least you're expressing your emotions."

"I admire how that should've been a compliment, but you've managed to make it an insult."

"That's my best talent."

I didn't see that he was slowly inching forward until he was sitting by my side, our knees touching. He took my binder away, and I was about to complain but then he spoke.

"I can think of a billion more fun things to do right now." His fingers gingerly tilted my chin up and then our lips collided to mark the I-don't-know-how-many-th time we kissed.

My legs straightened, and I angled my body so our chests were pressed together. Everything around us faded away, and our lips moved in sync. He ran his tongue across my bottom lip and my lips parted. He pulled my hips so that he was sitting up, and I was straddling his waist.

For the first time in my life, I wanted more.

I found my fingers fidgeting at the hem of his shirt and slowly tugging up. If it weren't for a voice interrupting the silence, I didn't know how carried away I would've gotten. I popped out of Ashton's lap like one of those plastic poppers I'd had in second grade.

"Ashton, are you planning on staying in for dinner? If, so, I need to know so I can start making—oh hey, Ariel. Are you planning on joining us tonight?" Roseanne asked.

Jumpily, I ran my hands through my hair to straighten out any knots that could've formed. I pulled my knees back to my chest and hoped that it was hiding how red I probably looked.

I cleared my throat, and when I felt like I wouldn't stutter, I opened my mouth. "I would love to, but my Aunt Stella is going to be home from work soon, so I better eat with her."

In the edge of my vision, I could almost have sworn that Ashton looked a bit disappointed.

"Of course, dear. Another time, then?" Roseanne leaned against the doorway.

"Definitely,"

"Ashton? Are you staying?"

"Yep," Ashton replied.

"Then I better go get some more groceries unless you want a few pieces of lettuce for dinner." She checked the watch on her left wrist. "I may not be back by the time you leave, so I'll see you soon, Ariel."

"Bye," I waved.

As soon as she left, I turned back to Ashton, unable to form words with my mouth.

"You are actually the prettiest thing when your face is all red."

Okay, I understand my face is red. No need to keep on reminding me about it.

"Uh, thanks."

I was never a person who always played with her hair, because it was always pulled back, but after coming to Lincoln Bay and letting my curls fly free, I couldn't stop. It was a habit I had developed after coming here.

I never knew why people did it before. Technically, I still didn't know why people—including me—did it. It wasn't like my hair had grown thorns in the five minutes that it wasn't whipping me in the face.

I also never knew how hard it was to balance only on my left butt cheek until Ashton's arm wrapped around my shoulder, and I tipped left, my face smacking into his chest.

Ash chuckled, but I didn't find it as funny, though I did have to admit that his shirt was soft—in the least stalker-ish way possible.

It was quiet for a moment, but for some reason I didn't even know, I ended the silence with a ridiculous question. "So, do you—are you planning on going to homecoming?"

I knew it had been a bad thing to ask when he tensed. "No."

I made the mistake of pushing it.

"Why?"

"I don't go to homecoming. Ever." His voice was cold.

"If you don't want to go with me, you don't have to."

"Trust me," he said with such intensity that I couldn't look away from those blue eyes, "if I did go, you'd be the only girl I'd ask to come with me."

And I believed him.

He kept his word.

That was the last he talked about homecoming, but that didn't stop me from idiotically asking about it again over the next two weeks. I didn't know why I cared. I shouldn't've. It was going to be a letdown.

Excluding that day, I had brought up the subject of homecoming twice, and each time we fought because I didn't have the ability to stop talking when I was around him.

Fighting with him made me remember why I didn't do relationships. It reminded me that this could easily go downhill.

But what if it won't? Was what I had begun thinking not too long ago. It was like my brain suddenly couldn't see more than a month into the future because what I should've known would eventually end felt the slightest bit unlikely to happen. And before I knew it, I was accepting Ashton's apology without a single regret in mind.

I figured if Ashton wasn't going to Homecoming, then I had no reason to, but Flora thought otherwise. Something about how he'd eventually change his mind. Even though I wasn't that dense, I listened to her, and we got our dresses. I began to wonder why I really had agreed to get a dress and go.

Right. She had promised me food.

The dreaded day arrived faster than I thought, and, in the blink of an eye, we were in the salon getting our hair done. Part of the "experience."

I didn't consider myself excited to go to homecoming. I suppose I only wanted to go because Ashton would be there.

But was he going to be there?

No.

Did I kind of want to go with him?

Just a little.

Did he want to go with me?

Nope.

"What do you mean that Ashton isn't going? I thought he'd get over it by now," Flora complained. She wasn't looking at me, though, because a stylist was working on her hair.

"How am I supposed to know? I don't even want to go anymore."

"It'll be fun. If you embarrass yourself, then it's like you have a freebie, because you'll be gone in May."

"Or I could just skip, and we can go eat ice cream and pizza?"

"As tempting as it sounds, I'll pass."

"Suit yourself."

"You're going."

When we had finally finished getting our hair done,

there were only a couple of hours before the torture would begin. Pizza and ice cream was sounding better by the second. I did have to admit that Sandra was damn good at what she did. In my brunette locks, she managed to sneak in some skinny braids that were camouflaged into the rest of my hair. At best, I knew how to braid. And not well.

"Thank you so much, Sandra. You've worked miracles. Again."

"No problem, darling. Now go make all those high school boys drool."

I caught up with Flora as we walked out of the store. We wound our way to the exit and piled into my car. We were both heading to my house to get ready. She preferred my home, and I didn't complain.

I shoved the keys into the ignition, starting up the engine. "Do you mind if I drop you off at my place and then head off for a bit? I think I'm going to stop by Ashton's."

"Of course you can. I think I'll survive at your house alone for a while. Besides, there's a chance Stella will be there and then it'll be like you never left."

"Gee, thanks, best friend."

"No problem, best friend," she said with a wink.

I rolled into my driveway, parked the car, and motioned for Flora to get out. "Don't set the house on fire," I warned.

"No promises," She replied with a mischievous smile.

I pulled out of the driveway and made my way toward Ashton's house. When I arrived, I suddenly regretted even thinking about coming, but on impulse, I rang the doorbell.

I heard the sound of the doorbell echo through the

house and then thumps of someone stomping growing louder. When the door creaked open, it revealed a confused Ashton. Not to mention that he looked like a mess. He was dressed in a pair of sweatpants. Only sweatpants. But still, sweatpants. His hair was all ruffled up, like he hadn't even bothered to brush it.

He looked the exact opposite of when we went to get lunch together at noon. In fact, when we went for lunch, he was the bubbly boyfriend I couldn't stop thinking about.

Boyfriend. I still couldn't believe it.

But good Lord, the boy has abs, all right.

The thing that kept me from ogling at the fact that he was shirtless was the dark circles around his slightly reddened eyes. They were signs of crying.

"Ariel? What are you doing here?"

He motioned for me to enter his home but it felt like he was only doing it out of politeness. His fingers laced with mine, leading me to the living room. We sat down on one of the couches, and he turned to look at me.

"Where's Roseanne?" She had to be a least a little concerned about his state.

"She has the day off."

"You sure you're not going to homecoming?"

He let out a sullen sigh before leaning back so he was pressed against the sofa.

"Ariel, I'm not going to the dance tonight. I told you that," he stated simply. "Your hair looks pretty, though."

"Are you just going to be a bum tonight then?" It was like he wanted to be miserable.

"I'm just not going," Ashton snapped defensively.

"Why?" I protested.

"I want to be alone tonight."

211

"Why on earth would you want to be alone?"

"I just do. I told you I am not going to that stupid dance, and that's final." His voice was low and stern.

I shrank back.

"But why are you so—"

"Ariella, I think it would be best if you went home now," he said grimly.

It didn't go unnoticed that he called me Ariella. I was pretty sure he had never called me Ariella before.

"I'm sorry. I just want to—"

"Ariella, please leave." Ashton's voice was getting harder.

"Ashton, please—"

"Ariella, *leave*!" Ashton shrieked. His voice echoed through the house, and my mouth shut.

I cowered, completely unsure of what to do.

"I'm sorry," I whispered before sprinting out of the house. I slammed the door shut, breathing hard. I ran down the driveway, climbed into my black Sedan, and just sat there.

I guess I had a sliver of hope that he'd come outside. I sat there for a good five minutes watching his front door like a hawk.

He didn't come out. Finally I started the car up and drove.

When I reached home, which felt like forever, all I wanted to do was sit in my room and read. Aunt Stella was in the kitchen fixing up something to eat but before she could even notice I was home, I ran upstairs as quietly as possible.

In my room, Flora had laid her makeup out on the floor.

"He's not coming." I sighed. I didn't know why he

212

wasn't, and I felt guilty for not knowing why. Weren't good girlfriends supposed to know what was wrong?

"What's wrong?" She got up and walked over to me.

"Nothing—more than nothing—I don't know. He's not going." I said it like it was.

She placed her hands on her hips. "Well, you're just going to have to hang out with Elliot and me then."

I stared at her, annoyed. "I still have to go?"

"Duh. You've already spent money on your dress and hair. It's a waste if you don't."

"I think I can still return that dress—"

"In your dreams."

I pinched the bridge of my nose. "Let's get this night over with then."

We did our makeup, or she did mine because she said I sucked at it, and then I grabbed my dress and went into another room to change.

I had chosen a light-pink gown, and it was the prettiest dress I had ever seen. The straps as well as a portion of the middle of the gown were embroidered with silver sequins. The dress cut right above my knees, the bottom of the gown laced neatly. On the back, there was more of a revealing area as the dress had a large cut-out diamond, the edges of which were also lined with silver sequins. When I'd spotted the dress, I thought it was a bit too revealing, but Flora absolutely adored it. When I tried it on, I fell in love with it.

I made some final touches to the dress and left to go find Flora. When I entered the room, I spotted Flora fiddling with the bottom of her dress. She looked drop-dead gorgeous.

She had chosen a royal blue strapless dress that cut at midthigh level. Each side of her hip had a bit of cloth cut out, which made the upper part of her gown form a heart shape. The heart shape was covered in royal blue, black, and silver sequins. There was one line of silver sequins under the heart shape, which was the cut between the two halves of the dress.

"You look absolutely amazing." We both gasped at the same time.

Right at that moment, someone knocked on the door and peeked her head in.

"Ariel? When did you get home? Oh my, the two of you look stunning." Aunt Stella gushed. Flora beamed while I blushed.

"I got back not too long ago," I told her.

"I see. My, oh my, Ashton is in for a treat," she cooed.

"Something like that." I waved my hand.

"Well, I just came to tell you girls that I gotta go. My job awaits, but I just wish I could stay and see the look on those boy's faces."

"See you later," Flora and I said at the same time.

Aunt Stella gave us both a thumbs-up and headed out the door.

"Stella's right. If Ashton saw you, he'd be drooling. He's missing out." Flora crossed her arms.

"Yeah, yeah," I said, waving her off.

"I'm serious."

"And I'm serious when I say Elliot is a lucky guy. Unless he hurts you. Then he's a dead guy."

We sat on my bed for a bit until the ring of the doorbell sounded throughout the house. Flora and I got up and went downstairs. I let Flora open the door because the only possible person it could've been was Elliot.

As soon as Elliot laid eyes on her, his mouth gaped.

He stuttered a lot, but the one thing that stayed constant was the smile that played on his lips. He leaned down to give Flora what I thought was just a kiss but turned into a full-fledged make-out.

"Jesus Christ, don't you two have a little mercy to not do that in front of me? And in my own house, too?" I whined, and God help me, they didn't pull away. Flora smiled and tangled her fingers in his hair. "Seriously, my eyes are burning. Flora, come on. I'm telling your mom that you and Elliot were fornicating instead of going to homecoming."

When they finally (emphasis on the *finally*) pulled apart, I was fake gagging.

"That's not a bad idea. What do you say, Flor?" Elliot winked.

"Well, Elliot—"

"That sounds like a conversation that should only be heard between the two of you," I blurted out.

They both laughed. "I'm kidding, even though your suggestion is becoming more appealing by the minute."

Flora rolled her eyes. "Keep on dreaming, Elliot."

"I will. Anyway, Ariel, you look great. Ashton's really missing out. I really thought he wouldn't be a no-show again," Elliot commented.

"Thanks, Elliot. You don't look too bad yourself," I said shyly.

"Ashton's a dumb ass."

"Why isn't he going, anyway?" I tried to ask as casually as possible.

His face fell a bit, and there was a long pause. "Ashton never goes to the dance."

"He's told me that enough times."

"Didn't he tell you about Amelia?"

I nodded.

"And how she passed on his birthday?"

"Yeah, but how does that have to do with anything?"

"Today is Ashton's birthday."

And then it all came together, along with my stupidity.

"What?" I choked out.

"Yeah, today's April 2nd. They always have the dance every year on this day. No one ever celebrates with Ashton because he always wants to be alone. He spends the night on his own, grieving. He doesn't even talk to me. He really does think that it's his fault that Amelia got into that accident so he spends the day making himself miserable."

"But he seemed fine when we had lunch today."

In fact, he seemed great.

"That's only because you were with him. Normally, he never leaves the house. He really does like you. You've managed to make him feel like he did when Amelia was still here. He forgets."

"He's never gone to the dance once? How does he even dodge the number of girls hoping he'll ask?"

"It's not that bad. Everyone catches on that he's hopeless, so they don't even try."

"Doesn't anyone question it?"

"People still respect him."

"But—"

"Ariel," he said softly. "He's still human. He can break."

If I had really done all that to Ashton, then I had to be able to cheer him out of his misery, right? Well, it was worth a try.

Homecoming was lame no matter what, but

compared to Ashton, it was even lamer. There was no point in going, knowing that Ash was at home, grieving over something that wasn't his fault.

I only had one priority tonight: mending Ashton's hurting heart.

Chapter 17

I hadn't bothered to change before I headed to Ashton's house. It had been hard enough to get into the damn dress. I wasn't about to spend ten minutes trying to get a hold of the zipper on my own.

It occurred to me that Ashton was alone for a reason and that me going there might've annoyed him to no end. But I couldn't get his face out of my mind. I hadn't actually seen him cry, but I could tell he had, and it was heart-wrenching.

It also occurred to me that I had forgotten to change my shoes. Heels weren't my number one choice of footwear, especially because I had a tendency to trip and fall around Ashton.

If I do fall, I hope my pain will at least make him smile.

By the time I reached Ashton's place, the moon was the only source of light available, other than my black sedan's headlights. Once I parked and shut the car off, my phone lit up to tell me that it was 7:30 p.m.

I took small steps up the driveway making sure to watch where I was stepping in these bone breakers, a.k.a. heels. *Slow and steady may not be very productive, but as long as I'm not dead, I don't mind.*

The only sound as I walked was the clinking of my shoes on the cement and a light breeze that caused the leaves to rustle against each other. That is, until I heard the clicking of a door, and my head snapped up. I could only make out the small movement of Ashton's front door. *Maybe Roseanne's here.*

Or a robber.

I hope it's Roseanne.

But she has the day off.

I started to walk a little faster toward the house, which created a new annoyance: the tightness of my dress.

My eyes automatically locked back onto the point at the tip of my shoes but before I knew it, my forehead bumped into something firm. It was Roseanne/the robber. I took a step back, embarrassed.

"Oh my goodness, I'm so sorry." I began. "It's just that I wasn't looking, and it's a stupid explanation, I know, but I really am sorry that—"

"Ariel? What're you doing here?"

I was wrong.

It was neither.

It was the boy that I was looking for.

"Well, I was coming to your house to see you, but I guess you're already here." I shifted back and forth.

Ashton must've shifted too because suddenly the moon's rays reflected onto him so that I could see him just a little bit.

Holy mother of all things perfect.

Ashton had on a tux that was similar to Elliot's, but for some reason, a chill went down my spine. He was wearing black dress shoes and his hair had been gelled up a bit, though it was still floppy enough to droop over his forehead.

We need a fire extinguisher over here because no human should ever be allowed to be this hot.

And I should go to jail for even thinking that.

Ashton must've noticed my stupid expression, because he smirked.

My arms, which had been covering my chest, suddenly went limp and swung back and forth at my sides. As they swung, Ashton's mouth dropped open. He blatantly looked me up and down, his eyes drifting down to my black heels and then back up to my face. I was confused why until I remembered that I had a dress on. And very expensive bone breakers, a.k.a. the high heels.

The moon may have given a faded glow, but I could see the flash of color in his cheeks. "Wow. You look beautiful," he breathed.

"I could say the same to you."

"Good thing you didn't, because that's my line." He took a step closer and linked his right hand with my left.

"Oh really?"

"Yeah, and I was planning to find you at the dance to apologize, but you're already here."

"I've made it really convenient then, yeah? And you have nothing to be sorry for. I'm sorry." *Cue the word vomit.* "I didn't know that today was your birthday. None of this was your fault, and I feel absolutely terrible, and I was so inconsiderate, but sometimes I'm just so oblivious to everything, and I promise I'm not like this to everyone. And I'm not as stupid as I look right here.

Aunt Stella has a problem with rambling so I think it's genetics maybe. But she's my aunt so I'm not quite sure—"

"Do you always talk this much?" Ashton beamed his cheeky smile.

And I loved it.

"No." I decided to take a step that could have gone really good or really bad. "Would it be terribly rude to say happy birthday now?"

"Not rude. A little saddening maybe, but I don't mind when it's coming from you."

"Well, that's all I wanted to say, so—"

"Let's go somewhere. There's a place that I've wanted to take you to for ages but I didn't want to scare you off." Ash took my hand in his, and my stomach churned.

"A little bit of spontaneity, I see."

"All part of the package you involuntarily accepted when you agreed to be my girlfriend."

"I like it."

"Good, then. And as much as I want to just stand here and stare at you all night, I think we should get going. It's a bit of a far drive."

And that's all it took for me to turn beet-red.

"Yeah, I guess so."

"Well, that is, if you don't mind skipping homecoming. I understand if tonight is important to you. Most girls find this dance really important, so I get it if you want to go."

"Am I most girls?"

His mouth opened and shut. "No, I didn't mean it that way I just—"

"I didn't want to go to homecoming anyway," I reassured him.

He let the words sink in and then his lips drew upward.

"And that's why I like you so much."

He unlocked his Acura.

"Do I just leave my car here?" I pointed to the car that was parked in front of his house.

"Yeah. I'd rather you sit next to me."

I got into the passenger's seat and put my seatbelt on. I slipped my phone in the cup holder, and Ashton started up the car. As soon as he backed out of the driveway, his right hand locked with mine.

And I prayed to God that my hand wasn't clammy.

There was a comfortable silence that lingered for a good fifteen minutes other than the quiet hum of the songs that were playing on the radio.

Ashton's eyes were focused on the road, never glancing my way. He didn't look very sad, which was probably a good thing. It was hard to believe that the Ashton I was looking at now had appeared so tortured a couple of hours ago.

As fifteen minutes turned into twenty minutes, and twenty minutes turned into thirty minutes, I noticed that we were going into a part of Maryland I had never seen before. The number of trees drastically increased around us as he kept driving. I checked the time on my phone. 8:10. *Oh look, no signal.*

"You're not kidnapping me, right?" I joked, but really, I wasn't completely joking.

Ashton chuckled, shaking his head. "No, gorgeous, I'm not kidnapping you."

"Somehow, I'm not totally convinced." I squeezed his hand a little harder.

"If I kill you, I won't be able to see your pretty smile anymore."

The car ride felt like we were just driving on a giant treadmill. There were very few homes along the road, and the road lamps seemed to get dimmer and then completely vanished from sight. Ashton looked so much calmer as we went along. I, however, wasn't as calm.

I trust him. I trust him. I trust him.

The fact that Ash squeezed my hand lightly about every two minutes made it a bit better. But that didn't stop the endless chatter that was flying out of my mouth.

"You know, I really am sorry. I don't know why, but it's like a can't not be stupid around you, and I may come off as a bit insensitive but—"

"It's cool." Ashton cut me off.

"I should have known something was up, and I honestly didn't think about it, and I was selfish and you know—"

"Ariel—"

"I really hope you don't take this to heart because I'm an oblivious person sometimes, and I think it may be an issue I have, but the doctors haven't said anything about it, so I want to assume it's all okay. I'm not always that inconsiderate, well, most of the time, so I genuinely believe that there's something wrong with me, but the doctors continue to tell me that they're sure I'm fine, but doctors can be wrong, you know—"

"Ariel—"

"I just want you to know that I haven't had much experience with people, and I've had quite a boring life so I don't know very much but—"

"Ariel!"

I jumped when Ashton yelled. I thought he was angry, but when I peeked an eye open, I saw that he was chuckling.

"It's fine. By the way, do you always talk this much?" he asked again.

Was this question going to stick around?

I could've come up with a witty reply, unlike last time, to make him laugh, but I didn't. To be completely honest, I didn't exactly know why I said the thing that I said next. It just came out.

"Only around you."

And just like that, Ashton stepped on the brakes and pulled off to the side of the road. He turned on the emergency flashers, even though the car seemed fine. He turned to me with a smile that reached his eyes.

I couldn't even look at him. Since when did I say things like that? Suddenly, Ashton's fingers slipped underneath my chin, tilting my head up so I stared directly into those mesmerizing blue eyes of his.

"I'm sorry. Jesus, that was really embarrassing. I take it back. Forget I said it. Lord—"

Our lips collided, and I slipped into temporary bliss. His left hand was cupping my cheek while his right was still holding my hand. Luckily, I was sitting so I didn't have to worry about my limbs turning into gelatin.

He ran his tongue against my lower lip and without thinking, my lips parted. His tongue slipped in, coming into contact with mine. Our lips moved against each other slowly but sweetly.

Before, I never understood why people French-kissed, because it sounded like the grossest thing ever, but now it was a whole other story. I couldn't pull away, even though I was sure my lungs were running out of air.

Well, fuck it. If I died, I would know I died while kissing Ashton Walker, and it was heaven. Ashton clearly didn't think the same thing because he pulled away, gasping for air. The warmth in my cheeks turned to boiling hot in seconds.

"What are you doing to me? Sorry, I couldn't not do that and remain sane," Ashton breathed.

"It's okay," was the only thing I could manage.

Ashton pecked my lips once more before turning off the emergency flashers and continuing our drive to nowhere. After that kiss, God help me, my brain went blank, and a warm feeling surged through my entire body. Ashton still held my hand as he drove, and I sat there like an idiot, smiling to myself. I was pretty sure that if Ashton had even glanced at me, he would have thought I was crazy.

When the car came to a halt once again, my eyes widened a bit. We had stopped near a small pond. If I squinted, I could barely make out the outlines of a diminutive building that looked like a cabin. The stars and moon were the only sources of light.

"We're here," Ashton hollered.

"This better be worth the drive," I joked.

"Oh, it is. You just wait. Especially since you're into photography." Ashton got out of the car, and I took his gesture as a sign to get out as well.

As soon as I stepped out, I felt immersed in nature's wonders. The air was fresh, and I breathed it all in. The stars twinkled luminously, each one slightly different than the others. The weather hadn't been too cold, but there was a slight breeze. It seemed like the perfect time of year to come to a place like this.

Ashton popped the trunk and grabbed a blanket. I raised an eyebrow.

"I'm 99.9 percent sure you don't want to sit down and get your dress dirty."

"We're sitting?"

"Or we can stand all night, your pick."

I stared at my toes until I felt a warm touch on my hand, and my mouth twitched into a smile. I looked up at Ash to find him a bit more fidgety than before. I gave his hand a comforting squeeze, and he squeezed back. We walked over to the house like structure. I waited for my eyes to adjust, trying to figure out what the small structure was.

Finally I had a good image of it, and it appeared to be a small, flat-roofed cabin. Clearly, the shack was pretty ancient, and it was easy to tell that no one occupied it. But I liked it. I admired the structure's simplicity. Even though it wasn't a mansion, it was probably pretty cozy. At least, it probably had been when it was suitable for living.

"You know, my parents bought a little cabin less than half a mile away. We never really ended up camping, but during the few times we actually went up to the cabin, Amelia and I came here. She discovered it. We asked someone who was in charge of a lot of the cabins, and they said that they didn't rent it anymore. Said that we could come here all we wanted. After that, sitting on the roof at night became my favorite thing to do, even though I didn't come here a lot." Ashton exhaled. He tugged at my hand, pulling me to a small ladder against the cabin, motioning for me to climb it.

"I'm supposed to climb this?" I asked skeptically.

"I forgot about your current look."

"That might've been something to remember." My eyebrows drew together.

"I'll catch you if you fall," he tried.

"Are you sure it's safe?" It didn't look like the most stable thing I had ever been on.

"Yep. At least I think so."

"You think?"

"Just wait till you see the view."

Eventually, I took off my heels and dropped them on the ground. I shook the rung closest to my hand and stepped on another. Slowly but surely, I crawled onto the roof, which, frankly, wasn't that high up. I was pretty sure Ash saw my underwear, but I knew for a fact that I wasn't about to bring it up. Ashton climbed all the way up after me and set the blanket down in the center of the roof. I took a few steps, a couple of leaves crunching under my bare feet. I hadn't even sat down when he pulled me so close that his lips were right next to my ear.

"By the way, I was totally looking up your dress. Nice ass, by the way."

I shoved him back, and he cracked up. "Asshole."

"I'm your boyfriend, so technically I'm allowed to do that."

"Because that's so logical."

"Come on." He sat down, patting the spot next to him.

I crouched down a lot slower than he had, since my dress was starting to tighten. It was one of those awkward moments when I couldn't just plop down or he would see my underwear … again. It was more of a slow, escalating motion downward.

Ashton must've felt my awkwardness too because he reached out and pulled me right onto his lap. His arms wrapped around my torso, and I gave him a small smile, my cheeks heating up for the tenth time tonight.

"Thanks," I said softly.

"I should be the one thanking you. I mean, I have

a hot girl in my lap right now." He gave a little squeeze around my torso.

"You never stop, do you?"

"It's all in the package, gorgeous. Now, as much as you like staring at my face, you should really consider looking up."

I did as he said and saw possibly one of the most magnificent things I had ever witnessed. It wasn't like home, where I had limited space to look because the trees blocked most of the sky. Here, it was completely open, and it felt like at any second I'd just start floating up into the endless beauty. Okay, there wasn't a constellation that I could detect, but it wasn't needed.

My gaze traveled from the stars to the slight glow of the pond, as I scanned every inch of nature that was visible. The environment had always been an intriguing topic, but this was the first time I had truly witnessed such perfect scenery. I couldn't even imagine what it'd look like at sunrise, when I'd be able to really see everything.

"I wish I'd brought my camera. It's really beautiful out here."

"Not as beautiful as you."

"Cheeeeeeesssyyyyy!" Was the first thing that came to my mind.

Ashton feigned being hurt. "You ruined my moment."

"You got to admit that it was way too sappy."

"But you love it." He tapped my nose.

I said nothing. He was a little too right.

I leaned into Ash, and his arm tightened around my waist. I could have fallen asleep right then and there, but that would have been weird, so I just admired what was above me.

It was times like these that I wished I could just bottle up and keep forever. When everything—as clichéd as it was—just felt right. Nothing was certain, especially with relationships, which made these moments even more extraordinary.

I may have been head over heels for him, but I wasn't picturing a marriage.

It was a million-to-one chance. We were in high school. We were probably interested in different colleges. I would be gone at the end of May.

But even though everything pointed to the fact that we wouldn't last, I really wanted us to. Really, really wanted us to.

I wanted to have him be a part of my future. I wanted for him to be more than just a memory, and it was at that moment that I really started to feel like it would be more than just luck for us—it was a possibility. Maybe even a pretty good possibility.

There was no doubt that things weren't always going to be as great as this, but in times like these, I could easily buy into the lie that everything would be okay.

I didn't recall ever believing that high school relationships lasted.

But being with Ashton had changed that, and I was still figuring out whether that was good or not.

It certainly felt good.

"This is a lot better than homecoming," I said, breaking our perfect little silence.

"I'm not denying that."

"I just wish I'd brought my camera."

I shifted out of his lap and leaned back until my back

hit the blanket. Ashton did the same, positioning his arm so it was right under the back of my neck.

"We can come back. You should see this place in the summer."

Summer.

He'd know by then that I hadn't moved here. That I only got to know him in the beginning for a project. Sure, that had changed, but it probably wasn't something that anyone, not even me, could just be okay with.

Maybe I was wrong. Maybe Ashton wouldn't care, and he'd still take me here in the summer.

I took a deep breath and draped an arm over Ash's torso. The warmth of his body traveled to mine, an involuntary tingle creeping up my spine.

Take in the sunshine while it lasts, because it won't wait for you forever was what Stella always told me whenever she visited. So that's exactly what I did. *Thanks, Stella.*

Chapter 18

I was deep into the land of pizza and cameras when I felt something stroke my stomach. My eyes flew open, but it was a mistake, considering that I was greeted with a blinding ray of sunshine. Not ready for another day to begin, I cringed.

That is, until I realized that the thing that had stroked my stomach was an arm. Ashton's arm.

Our legs were tangled together, my back glued to his chest. We were under what felt like the softest duvet I had ever slept under.

When we finally left what was the prettiest place I had ever been immersed in and arrived back at his place, it was 1:00 a.m. I sent a quick text to Stella that I'd be out for the night. In fact, the only house I really ever stayed at was Flora's, which is why Stella probably didn't question exactly where I was staying. I should've gone home. Staying at a boy's house wasn't something that I just did. I don't exactly remember how our conversation went from driving me home to staying overnight, but it had happened, and here I was in his bed.

Fully clothed, of course.

Except that I wasn't in my dress from last night. Ashton had lent me a huge T-shirt and sweatpants, and I had taken them immediately. Anything to get out of my dress.

My old routine of waking up, eating, and studying was suddenly feeling very dull in comparison to being wrapped in Ashton's arms. As subtly as possible, I turned so that I could face him. When he didn't stir, I took it as a sign that I had succeeded.

Ashton's disheveled hair flopped right over his eyes, and I had to fight the urge to run my hands through it. Then I realized that he didn't have a shirt on.

I mean, the boy was sleeping. How did he still look good?

I suddenly wanted to wake up next to him every morning.

Obviously, that wasn't logical.

We were seventeen, for one.

"I can feel you staring at me, gorgeous," was what escaped his mouth. One side of his mouth tugged up lazily. *Did I mention that his voice is really hot in the morning?*

Since I couldn't escape how hot my cheeks were getting, I burrowed my head into the crazy-soft duvet.

There was no doubt that my hair was a knotted mess and that my breath smelled like moldy cheese. In my opinion, I was saving him.

From my face.

I felt him pull on the comforter, but my death grip on it didn't let him take it all the way off.

All of a sudden, I remembered the emergency toothbrush, toothpaste, and makeup kit Flora made me put in my car, and I was thankful that she had. Facing him with fresh breath would certainly make me feel better than facing him while looking like an ogre.

Before he could see what I was doing, I swung my legs off the bed and was about to get my keys but an arm pulled me back so hard that my back hit the bed with a thud. Rapidly, I grabbed the same piece of fabric that I'd let go of and covered my head.

"I need to go get my toothbrush from my car," I shouted from under the blanket.

His chest vibrated. "English please, gorgeous." Ashton's voice echoed through the material of the blanket.

"I have to brush my teeth! My toothbrush is in the car." I was speaking louder than I had before.

His arm didn't leave my waist, however; instead, he burst into laughter.

"Ha ha. So funny," I grumbled but he was laughing too loudly to hear me.

His grip loosened as he tried to tame his laugh, and I took the opportunity to dash out of his arms, but not without shoving him on his back first.

"Jerk!" I whined and rushed to my dress, which was thrown next to the door. I picked up my keys and sprinted out of the room.

Barefoot, I ran out of the house to retrieve my kit. Once it was safely in my hands, I went back inside. Instead of going upstairs, I just slipped right into the bathroom closest to me and locked the door.

I took a deep breath before looking in the mirror. I let out a silent shriek at what was in front of me. My hair was more of a mane by now. My eyes were puffy from just waking up. I ran my fingers through my hair, hoping to get rid of as many tangles as I could. I splashed some water onto my face until the puffiness went away, and I wet my toothbrush.

When I felt decent-looking, I went back upstairs. I stopped dead in my tracks when I was confronted with Ashton's bare back. Embarrassment flushed over me, and I forced my gaze to the bed. Clutching the kit, I stepped right in front of his mirror and pretended that I had not just ogled at his shirtless state. I began to conceal the awful bags under my eyes.

"I don't think I'd mind having to wake up next to you every day." Ashton spun around and stood right next to me.

"Uh, same."

"Why are you putting that on?" Ashton pointed to the concealer stick.

I shrugged, not quite sure how to explain. I had a mixed relationship with makeup. It was something I wish didn't exist but at the same time, in front of Ashton, I felt a need to put some on.

Probably because he'd wonder why he even liked me after staring at my bare face for so long.

"So I won't look like a zombie."

Ashton furrowed his eyebrows and grabbed my makeup back, along with the concealer, out of my hand. *Okay. I get it. My jokes aren't that funny.*

"You know, you look fine without makeup. In fact you look beautiful."

Blushing in three, two, one, go.

"Do you just like seeing my face red, is that it?"

"Maybe."

"So what's the plan today?"

Ashton's eyebrows lifted, and a smug smirk made its way onto his face. I fought the urge to roll my eyes at his stupid expression. He inched closer, which made me step back.

The closer he got, the more I stepped backward, but I couldn't keep walking forever, and in seconds, my calves bumped into the bed frame.

"How about this?" Ashton's minty breath smacked me in the face.

I suppose I had given him more than enough time when I was running for my life to my toothbrush.

He was instantly centimeters away from me. His lips grazed mine, and then all at once, my arms flew around his neck, and his slid around my waist. Everything felt right again. Our lips moved together, at first softly, then intensely.

I didn't notice that he was easing me back until my body was buried into the soft covers. His forearms were placed right outside of my shoulders holding him up so I didn't get squished. This was more of a rushed kiss—like we just couldn't get close enough to each other.

Then I did the one thing I never thought I would do for at least years.

Without thinking, I ran my hands down his chest to his chiseled abs, stopping at the elastic waistband of his gray sweatpants. I didn't quite know what I planned to do afterward, but I didn't have to because Ashton's mouth left mine seconds after.

Shit, why did you do that?

"I-I," I began to explain.

"You're not ready. And if you go there, I won't be able to stop. Besides, I intend to be with you for a very long time, so we don't need to rush." He pressed a feathery kiss to my mouth, and I found myself trying to swim out of a pool of blushes but ultimately failing.

"We should, um, go downstairs because, um, where's Roseanne?" I stuttered through my most likely swollen lips.

"You know I'm not ten. Roseanne doesn't have to be with me every minute of every day. I give her my birthday week off."

Our chests were still pressed together.

And I became very aware of my braless state.

"Doesn't she want to see you on your birthday?"

I'm just an insensitive person aren't I?

"I never let her. And she understands why I force her to go."

"So you're alone all week?"

A grin made its way onto his face. "Not anymore. I've got you."

"I'm dumbfounded at how cheesy you can be."

"And I'm dumbfounded at how easy it is for you to ruin any cute moment I plan on creating."

"It's what I do best."

He rolled his eyes. "I guess I have to deal with that the rest of the day because you're spending today with yours truly."

There went my social plans for the day.

Like you had any in the first place.

"Thanks for choosing what I'm doing today," I said with a snort.

He tapped my nose. "You're welcome. Now come on. I'm craving some omelets by Chef Ashton."

He got up and pulled me up with him.

I had to admit that omelets sounded pretty good to me.

⭐

A giant omelet and a dirty kitchen later, I was in my happy place.

"I feel like I've just consumed my own body weight," I huffed.

"Good, because I was hoping that you wanted to clean this all up." Ashton pointed to the dirty pans and cutting boards we, or shall I say he, had used.

"So you cook, and I clean—is that what you're hinting at?"

"How about this? Let's play a game of Scrabble, and loser cleans up?"

I raised one eyebrow. "Why Scrabble?"

"I don't know. I like the game, I guess," he said with a shrug.

"Deal."

To be honest, I was fully okay with cleaning everything up before he wanted to play Scrabble.

"I'll go get the game, and you meet me in the living room." With that, he was gone.

I picked up both our plates and set them in the sink for now. In all my life, I think I had played Scrabble once, so I was fairly confident that I was about to lose.

Once I reached the living room, Ashton had already set up the game on the floor.

"Are you sure you don't just want to play because you're good at it?" I crossed my arms over my chest.

"You'll never know until you play." Ash winked.

"Game on," I sat across from him, cross-legged, and offered my most intimidating face.

"Hate to break it to you, gorgeous, but if there's anything you're not, it's scary."

I frowned. "I think I'm actually quite scary."

"Just like a guinea pig."

"Let's get on with this game."

He laid down the first word.

Latch.

I cocked an eyebrow. "That's very, very creepy."

He held his hands up in surrender. "It was the only thing I could think of."

I just shook my head and put down the next word.

Embrace.

Bake.

April.

Pee.

He stared at me like I had suddenly sprouted wings.

"What?" I held my palms in the air. "It was the only thing I could think of."

"Okay."

Escape.

Slice.

Ten minutes later, I was winning.

I know. I was surprised, too.

I was at 130, and Ash was at 101. Maybe I was better than I thought. And the game was pretty much over.

Ashton was stroking his imaginary beard as he looked intently over the board.

"You know, I'm probably just better at Scrabble, Ashton. You need to face it—"

"Got it!" Ashton shrieked.

Love.

Fifty points right there.

It brought him to 151 points.

It happened so fast that I was suspended for a moment.

"H-how did you?"

Then I felt an inexplicably warm feeling spurt flow up my spine. *He only wrote love because it was the only way he'd win. He's too young even to know what love is.*

"What were you saying? No wait, don't reply. Go clean the kitchen while I sit on a chair and watch you." The sides of his mouth lifted cheekily.

"I-uh," I stammered, unable to formulate a decent reply.

Instead, I lifted myself up, ashamed, and trudged into the kitchen.

"Who's the winner? Me. That's who. High five, Ariel." Ashton snuck up behind me and held up his hand. I went to high-five him, but right before our hands touched, he swiped his away. "You wish."

I pushed him away as hard as I could, which was about six inches. Who said running required a lot of arm strength?

"You're a jerk."

He chuckled. "I'm sorry. Here, give me a hug."

He opened up his arms, and reluctantly, I stepped closer to hug him, but just as our chests were about to touch, he spun around so that my face nearly smacked into his back.

"In your dreams," he said quickly.

I set my lips in a thin line and narrowed my eyes. "You suck!"

He must've thought he was just hilarious because he burst out laughing.

"I-I'm s-sorry but you should've seen your face. I wish I could've caught that on camera. Now that's a picture I would frame," he said between laughs.

"I hate you."

"Aw, come here. I'll give you a hug."

He opened his arms yet again, but this time I just stayed right where I was.

"I don't want a hug anymore."

He jumped up right in front of me and pulled me into him. "Don't be a sore loser, gorgeous. I still like you."

Ashton pressed a feathery kiss to my forehead, and I smiled into his T-shirt.

"But I'm still making you clean up because I really don't want to," he whispered right in my ear.

I placed my hands on his chest and took a step away. "Sometimes I really don't like you."

"Key word to what you just said is *sometimes,* meaning not all the time, meaning most of the time you like me, and that's good enough for me." He sang.

I made my way to the sink and pulled open the dishwasher. "Your logic never ceases to amaze me."

"What can I say? I'm just a genius. I'm lucky you aren't using me for my smarts. Well, technically I don't know that, but I'm just gonna trust you." He patted his heart.

"Yes, I'm attracted to your smarts. You want the truth? You have the face of an elephant and a chameleon combined."

His nose scrunched up. "That's not a pretty thing to imagine."

My mouth dropped open. "Thank you! Now you finally understand how I feel whenever I look at you."

"Hey!"

"Joking," I said, beaming, as I scrubbed the dishes and slipped them into the dishwasher.

"You better be. Now wash those dishes, loser."

"Now I know how Roseanne feels."

"Roseanne loves me."

"How do you know she doesn't secretly spit in your food?"

He switched from smug to disgusted in a millisecond.

"That's awful for you to say."

"Exactly. And ta-da! Dishes are done." I closed the dishwasher with my hip as I dried my hands with a paper towel. "Now I want a rematch in Scrabble."

"Bring it on."

Chapter 19

School was always something I looked forward to.

I always thought of it as one step closer to completing my checklist. I didn't mind getting up early, considering a good job in the real world would probably begin even earlier and end later. Even if I was tired, I never complained. There was no point in telling everyone I knew that I was tired.

But today was different.

I was abnormally tired, even though I had a solid seven hours of sleep.

Monday morning. My bag was slung over my shoulder as I walked to precalculus. There weren't many people at school, but the ones who were waved at me, and I waved back. It was still crazy that most of the school knew who I was. And they didn't hate me. At least, I hoped they didn't hate me.

As I entered the classroom, Mr. Blair was already sitting at his desk, and, for once, Ashton wasn't there.

He was probably tired. Monday wasn't my favorite day of the week, either.

"Morning, Mr. Blair," I greeted him.

"Good morning, Ariel. How are you?" he replied, writing on something that was on his desk.

"I'm doing great. How are you?"

It was always a habit of mine to ask how someone was. I didn't know when it started, but I never really thought much of it. It wasn't a bad habit, anyway.

"I'm very well. Are you getting sick of sitting through this class yet?"

More than you know.

"Just a little bit. I mean, I still have packets of work to do from Easton."

He put down his pen and smiled.

"Well, I'm very impressed with how well you're handling this experience. I'm sorry to say it, but you and those five other students are kind of like the guinea pigs in this assignment."

"I guess I should be proud?"

"It's all in perspective, but I can imagine how boring it all is."

"I don't really mind now. I mean, I did a little when I first got here, but it's really been an experience."

"I'm glad."

But before I could respond, Ashton strolled in. A jolt of electricity surged through me, and I just accepted that it wasn't going to go away.

He was in a faint-red T-shirt and light-green trousers. Only he could pull that off without looking like a watermelon. When he caught my gaze, the toothy smile I loved was etched on his face.

As he sauntered over to his seat, he spoke. "Good

morning, gorgeous." His morning voice was regrettably my favorite voice of his.

"Morning," I squeaked, face-palming for sounding so stupid.

Ashton just chuckled, placing a small kiss on my cheek. Mr. Blair was no longer looking at me, and his face was turned toward the computer.

He took his seat right next to me, and we continued to talk until everyone filed in, and the late bell rang.

After that, I immediately directed my attention to Mr. Blair. I could feel Ashton watching me for the first few minutes, and I had to force myself not to give in to his stare.

Of course, Ashton just had to win at everything.

"You're beautiful," he whispered into my ear when I was looking in the opposite direction.

I snapped my head around, turning beet-red. After that, Ashton directed his attention to the front of the class room, satisfied, as I recovered from the small gesture. *Why can't I hold my composure just once? No one should be this affected by two words.*

The class passed by fairly quickly, and when the bell rang, Ashton immediately got up and hung his arm around my shoulder. I raised an eyebrow at him.

"What?" he asked with emphasis. "Can't I walk my girlfriend to class?"

"But we have the same classes."

"Which is why I'm the luckiest guy ever."

"Why? Because you get to spend the day with a goddess like me?" I tilted my head to the side and smiled.

"Don't flatter yourself."

We fell into the rhythm of Ashton holding my hand or draping an arm around my shoulder every time we walked to a different class, and I didn't mind at all.

The next three periods were fairly fast, mostly because it was all so easy, but when the lunch bell rang, I wasn't lying when I said I was relieved.

Ashton stayed back to talk to the teacher, so I just went to our lunch spot. On the way, I noticed that there was a rather large scuff on my right shoe, but in that short span of three seconds, I bumped right into Elliot. And by bumped, I mean I literally bumped into Elliot.

"Well, hello there, Ariel. Still as clumsy as always, I see," Elliot greeted me.

"Hey there, Elliot. Still as tall as always, I see," I huffed, tilting my head up to make eye contact with him.

"Nah, you're just short." He ruffled my hair.

"There's nothing wrong with being short. Your girlfriend is like the same height as me."

"I didn't say there was something wrong with being short."

"Speaking of Flora, how's she doing, seeing as you've stolen my best friend from me?"

"I could say the same about you, Winters." He narrowed his eyes, but he didn't hide the playfulness in them.

As we walked toward the popular hallway, something unusual happened. Tara was staring right at me. No one with eyes could've missed it.

"Where's Ashton?" Elliot asked casually.

"Talking to a teacher about something," I whispered.

"Why are we whispering?"

"I don't really know," I said, returning to a normal volume.

I looked around for Erika, hoping to find a distraction from Tara's beady eyes. Erika wasn't the greatest friend, and we hadn't exactly bonded in the months that I'd been here, but she was nice. Much nicer than I expected, to be honest. When I found her, she was sitting next to Tara. I waved at her, but she pretended not to notice me, and it hit me as a pang of rejection.

"Are you seeing that killer stare Tara's giving you or is it just me?" Elliot said, poking me in the shoulder.

"Oh, I see it."

"That girl needs to move on."

"What do you mean?"

"She probably just found out that you and Ashton are a couple. She thought you were another one of his hookups, but you're not, and she's pissed."

"Can I sit with you guys today?" I eyed the seat where I normally sat and where I had been replaced with a backpack.

"Like you even have to ask."

I followed him and sat right in between him and Jarod, which just happened to be right across from Tara.

I didn't expect Tara to say anything, but as I pulled an apple out of my lunchbox, I was proven wrong.

"So, you and Ashton are together now?" Tara blurted out.

"Uh, yeah."

"How long have you been a couple?"

"Is this an interrogation?"

"You know, Ashton doesn't like you."

Was it unhealthy to picture Tara falling off a mountain? "And he likes you?"

Tara narrowed her eyed into slits. "Yes, he does. He would never like you. You're ugly, fat, and you don't deserve him. You're just playing hard to get. And when you give in, and he realizes how much time he wasted on you, he'll come running back to me," she spat. It was the longest thing she had ever said to me. I could feel her jealousy, and it did not feel great.

Still, I wasn't about to let her think that I was a doll she could just yell at any time she wanted. Did she even know what she was really saying? All it really did was bring me back to Caroline and how much I regretted not standing up for myself, just to lessen the commotion.

"So you're telling me that he's interested in you? Well, I recall him telling me that being with you was a mistake," I sneered. "Maybe you should learn how to dress properly before you start calling people ugly."

"My taste in clothing is perfect."

"Oh, please. You could come to school butt naked, and there wouldn't be much of a difference."

I don't know what I'm doing, but it feels pretty awesome.

"Bitch," she replied.

"Whore," I retorted without a single hesitation.

"What did you call me?"

"If I'm a bitch, then you're a whore," I explained extra-slow, just for her.

"Take that back."

"If I wanted to take it back, I wouldn't have said it, genius."

"You are going to regret that, Ariella Winters. Just you wait, because Ashton's going to leave you and come crawling back to me."

I simply scoffed. "In your dreams."

"You are going to regret saying that to me," she screeched, and I really wanted earplugs right about then.

If only she had a mute button. If she were a guy, it would have been much easier. I could just kick him in the balls and call it a day.

"And what could you possibly do?"

She stood up so that she was towering over me. "I'm warning you now to watch your back."

Tara didn't give me any time to respond, and she yanked Erika by the arm and strutted away. I blew on a strand of hair that was poking my eye.

"Ding, ding, ding, smack down!" Elliot called out.

"Whoa," Jarod breathed.

I turned around to find Elliot, Xander, and Jarod staring at me, wide-eyed and grinning. The other girls had all left with Tara.

"What?" I snapped.

"That was awesome," Jarod said.

"She deserved it."

"Well, yeah, she did, but I've never seen her so pissed before, and it was the best thing I've seen all week."

"You might want to watch your back, though. She really likes Ashton, and you're the first person who has really taken him away from her," Elliot warned, completely serious.

"Whatever."

"I'm serious," Elliot emphasized.

"What are you serious about?" A new voice spoke as someone sat down next to me. An arm landed around my shoulders, and I immediately relaxed.

"Nothing," I told Ashton. "What were you doing?"

"Teacher accidently gave me a zero on something. What did I miss?"

"Noth—"

"Dude, you missed it. Your girlfriend got into this crazy cat fight with Tara, and it was the best thing ever," Elliot exclaimed.

Ashton raised an eyebrow. "Really?"

"I wouldn't call it a fight," I said

"What would you call it, then?" Elliot challenged me.

"A small confrontation with the devil," I said in all seriousness.

Xander choked on his water and began cracking up.

"And I missed it? Damn it. I would've loved watching my girl pounce on Tara," Ashton cooed.

"You didn't miss much. Besides, she prevented me from eating my apple. The girl deserved to be yelled at."

"You're amazing, you know that?" he whispered when Elliot, Jarod, and Xander started talking about the Modern World test they were going to take next period.

"I know."

"And modest, too."

Chapter 20

ove.

It was one four-letter word that had managed to drive most of the human race absolutely mad.

One syllable that was arguably the only way to achieve true happiness in this world. And I never understood why.

To me, the whole idea of love had oozed dependence on someone else. Weakness. Happiness shouldn't be caused by another person's presence. It should be caused by success, or at least that was what I had always thought. Getting an internship, receiving a full score on a tough exam, getting accepted into a great college. That's what I always considered my happiness.

And it still was. But when I was with Ashton, there was a different kind of happiness. A kind of happiness that made my stomach rise and fall all at the same time. A kind of happiness that made me all bubbly inside. One that could make me think for a split second that everything else didn't matter.

Was it love?

I wasn't sure.

Or maybe I just didn't want it to be.

It could've been. Mom had always taught me that I'd know if it was love. That the feelings would be so overwhelming that there wouldn't be any alternative explanation except for love. When Princess Ariel first saw Prince Eric in *The Little Mermaid*, she just knew.

Of course, it never worked like that because there was no way she could fall for someone that quickly. And fairytales don't exist. But then again, they could come pretty damn close.

There were things I loved about Ashton, though. For one, I loved how his eyes sparkled when he laughed. I loved his dimples. I loved how much he loved soccer. I loved how sweet he could be. I loved the way his smile could make a room full of crying babies pause and grin. His smile was that contagious.

All I really knew was that whenever Ashton was with me, I didn't want to let him go. I wanted to feel his arms wrapped around my waist. I wanted to feel his lips on mine and let the butterflies in my stomach go wild.

And if I was wrapped up enough in him, I'd truly believe that we had a good chance of lasting. That maybe we'd be like my parents and defy what was bound to happen. There was a slim chance, but that chance still existed and was becoming more and more possible with each day.

Perhaps my newfound hope was utterly detrimental, but it certainly didn't feel that way. In fact, it felt way too good to be healthy.

Saturday had finally come around, and we were sitting in my living room, our legs tangled together, and

I can safely say that I didn't have the tiniest inclination to study or run.

Stella was working, and I didn't blame the people who asked her to teach. If someone gave me a paintbrush, I could have a whole year and never be able to whip up what Stella could do in one week.

"You know, Ariel …" Ashton trailed off, "there's this party going on tonight that we could go to. If you want to, of course."

Ash looked at me with hopeful eyes, and I cringed.

Parties weren't my idea of fun. Period. Especially high school parties.

A while ago, I had come to the conclusion that when a large number of hormonal teenagers were shoved into a confined space and given generous amounts of alcohol, bad things tended to happen.

And I had no desire at all to test my theory.

"I'm not sure that's a great idea," I said.

But it was a lie, because I knew full well that it was a bad idea. I knew Ashton didn't really agree with me about parties—hell, he was probably the life of the party.

"But it'll be fun."

He shouldn't've been held back by me. So maybe I didn't like the idea of dozens of girls throwing their intoxicated selves at him. Okay, I really hated the idea, but I trusted him to not go there.

"Why don't you go with Elliot? I'll stay home. Go have fun."

"But Ariel, you're my girlfriend."

"And your point is …?"

"That means without you, other girls will annoy me," Ashton wailed.

"That doesn't mean I have to go. Besides, you should

be happy that I trust you not to hook up with those sluts."

His smile could've stretched up to the ceiling. Ash pulled me tighter against him, and I took it all in. "I wouldn't even think of it. I don't think I'd ever forgive myself if I lost you like that." He slanted his lips over mine for a quick peck, and I almost lost control and yanked him back into me. "And for the record, I just really want to see you in a minidress."

"You can do without that sight."

"Please come," he tried.

"No, thank you."

"Pretty please?"

"No."

"Please?"

"No."

"You'll be jealous."

"Nah, I already said I trust you enough to not cheat on me."

"What if I do?" he challenged me.

"Then you won't have a girlfriend anymore. And I will kick you in the balls so hard that you will collapse and crumble into a little ball of pain," I said, emotion drained from my voice.

"You really are something special, aren't you? And I already told you I wouldn't dream of doing that shit to you. I might've lost myself for a couple of years, but cheating is where I draw the line." His index finger drew small circles on the palm of my hand.

"I know that you wouldn't, 'cause you know exactly what'll happen if you do."

"And I would miss having you around too much,

gorgeous," Ashton said sincerely, and I almost pressed kisses all over his face.

"I'd miss you, too," I said with a grin. "But that doesn't mean I'm going to that party."

"Ariel," he whined like a little baby.

"Ashton," I echoed, mocking him.

"If you cared about me in the slightest, you'd come with me."

"You can't play that card."

"Oh, yes I can, and I will."

"Why can't you take Elliot with you?"

"I wanna show off my beautiful girlfriend."

And that was all it took.

"Fine."

I hadn't realized what I said until after Ashton fist-pumped the air.

"Yes. You are the best girlfriend ever. By the way, can we leave in five minutes?"

"What?" I pointed to my sweatshirt and yoga pants.

"Fifteen minutes?" he offered.

I said nothing and ran to my room as quickly as possible. I thought I was pretty fast, but Ashton caught up to me with ease. I had no idea what to wear. Was it too late to change my answer?

As we entered my room, also known as me going in and him following, I pulled open the closet door and just stood there. After a solid minute during which I didn't move, Ashton spoke.

"Are you going to pick something or are you going pretend you're a statue for the rest of the night?"

"Idon'tknowwhattowear," I said all in one breath.

"Huh?"

"I don'tknowwhattowear."

A smug smile crept onto Ash's lips. "Then you need some of my expertise in your life, my dear."

He rummaged through my closet, and I was thankful that I kept my underwear in a drawer and out of plain sight.

"Are you—"

"Perfect!"

He held up a black minidress that I could've easily mistaken as an oversized yet skin-tight shirt. It wasn't even my dress. I was pretty sure it was Flora's, and which had come with the pile she stuck in my closet so I'd wear them. I'd thought the thing was pretty camouflaged with the rest of my clothing. I was wrong.

There was no doubt that the dress would cling to my body like plastic wrap. It was the type of dress that cut just below my butt and showed way too much cleavage. It was the dress I always hoped I would never have to wear.

"How about no?" I asked as Ashton wiggled his eyebrows at me.

"Please?"

"I hate it," I groaned.

"You're gonna look beautiful."

"I don't like it."

"Please? For me?" That was when he decided to throw on his famous pout.

"I'm not going in that puny piece of cloth."

"How about I buy you whatever food you would like?"

Food. They always go for the food.

"Fine."

My theory was correct, in case anyone was wondering.

Actually, everything was ten times worse than I anticipated. The stench of alcohol was overwhelming, not to mention that it felt like I was in a furnace. I never got why people thought it would be fun to rub up against each other in a small space.

It didn't feel nice at all.

And what if I had a bad case of claustrophobia? The red flags were everywhere.

Not to mention that I could've gone to jail. The police could have come and arrested everyone for underage drinking. I could already see the police officers handcuffing me and telling me I had the right to be silent. *Stupid, damn party.* I didn't even know whose party it was.

I shoved past a group of guys who oh-so-intelligently thought of the idea to have a belching contest, which made the stench twenty times worse.

Great. Just great. So this is what I've been missing all this time. At least there would be no regrets in the future. To say this was hell was an understatement.

The stereos were blasting some random Justin Bieber song to make everything just oh-so-much better.

And could it get better? I didn't think so until I told Ash I needed a drink.

Then I did the best thing I could think of.

I went into the kitchen.

And when I finally found it, I was so thankful there weren't any people there. I sat in one of the chairs randomly placed in the middle of the room.

Yup, this was definitely a great idea. Way to remind yourself that you don't have a social life.

And I was happily staring at a blank wall when Tara

stumbled in and decided to ruin it all. It didn't take long for me to notice that she was drunk. I was seven feet away from her, and I could smell the stench of alcohol reeking from her body.

"Did Ashton dump you already?" she slurred. Even when she wasn't herself, she was a bitch. *How lovely.*

"For your information, no, he has not," I snapped, not wanting to deal with all her bullshit now.

If I poked her shoulder, would she tip over and fall?

"Y-you don't deserve him. He loves me," she stuttered.

"Go away, Tara. You're drunk," I said calmly.

"Your face is drunk."

The wise words of Tara Cunningham. Everyone take notes.

"Thanks for that."

I slowly backed out of the kitchen, and the most amazing part was that she didn't even notice.

Thanks for taking away my one hiding spot, Cunningham.

"Ari!" I snapped my head around to find that it was Flora shouting my name. She ran across the dance floor to my side.

"Hey, Flora."

"I didn't think you would come here," she said admiringly. "And in that dress, too. I told you it would look fucking hot."

"Who said I wanted to be here? I was bribed with food and movies," I muttered.

"Now that's the Ariel I know." *What was that supposed to mean?* She must have noticed my discomfort because suddenly a concerned look crossed her face. "No, I mean that I just thought you hated parties. Too loud, too noisy, blah, blah, blah. By the way, food and movies would've persuaded me to come here, too."

"And that's supposed to make me feel better?" I rolled my eyes.

"You know I love you."

She pretended to blow me a kiss, and I didn't catch it.

I waved my hands as one would do when one sees a bug flying toward one's face.

"That's truly touching, best friend." She placed a hand on her heart and beamed.

And before I knew it, we both burst out laughing. When the laughter subsided, she sucked in a breath and leaned closer. "Oh by the way, who's the blonde bitch who's staring at you like she wants to burn you in flames?"

"How do you know she's a bitch?" I teased.

"Firstly, she's staring at you like you've taken everything she's ever loved. Second, her boobs are flailing around practically asking to be punched. And finally, she looks like she's been manufactured in a Barbie company."

I snickered. "That, my friend, is Tara Cunningham, Lincoln Bay's Caroline. But somehow, she manages to be even worse because she hates me."

"Why does she have any reason to hate you?"

"Ashton."

And just like that, she understood.

"Don't worry. I've had my fair share of crazy ex-girlfriends coming after me, too." She nudged my shoulder.

I was suddenly reminded that Elliot was here too. Of course he was here. Elliot wasn't the kind of boyfriend who would just let Flora go to a party like this where guys wouldn't ever stop hitting on her.

"You should go find Elliot," I told her.

"What about you?"

"I think I'm going to go home," I said, actually fearing that the blasting music was giving me hearing problems.

"Ariel ..."

"I don't feel well." I faked, placing a hand on my forehead. Flora eyed me suspiciously and then she sighed.

"Fine," she finally said. Before she left, she turned to me. "By the way, I know you're faking, but I can tell you don't want to be here so I won't force you."

"You're the best," I shouted.

"Yeah, yeah whatever. I'll walk you out, yeah?"

"Nah. I have to find Ash anyway. I'll catch you later?" She nodded and wiggled her eyebrows at me. *Perv.* And with that lovely gesture, she left to search for Elliot.

I shoved past random people, looking for Ashton when someone grabbed my wrist and pulled me back. I looked up to see one of the guys from Easton. I was pretty sure he was on the football team. I didn't recognize him, though.

"Hey, you're really hot. You want to get out of here, darlin'?" he garbled.

I slapped his hand away and took a step away from him. "No, thanks. I have a boyfriend." I tried to walk away but he gripped my shoulder again.

"He won't know," he whispered.

I put on a fake smile. I signaled for him to bend down to my ear level. He seemed satisfied. I put my mouth next to his ear.

"But I will so you have ten seconds to walk away

259

before I kick you in the groin and make you unable to ever have babies," I said softly.

His eyes went wide as I pulled away. After that, he scrambled away from me. I smiled and continued my search for Ash. *All hail the mastermind, Ariella. Boom, boom, POW.*

I finally found him goofing off with Elliot. *Figures.* At least it wasn't a swarm of girls. He hadn't seen me yet, so I took time to look at him. He really did look like he was having an awesome time. I sighed.

"Ashton?" I asked, tugging on his shirt. When he saw me, Ash slung an arm around my shoulder, and my face hit his chest.

"Oh hey there, babe. Did you get that drink?" Ashton asked. He placed a sloppy kiss on my lips. The taste of alcohol lingered on my lips. I wiped it off with the back of my hand. I never could understand why people liked to drink.

"Yeah. But I think I'm going to head home. You stay here and party, okay? I'm not feeling too well," I told him.

Ash's eyebrows knit together, concerned.

"I'll come with you."

"No, you stay here. I'll be fine."

There was no reason that I had to drag Ashton with me. It's not like I'd had any drinks, anyway.

"Are you sure?"

"Positive."

"See you later, gorgeous. Be careful, okay?"

It was then that I realized I was in love with Ashton Walker. There was something about how sweet he was, even when his brain was clouded with alcohol. It somehow made me see how much I loved every single aspect of him.

I know, an overcrowded party where ninety percent of the people are drunk wasn't the most romantic place for this realization, but Mom never told me that my moment would be in a field with rainbows and unicorns. I almost blurted out those three words, but I stopped myself, letting it sink in that not everyone was having this same epiphany as me.

I felt like I had enough adrenaline coursing through my veins to run ten miles.

"Oh and Elliot, Flora's looking for you," I shouted over the music.

"Okay, Ari."

"Bye, Elliot."

"See ya later, girly," Elliot said in a high-pitched voice. *Intoxicated idiot.*

I weaved my way through the crowd of people, taking a deep breath when I got outside. It felt nice to be free. I walked toward my car, giddy about getting home.

When I turned the engine on, I noticed Tara stumbling out of the house toward a car. She wasn't planning on driving, was she? Either way, I didn't want anything to do with it. I drove off, not sparing a second glance in her direction.

When I glimpsed in my rearview mirror, I noticed that Tara was following me. I frowned, not quite sure what the hell she could be planning at this time of night. The path of her vehicle was nothing close to straight. The car weaved left to right, speeding along. Suddenly, she started to speed up, coming extremely close to my car.

On instinct, I drove a little faster, not wanting to

have a collision. The speed limit wasn't exactly my main concern at the time.

My main concern was the drunk, crazy girl following me in her car. It didn't seem to do much, however, as Tara just kept getting closer. As I reached a red light, I slowed down to a stop. I turned to see whether Tara was gone, but she was still there, and she wasn't showing any signs of stopping for the red light. It seemed that she was increasing speed by the second, even though she was already driving at a solid forty miles per hour.

I gasped, trying to swerve out of the way, but it was too late. Her car rammed into mine, sending me spinning in circles. Maybe I even flipped, but I couldn't tell. My head banged against the window a couple of times, and I felt a liquid, most likely blood, trickle down my cheek. Everything around me was spinning. Suddenly, my eye lids felt cemented.

I'll just close my eyes for a minute.

At first, a million things were happening. Police sirens were blasting in my ears, I could taste my own iron-filled blood, which had dripped onto my lips and into my mouth, I could feel my seat belt digging into the side of my neck way more than a seat belt should've been able to. And then, there was nothing.

Chapter 21

'm sorry, I'm sorry, I'm sorry, I'm sorry, I'm sorry ..."
A voice continued for what seemed like forever.

My eyes were still shut tightly, and a growing pain in my head was spreading. It had been that single voice that hadn't stopped for what felt like ages. It took me a while to pinpoint it as Ashton's, but even when I knew, I didn't move from my position on what felt like a bed.

Instead, I enjoyed the sound of his voice. It was almost as though his sound could distract me from the excruciating pounding in my head. I didn't know why he was sorry, though.

"This is my entire fault. I'm so sorry. I can't believe I almost lost you. I love you, Ariel," Ashton wailed.

"I love you too." I said the words before I had even processed what I said.

He didn't respond. I'm pretty sure his breathing stopped too. *Did he run away? No, he wouldn't do that.* I fluttered my eyes open, flinching at the bright light. It took me a while to notice that I was in a hospital room.

My eyes settled upon Ashton's adorable face staring at me like a deer caught in the headlights.

And then the memories of last night flooded back. *Party. Really tight, no-good, black minidress. Hot. Smelly. I love him. Tara. Tara being intoxicated. Tara following me with her car. Now what happened after that?*

"You're awake!" Ashton finally exclaimed.

The grip he had on my hand tightened slightly, but at the same time, it didn't feel tight at all. He squeezed as if I were a thin layer of ice that'd break if he used more than five percent of his strength.

"Thanks for that, Captain Obvious."

He scoffed. "Well, it's nice to know that you've kept your sense of humor."

"Now, now, Ashton. You should know that will never go away."

He lifted my hand and pressed a delicate kiss to each knuckle. "Good. I'd miss it way too much. How do you feel?"

"My head hurts like hell, these lights are way too bright, I'm not quite sure what's happened, I kind of need to pee," I said, trailing off when I noticed Ashton wince. "But you being here, despite your probably-really-shitty hangover, is making this situation oddly okay." And then my cheeks warmed up, and I had that same urge to grab his face and slam my lips into his.

"I'm sorry."

"You have nothing to be sorry form but that brings me to the question of how are you here? Why are you here? What am I doing here? What happened?"

"Stella called me last night. Apparently, mine was the first number that she could find. You were in a car accident. Tara's car hit yours. When I got here, you were sleeping, so I just stayed."

He didn't look me in the eyes, and it became plain stupid how much I wanted to see those blue orbs looking at me again.

"Where's Stella?" I wondered, secretly trying to get him to lift his head up.

"She went home to take a shower. She left twenty minutes ago, so it should be a while until she comes back."

Was there something unordinary about his shoes? Is that why he didn't look at me?

"How long have you been here?"

"Seven hours," he mumbled. "But it's nothing. I would've stayed here for days if I had to."

"You are too sweet," I said, grinning.

"Only to you."

And then I was happy his head was down so he couldn't see how flustered those three little words gave me.

"So," I trailed. "You love me?"

And then I was met by those blue orbs that I was waiting to see. "Yes. I love you. I love you a lot, actually. I wasn't going to tell you because it might be too early, and you weren't supposed to hear me. And I'm sorry."

"Don't be sorry. It wasn't your fault." I lifted his hand to mine and pressed a kiss to his thumb.

"You could've died." His face went pale, and his lips quivered. "I don't know what I'd do if you weren't with me right now."

"But I'm still alive." *And hungry.*

"I'm sorry."

"Stop apologizing." My eyes closed for a couple

seconds when it felt like a grenade exploded in my head. "Hold on for a second."

After a minute, Ashton's voice rang out. "Hey, Ariel?"

"Mmmmmm ..."

"Can you say that you love me back?" Ash said it in the most tentative voice, and I just wanted to melt into a puddle.

"I love you." And I really meant it.

"Can I kiss you now?"

But he didn't let me answer before his lips fitted right over mine, stealing a kiss. When we pulled apart, I had that same tingle flowing through my lips as the first time we kissed.

"So are you going to tell me what exactly happened with Tara and whether she's hurt, or is that just minor information?"

And then the emotions drained from his face. There was fire in his eyes, and I would have hated to be the one causing it.

"When the police found her, she was trashed, not to mention not really injured in the slightest. Actually, I feel worse for her car than her. She owned up to everything right after she threw up on the street." His left hand balled up into a fist.

My lips formed a pout as I thought over what he had said.

"I'm gonna sue her."

"What?"

"I'm. Gonna. Sue. Her," I repeated slowly.

Just like that, Ashton's fury seemed to vanish. Instead, it looked like he was about to burst out laughing.

"Why are you laughing?" I demanded.

"Your only reaction is to sue the damn girl?"

"I told you I've always wanted to sue somebody. It's on my bucket list. This is my chance!"

"I really love you." His eyes twinkled, and my heart melted a little. "But I'm not sure how successful you'll be. Her parents are lawyers, and when they found out, they pulled her out of Lincoln Bay straight away so as of now she's homeschooled, I guess."

"So she's gone?" He nodded, and I was about to cross my arms over my chest, but I noticed an IV needle taped in my right arm, restricting me from doing so. My smile faded as I stared at the needle with a burning hatred that couldn't be controlled.

"What's wr—"

"There's a needle in my arm."

"And?"

"I hate needles. And there's a needle in my arm. See the issue?" My arm stayed completely still, making sure that devil of a needle didn't move.

"Ariel, it's a needle."

"But …" I thought of countless things I could say, but they all made me sound like a baby.

"Don't tell me you're afraid of a teeny needle."

"Well, what if I am?" This time, instead of crossing both arms across my chest, it was only the left.

"Then that just makes me love you more." Ash's pointer finger tapped my nose.

"Ah, Miss Winters, I see you are awake. How are you feeling?" A man in a white coat walked in. I assumed he was a doctor, considering he had a name tag that read "Dr. Perry."

"I'm okay, but my head really hurts."

It truly felt like there was a party going on in my

head. I hated parties. That hadn't changed. And now I had a rational reason for why I hated them.

"Well, that's to be expected. We can give you some pain medications for that. Thankfully, you don't have any internal damage, but, unfortunately, you do have a slight concussion from the accident," he explained.

"Oh, great." I blew a strand of hair from my face.

"But don't worry; the pain medication will numb the feeling. Once you take it, try to get some sleep. Stay in bed. The concussion is mild enough that we can let you go home tomorrow to heal."

"Thank you," I replied gratefully. Dr. Perry gave a warm smile as he turned around to leave. I began to shut my eyes, but they snapped open when I heard Dr. Perry's footsteps get louder again.

"I almost forgot. We have contacted your parents, and they are getting here as soon as possible."

What he said didn't even sound real.

"When are they coming?"

"I'm not sure, but I will inform you when they get here, and I assume your Aunt Stella will tell you." Dr. Perry smiled at my reaction. "Now get some rest, and one of the nurses will bring you the pain medication."

After that, I seemed to forget that Ashton was by my side and drifted back into sleep.

My eyes snapped open when I heard the door slamming. Ashton shot up out of his seat as we both turned our heads toward the door. Aunt Stella was standing in the doorway and then she began running toward us.

"My God, Ariel, I am so sorry that the damn traffic held me up. I was ready to punch someone."

It definitely felt different having people talk to me while I sat in this plain hospital bed. For one, no matter how hard they tried to hide it, there was always something holding them back. Whether they were too nervous or terrified that I would collapse right there, they were never their full selves.

"It's okay, Stella. Ashton's here." I gestured to Ash. Stella's worried expression flashed to a smirk.

"Well then, I'm glad I called the right person." She dropped her purse on an empty chair and walked to the opposite side of the bed from where Ashton was sitting. "So how ya feelin', sweet pea?"

"I don't know. About as good as someone with a concussion feels, I guess?"

"Yeah, about that ..." Her nose scrunched up. "Maybe we lay off the parties for a while?"

"No problem with that," I said, but my eyes were trained on the damn IV needle penetrating my skin.

I was awake, I was breathing. Was this needle really still necessary? But my concentration was interrupted by Stella stifling a laugh.

"You and those needles, darlin'. I suppose that fear is never going away." She pointed a finger at Ashton. "Ashton, dear, did little Ariel tell you about the time she hid in a bush for a good forty-five minutes to avoid getting a shot or when she nearly punched the doctor because he was holding a needle? I remember your mom having to hold you down."

I groaned, wishing I could hide how red I was probably getting.

"Oh, that never came up."

"Stella," I said with a frown. "He didn't need to know that."

"Oh, don't be silly. It would be a crime if I didn't embarrass you in front of your boyfriend. You know your mom would do the same. Oh, and that reminds me. Your parents should be here any min—"

Stella was cut off by the door creaking open. My mother came rushing in, tears in her eyes, while my dad trailed behind. As soon as she saw me, Mom ran up to me, wrapping me up in a hug. I noticed how careful she was not to touch my head, for which I was thankful.

I hadn't seen them for months, yet when her face popped through the door, it was like she had been with me all this time, partly because she was basically identical to Stella. She hadn't changed a bit—well, except for the tears streaming down her face. Dad hadn't changed, either. And it kind of made me glad I had gotten into this accident. *No, wait. What?*

"My poor baby," Mom wailed.

"Please don't cry," I pleaded. There was just something gut-wrenching about seeing my own mother cry, and I hated it.

"I'm just glad you're okay."

"Me too."

"I don't need another person in the family to be sick," Mom said with a chuckle.

"I reassure you I will be all right."

She turned her head and pointed in Aunt Stella's direction. "Has this crazy woman been taking good care of you, sweetie?"

Aunt Stella crossed her arms. "I missed you too, dear sister. I'll have you know that I've been mighty fine, if I do say so myself."

"Katie, Stella, you've got all the time in the world to argue. Now, if you don't mind, I think it's time for me to hug my baby girl," Dad interrupted.

"Fair enough, Richard," my mother said as she straightened her back, stepping aside. "She's just mad cause I'm the older one."

"Only by one minute!" Aunt Stella protested.

"I'm still older than you, no matter what your logic is." Mom grinned mischievously. Instantly, Dad took her place, embracing me in a warm hug.

"How are you doing, Pumpkin?" he mumbled into my hair.

"I'm actually feeling pretty good. The pain medications are starting to kick in."

"I am so sorry we couldn't be here," Mom choked out. Her eyes glistened, and the last thing I wanted to see was her crying again because of me.

"I'm okay. Really." I held my mom's hand in mine, giving it a gentle squeeze. I suppose she took the hint because she wiped her eyes, eliminating any trace of tears.

"Your mother and I decided to move back for the rest of the school year and then we'll all go visit Grandma in July." Dad patted my head lightly. "No more accidents for you."

I could feel my lips twitch into a full-on grin as I pulled my dad in for a hug. "Thank you," I mumbled.

"You never have to thank me for that. We missed you too much anyway. And besides, we need you to keep your crazy mother in check."

"I think I've already got my hands full with Aunt Stella."

"*Hey!*" two voices shouted. Mom slapped Dad, and

Aunt Stella gave him her best intimidating face, though anyone could see a sparkle in her eyes.

"The first time we see our daughter in eight months will not be filled with you making fun of me, Richard."

"Sorry, honey." Dad pulled Mom into a hug, and that's when I realized how much I missed having those two in the house. Aunt Stella was wonderful, but nothing compared to parents.

"As much as I love watching this unfold, the poor boy should be acknowledged." Aunt Stella's voice butted in.

I glanced over at Ashton to see him shifting back and forth on his toes. At that moment, he looked as vulnerable as a puppy. I could practically sense his mind flying in all directions. Then again, mine would have been, too, if I had had to meet his parents.

"Well, Mom and Dad, this is Ashton." I gestured. "Ashton, these are my parents."

I rubbed the top of my head, which was beginning to hurt. Did it help? Not really. Did that stop me from doing it? No.

Ashton extended a stiff hand to my mom, but she pushed it away and pulled him into a hug. Visibly, Ashton relaxed a bit, hugging her back. When Mom finally let go, she grinned at Ash.

"So this is the famous Ashton that I've heard about. You're right, Stella, he is quite a charmer."

"Mom!" I truly felt the need to crawl in a hole and hide.

"What, honey?" she asked innocently. Before I could reply, Ashton cut me off.

"It's a pleasure to meet you, Mrs. Winters." Ashton said politely.

"Oh, call me Katie, dear," she gushed. "Oh Stella, you were right again. Ariel, this boy really is quite handsome."

"*Mom!*"

"That's enough, Katie. She's as red as a ripe tomato."

"*Dad!*"

"Ariel, I wasn't nearly as embarrassing when I met Ashton, right?" Aunt Stella cut in.

"Oh my God, Stella. I swear you all want to humiliate me. I have a concussion. You all should be catering to my every need." I grabbed an extra pillow to my right and covered my face in it.

"Don't be silly. No one is humiliated, Ariel. You're too dramatic."

"I've got to side with Ariel here—"

"Oh please, you embarrass her more than me," Mom protested.

"If you don't mind, I want to meet the boy my little girl is spending so much time with." Dad straightened up and smiled at Ash.

"It's a pleasure to meet you, Mr. Winters." Ashton held out his hand, but there was an ever-so-slight tremor.

"So, what are your intentions?" Dad stroked an imaginary beard. It would've been a real beard—that is, until Mom forced him to shave it off.

"Are you seriously going with the most clichéd question in the book?" I deadpanned.

"Hush, and let the boy answer this question."

"I just want to make her happy," Ashton finally answered, and I had never felt such a strong urge to kiss him to death.

Hmm, death by kiss. That's a new one.

"Well, any man who puts up with my Ariel, over here, automatically gets admiration from me." Dad patted Ash on the back, and I scrunched my eyebrows together.

"*Hey!*"

"You know, Ashton, you seem like a pretty nice guy." Ashton's face lit up like a kid's on Christmas. "But I don't want any hanky-panky going on. Just remember that I'm everywhere and that I can see everything."

"I am mortified. This is mortifying …" I ranted on.

"Oh please, it was meant to happen sometime. Given it wasn't the best circumstances, at least it's over with." Mom grinned.

"What? I am not allowing our daughter to be a teen mom. She's got too much going for her."

I watched as Ashton let out a sigh of relief as a grin spread across his face. "Thank you, sir. I assure you that will not happen."

"Call me Richard."

Mom stepped in. "Ariel, we have to go speak to your doctor about the details for tomorrow. We'll be back in a jiffy."

Aunt Stella stayed where she was, a smirk growing on her face until Mom dragged her away along with Dad.

"I'm sorry about that. I'm actually mortified," I said when I heard the click of the door closing.

Ashton shook his head, linking his long fingers with my tiny ones. "No, they're great. I wish I had parents as good as yours."

"Well, they really like you," I commented. "You can be a part of my family."

As I realized what I had just said, I froze. *Oh God. Really, Ariel? He's going to run away now because you said that.* Ashton placed a delicate kiss on the palm of my hand, and, for a moment, it felt like nothing could ever go wrong.

Chapter 22

I never liked hospitals.

No matter why I was there, I could always feel the constant dread lingering in the air. I hated that going to a hospital meant that something had happened. It meant that pain had been or was going to be felt. Someone breaks their arm and goes to the hospital because of the pain. Someone is going into labor and goes to hospital, about to be in a lot of pain. Even the friends and family who are there go through a type of pain. Whether it's the anticipation of waiting for a baby to be born or the fear that they might never get to see their close friend or family member again, it isn't a fun wait. Going to the hospital just isn't a fun trip to make, with the exception of the aftermath of giving birth.

For me, I was lucky. I didn't have a life-threatening accident, but it was enough to see Tara every time I closed my eyes. But having Ashton next to me somehow took those images out of my brain.

And weirdly enough, when Ashton went home the

next day, I was still okay. The only thing I really felt was boredom, which to me should've been a lucky emotion to have.

Maybe I was wrong to think so, but staring at a puny television wasn't my favorite pastime. I couldn't even check my phone. Something about it being bad for me, and I was banned from it for at least a week.

I couldn't complain about being alone, though. I practically had to shove Ashton, Stella, and the others out the door to get some rest. Ashton was the hardest one to persuade.

Being the stubborn guy he was, it certainly wasn't easy, but he needed it. The black circles around his eyes had become extremely prominent since the accident, and there was no way to hide it. I told him that if he didn't go home, I would never speak to him again. Of course, he and I both knew that wouldn't happen, but he left anyway.

When Ashton left, mom glued herself to my bedside. It wasn't like I would accidently have fallen out the window if they left. When Ash left, it was 8:00 a.m. By 8:01, Mom was already next to me. I was alone for a whopping one minute.

I was going home soon anyway and, although I wanted to leave this white-walled space, I wasn't as excited to experience the clinginess of the family.

I missed my parents, obviously, but I understood why they had to go. I respected it. It wasn't like I spent twenty-four hours a day missing them. Yeah, I wanted to catch up, but the consistent pounding in my head and my never-ending need to throw up were too overwhelming to be listening politely to how everyone was.

Luckily, Dad must have noticed my frustration

because, before long, he whisked my mom away, telling her that they needed to get home to prepare for my return. *Thank you, Dad.* My giddiness must have been apparent because even Mom agreed, after staring me down for a solid two minutes.

Now I just sat in my hospital bed, wearing a ridiculous hospital gown that didn't even cover my ass, watching the time tick by. *10:33.* My boredom resulted in my trying to find a paint chip on a wall. I hadn't found one yet.

Because that was a stupid thing to do, I let my eyes shut, but before I could be engulfed by the soothing, heaven-like comfort also known as sleep, the door creaked.

So close.

"Ariella, we have someone who would like to see you if you don't mind? She insists that you won't mind." A nurse in a white gown peeked her head in.

I was too confused by the painkillers even to try to figure out who it was.

"Okay."

The nurse backed away, and another figure replaced her. In came an apprehensive version of my best friend.

"Oh my God, Ari, you lunatic! Why didn't you call me? What happened? Are you okay? I'm so sorry I couldn't come earlier." Flora took three big steps and then she was right next to me.

"A: please be a little quieter. B: everything's fine, Flora. Sorry I didn't call. This was like the first ten minutes of peace I've gotten since I was checked into this hospital."

"When do you leave?" Flora sat at the edge of my bed, and I shifted my feet to give her more room.

"In like six hours, I think."

"At least you can get out of this place."

"Who told you I was here?" I nudged her with my toe, and she glared.

"Well, it certainly wasn't my best friend," she huffed. "Sorry, I'm not that mad. I understand how much concussions suck. Ashton told Elliot and then Elliot told me," Flora rambled. "That's not the point. Are you okay?"

"Fine."

"Are you sure?"

"Positive."

"You know you can tell me if you're not okay."

"I'm fine, Flora."

"Does your head hurt?"

"*Flora!*"

She stared at me with the same innocent puppy-dog face she'd pull when she wanted food.

"Yes?"

"My mom and Ashton have annoyed me enough. I don't need you to join in. I'm fine, really."

"Phew." Flora sat back down on the edge of my bed as she pushed a stray strand of hair out of the way. She spotted a clipboard, and a mischievous glint appeared in her eyes. "So it seems that the patient has a mild concussion. By the way, you can call me Dr. Flo," she said in her best formal voice.

"You are the worst doctor ever. I would never trust you to be my surgeon. God knows what kind of risks I would be taking."

"Please, miss, I am looking at something. I need a little quiet." She pretended to flip through the pages. I snorted.

"I would like to call in for a new doctor."

She narrowed her eyes. "Ungrateful hooligan," she muttered, and before I knew it, we were both giggling.

"You are exactly what I needed in this boring place."

"Why, thank you. Thank you very much," she said in an Elvis voice and bowed three times.

"Any time. So how is school?" I attempted to sit up. Even though everything around me was spinning, I couldn't keep lying on the bed, or I would fall asleep. And I couldn't fall asleep. Flora was the best friend that would draw a mustache on me while I was unconscious. Even in a hospital. Still, I liked that she wasn't treating me like a fragile painting or something like that.

"Oh, nothing's really changed here, but I hear your parents are back in town."

"Yeah, they are. And they miss you."

"I miss them. So how's life with the boyfriend?"

"I just got a concussion, and that's what you want to talk about?"

"I'm just trying to distract you from what looks like a killer headache."

"Thanks for reminding me." I shifted a little. "But he just left a while ago."

"That's sweet."

"You have ten seconds to say you told me so," I confessed.

"Why?"

"I like Ashton a lot more than I planned to. And I may or may not have said I love you."

Then came a series of high-pitched squeals, and I threw my pillow at her. *"I knew it I knew it I knew it!*

I called it, too. I was right, and you were wrong. I was right and you were wro—"

"I get it."

"You were wro—"

"*Ten seconds is up.*"

"Sorry." Flora tossed the pillow back in my direction. "I'm just excited. So I assume he knows?"

"Knows what?"

"About the project."

It was those three simple words that shattered my good mood.

"Um … well …"

"You haven't told him," she stated flatly.

"I just, I don't know."

"You know you have to tell him some time, Ari." Flora's voice softened. She scooted closer and put a hand on my forearm.

"I know."

"He won't be too upset. Just explain to him. It's not like the feelings were fake, anyway. It's really not too bad. At least you didn't try to act. You've only lied about minor things. What's so bad about that?"

"You know, I don't really know why I'm not telling him, either. It's like something in my body won't let me. Plus, what if he doesn't like me afterward? A guy like him wouldn't do a long-distance relationship with a girl like me." I pinched the skin on the bridge of my nose, which frankly just made my headache worse.

"Now you just sound stupid. It's not a long-distance relationship. You're like ten minutes away. You're just not with him for the first half of the day. Elliot and I do it."

"Kay, I was over the top on that one. Okay, but I exploited him. I became friends with him only for the purpose of using him for a project. That sounds pretty bad to me."

"Don't think like that."

"How can I not, Flora? 'Cause I'm pretty sure that once I tell him that I used him, he won't like me that much anymore."

"He loves you, doesn't he?"

"I think so."

"But—"

"You can't avoid it, Ari," she said. "You can prolong it for another week, but sometime you're going to have to face him. It's really not that big of a deal. You didn't cheat on him. You're just telling him what you weren't allowed to tell him in the beginning."

"I guess."

"It'll be okay."

"I hope so."

Chapter 23

Stress had always been a factor in my life. Whether I would do okay on a math test. Whether I'd do well on an English exam. Whether I had done enough to maximize my chances of getting into an Ivy League school. These things had always made me anxious in a way that made me want to hide away and cry it all out, and afterward, I'd feel perfectly fine again.

The type of anxiety I was feeling now wasn't even in the same category as what I used to—and still do—freak out over. It was one where I had no idea of the outcome, and if I had the choice, I would go back in time and change my actions. One where I hadn't stressed that much until it was real. Till I had no other option but to face it.

The moment I had been shoving in the back of my brain for the past four months was about to hit me like a tidal wave. It was now that I realized how idiotic I was for pushing it this long. Maybe he wouldn't have been as mad if I had told him everything earlier. But whatever was about to happen wasn't anybody's fault but mine.

It was two days after I had been able to leave the hospital. It was also exactly two weeks until I'd go back to Easton High. Back to the school I had taken a small break from, though for some reason it had almost felt like I was staying at Lincoln Bay for the rest of high school.

What terrified me the most was that nothing would change. Everything would remain the exact same as when I left. The popular crew would still remain the popular crew. The theater geeks would still be performing. The same teachers would still be teaching. I would still have my old schedule. Nothing should've felt different. I should've fit right back in. But in reality, everything would feel different because I was different.

I wasn't the same after Flora left that day at the hospital. It was obvious to anyone, especially Ashton, that something had changed in the few hours he left. He even tried to comfort me, which just made everything worse. *I didn't lie that much. I didn't lie that much. I didn't lie that much.*

Currently, I just sat on my bed with Ashton in an armchair beside me. There really wasn't much going on except for my mouth occasionally opening and closing because I was too chicken shit to spit it all out. He'd been by my side right after school for the past two days. If he wasn't there, mom was there, giving me never-ending bowls of soup.

I observed as Ashton obliviously scribbled down an answer on his AP Modern World homework. He ruffled his hair, his eyebrows drawn together, showing his concentration.

And I really did understand. I understood why

people got into relationships so early or fell in love. It was the butterflies in my tummy that neither movies nor books could elicit. It was the small kisses here and there that I became addicted to. It was the fuzzy feeling I'd get whenever Ashton would wrap his arms around me. And that feeling just never went away.

"You know I can feel your eyes so don't think you're being subtle." Ashton's lips tugged upward.

It's now or never.

"Come here." I patted a spot next to me on my bed. I grabbed my homework papers and set them on the nightstand next to me.

Ashton dropped his pencil and stood up. He plopped down next to me with a goofy smile that I loved way too much. I shut my eyes momentarily, enjoying the last few moment of happiness I would have. It could be worse. I could just leave without saying anything, but that would have been a terrible thing to do. Ashton deserved the truth. Hell, Ashton deserved someone a billion times better than me, but I had been too selfish to let go. In a way, I was setting him free to make his own decision— to change his mind. It would hurt like crazy, but I'd probably take a bullet for him—preferably a foam bullet, but still a bullet.

I put my hand over top of his, sliding my fingers into the little gaps between his fingers. "You know I love you, right?"

"Yes," Ashton replied, his free hand brushing a limp strand of hair out of my face. "Are you all right?"

I sucked in a deep breath. "Peachy." I crossed my legs, losing myself in Ashton's mesmerizing blue orbs for possibly the last time.

My next action was definitely not planned but I did it

anyway. I grabbed the front of his shirt and yanked him forward, placing a chaste kiss on his lips. He tasted like popcorn, and I savored it.

"What was that for? Not that I'm complaining by the way. You can do that more if you want." Ashton's loving smile almost sent me into a pool of tears, even though I had no right to cry.

"I have to tell you something," I croaked out. And then Ash's smile was replaced by a concerned expression. "I haven't been completely honest with you."

"What?"

"Before I say anything, I just want you to know that I really did fall in love with you. I still love you so much. Too much."

He didn't even flinch. "What did you lie about?"

"Why would you think that I lied?" *He knows. Holy crap, he knows.*

"You only look like that when you feel guilty about something. Now just tell me, it can't be that bad."

"Oh, on the contrary, well maybe, I don't know." I snorted but immediately regretted it.

"What have you lied about?"

"A bunch of stuff, uh, a few things," I choked out. *Wait to ease into it, smartass.*

"What?"

"Well, not that much. Just a little," I repeated.

"What do you mean?"

"W-we didn't exactly meet by accident."

How would you tell the boy you love that you were a scam?

"What the hell is that supposed to mean?"

"I'm not really from Colorado," I admitted.

"You said you were from Florida."

And presenting to you, Ariella Winters, Queen of Tact.

"Oh. Oops. Sorry." I was at a loss for words. "I actually go to Easton High."

The word vomit was on the tip of my tongue, threatening to spill.

"The private school like ten minutes from here?" I nodded. "Then what are you doing here?"

"It's a long story. Just please hear me out before you do anything rash. Just so you know, every date, every movie night, and every moment I've spent with you after that kiss was one hundred percent real." I took a deep breath. *Here it goes.* "Why don't I explain from the beginning?"

"Yeah, that would be nice," he spat out, scooting an inch away from me. His hand left mine, and I was on the brink of crying. *No, Ariel, you have no right to be weak.*

"I'm not really sure how to start it but um, yeah. I'm not popular. In fact, I would never be popular. If anything, I'm the opposite. Nerd, introvert, dork, whatever you want to call it.

"Frankly, I take pride in that name because I've completed all my high school credits so I spend most of my day at a county college. Easton created this small class with about five other students who are on or at least around the same level as me. I think they only did it because they had nothing left to offer."

"Okay, so why are you here?" Ashton cut in. *Well, straight to the point, then. That's okay, too.*

"Right, sorry. One day my teacher decided to give our class a special project. I'm pretty sure it was because he ran out of things to teach us, so why not ship us off to different schools? Each one of us was sent to a different school, and I was sent to Lincoln Bay to complete this project. We were told to change a social aspect of our life and wiggle our way into that social group. As you can probably infer, I got sent into the popular crew. Well, your crew, I suppose. The irony, right? Yeah, send the socially deprived dork to fit in with the ones who never stop talking."

My attempt at humor was not working.

"With the help of Flora, my best friend, who is now Elliot's girlfriend, I changed. So that's why you see Flora and me being so close. We've known each other for years. I got an entirely new makeover. I got rid of my glasses and replaced them with contacts. By the way, I still don't understand the concept of them. Why do I have to poke my eyes when I have perfectly good glasses with me?"

He didn't even crack a smile.

"After my transformation, I looked like, well, one of you, as you can see right now. When I got to Lincoln Bay, I was weird because I was trying to act, but I can't act, so I failed at that. I guess you didn't notice since you had much better people to think about.

"But then you said you liked me, and it changed everything. I admit I judged you when I didn't have the right to. You got under my skin, which is why you know more about me than I ever planned on you knowing. Like you were never supposed to see me without makeup on or with sweats.

"And now, the only thing I can say is that I'm sorry for not being honest. I really should have told you earlier, and I feel like an idiot for putting it off. I was selfish for wanting to preserve what we have. There's no way for me to sugarcoat this so it sounds okay. It's not. I'm just sorry." I felt as if I had been deflated.

Everything that I needed to say was over with. I buried my face in my hands and prayed that nothing would change.

For a few minutes, not a single word was uttered. It felt like hours, though. I almost wanted to shake him and force him to say something, but at that point, I couldn't do anything. I had been immature. I was stupid. It was entirely my fault.

"What exactly did you have to do for this project?" Ashton finally broke the silence. When I met his eyes, there was a mixture of emotions.

"We um … had to find some people, get to know them, and just learn what makes them tick. We were supposed to learn something about people or ourselves and present it to the class," I said.

Now that I played those words back, they didn't come out nicely. Yeah, I could have gone on and on and said "I love you" every five seconds but truly, it wouldn't have done much. It was all on him. And to top it off, the painkillers I took to ease the feeling of my head exploding were starting to fade away.

"So you used me?" Ashton's voice was firm, his lips set in a thin line.

"No, I didn't use you. I mean only a little bit in the beginning, but not after I got to know you." I felt like a mouse trying to reason with an elephant. Ashton scooted to the farthest possible spot from me on the bed.

"Did Elliot know?"

"Yes."

"Oh," Ashton puffed. Boldly, I scooted next to Ashton, laying a hand over the top of his. He stared at my hand, but he didn't pull away. *What am I doing?*

"That's only because he overheard his mom talking

to my teacher, though. I would never have told him," I explained, hoping that it would lighten the situation.

It didn't.

Somehow, it just made it worse.

"When are you leaving?"

"In two weeks."

"And will you just be going back to your old schedule?"

"I guess."

Silence. I just watched the second hand on the clock. *Tick tock tick tock tick tock. Nothing.*

"So why don't we sum up what you just told me, shall we?" Ash began, and I gulped. "So, basically you came to Lincoln Bay the polar opposite of who you really are. You pretended to be someone else in front of me and everyone else at that school. You used me for your stupid project so you wouldn't fail. My best friend knew about this the entire time. And now you're telling me two weeks before you have to leave and never come back?"

"I ... I ..."

He was right.

"God dammit, why didn't you tell me this earlier?"

Sighing, Ashton ripped his hand from mine and stood up. The tears were pouring down my face, and I didn't feel them until they dripped onto my fingers. Yes, I loved him, and yes, I wanted to fight, but now it was obvious that I had lost the game from the beginning.

"I'm sorry."

It was the only thing I could say.

No, it was the only thing that my voice box could formulate.

"Do you even love me?" Ashton shrieked.

"O-of course I do! I told you that!" I faltered. My voice came out cracked and shaky but the assurance was there.

It had to be.

"Why should I believe anything you say, *Ariella*?" Ashton demanded.

I bit down on my lip so hard I'm pretty sure I could taste the iron flavor of blood but I was past caring.

"Everything you've seen in the past five months was real. What I lied about was minor. I should've lied more, actually. But I couldn't. Something about you didn't let me." I sniffled, and I hadn't even attempted to wipe the tears away.

"Don't you get it? It's not about you lying. Did you even think about what would happen after the five months? Or did you just expect a happily-ever-after?"

"Of course I thought about it. But summer is only two weeks away and—"

"You're still fucking leaving, *Ariella*. We're going to different schools. Completely different paths. And, Jesus, was I not worth telling this to before?"

"No, it's just—"

"Well, *Ariella*, I'm not sure this is going to work out." Ashton gestured between us, his voice cracking near the end.

I knew it was coming but when it really came out of his mouth, it hurt a bazillion times worse.

"Please."

"Fucking hell, *Ariella*. You know this won't work out in the end. You should just give up now."

"It'll work. We can—" I cried. And for once, I yearned for him to call me "gorgeous" just one more time.

"What's the point? I should've seen this coming. Why can't I just be happy without there being a catch?"

"Y-you love me."

"Yeah, and I thought my parents loved me too, but clearly they don't give two shits about me, or they would call more than once a month."

"Ashton—"

"I really believed that you could've been the one, too."

The one. Which meant that Ashton could see himself growing old with me. With me. Then I didn't care that we were only seventeen. He still thought I was the one.

"Reall—"

"You know what the worst part is?"

I didn't answer.

"I'm actually not that mad."

"Huh?" *Wasn't he fuming a couple seconds ago?*

"I'm actually considering just forgetting it all and putting in a movie for us to watch."

"W-what?"

"I should be extremely pissed, right? Actually, I know for a fact that I should be pissed that my girlfriend, who I trusted, didn't care enough to tell me this shit except for when she's about to leave me. I shouldn't hesitate in leaving you right now. I should walk away. But you see, I can't bring myself to do that right now. Why? Because I made the fucking mistake of falling for you."

Whoever made that stupid saying, "Sticks and stones may break my bones, but words can never hurt me," lied because my head was pounding, yet all I could focus on were those last ten words. And believe me when I say they hurt.

I looked at Ashton long enough to see his eyes widen in the slightest.

"I think I should go." Without sparing me a second glance, Ashton stormed out of the room. I heard footsteps and then the slam of a door and then nothing.

I didn't go after him.

And then I became that girl. The girl who had fallen hopelessly for someone only to face the inevitable heartbreak. I was the girl I swore I never wanted to be, and it felt even worse than I had thought.

After that, I slumped back into the old Ariella. The one who only let her mind focus on grades. The one who had a plan and intended to complete it. The one who wasn't as stupid as what I had become. The one who didn't believe in love because there was no point.

I then realized that people didn't change. They just get off track for a while and before you know it, their "old self" would come haunting back.

He was right. I was leaving. We weren't going to work out. And he was the one who had reminded me of that.

He also reminded me that love was useless in the long run. It gave you pain that didn't need to be felt and also the regret of falling for that person like Ashton regretted me.

And love would ruin me for a bit, but eventually it would all be okay, and it wouldn't hurt.

This time, I let myself lie to my brain that it'd all be okay. Mom always told me to give love a chance.

I had.

And it sucked. I vowed to myself that day that once the storm passed, I wouldn't fall in love until it was appropriate.

But before that, I balled up on my bed and cried myself to sleep for the first time since I don't even know when.

Chapter 24

Nine days.

My calendar marked exactly nine days since Ashton and I broke up.

I wouldn't be lying if I said that I still felt pretty shitty.

And I was doing the exact thing I swore I'd never do. *Stupid heartache. Stupid people. Stupid world. Stupid, stupid, stupid.*

In my opinion, humans were always the weakest and most dependent species. That was a fact—well, in my book, anyway. I doubted any other animal suffered this badly from losing a significant other. Hell, some animal mates never see each other again after their babies are born.

People like to argue and say things like humans are mammals. Fine, humans are the weakest mammals, then. We feel the need to latch on to another, leading us to believe that nothing bad could happen. Then we are left surprised and sad when clearly it was coming to an end anyway. Then, when it all crashes down, there's not even a coping method that will help.

I hadn't touched my camera in nine days, either. Anytime I had an urge to grab it, a spiral of memories of Ashton would flood into my mind and then I'd end up feeling worse than before. My concussion was pretty much healed, which had its pros and cons. A con being that I had to go back to Lincoln Bay and face everyone.

School was even worse than I could've ever imagined. I understand it was probably a bit alarming when the new popular girl in town completely changed to wearing sweats, abandoning the makeup, putting on nerdy glasses, and just stopped making herself presentable.

Yes, that's how I see myself at Easton High. A bit too unpresentable. But for high school, it didn't matter. What really mattered was when I'd go to college. Then I'd have to worry about being presentable. And if this change of clothing was what Ashton wanted to see, then he got his wish. Little did he know how disappointed he would actually be.

It was a bit uncomfortable to have every single person turn their head when I walked through the hallway, though. But at that point, it didn't matter. And the only person I really wanted to look at me pretended that I didn't exist.

I tried to talk to him once on the first day I went back. My voice was like that of a mute puppy, and it was completely and utterly pathetic. It came out as a whisper, and I was pretty sure Ashton didn't even hear it. It wouldn't even have mattered if he had heard me, though. It was obvious he didn't even want to look at me, and I refused to be the girl who looked like she wanted to cry in front of her ex.

I couldn't be.

I wouldn't be.

So after that one failed attempt at sparking conversation, I stopped trying.

But it was so hard to not think about how differently this project could have gone. If I hadn't stopped in front of the graveyard and had kept walking, maybe I wouldn't feel so terrible. Maybe if I had just put my act together while I was alone with him, then I would still have completed the project, and my emotions would have stayed intact. If only I hadn't been so careless when I was with him, maybe there would be no pain to go through.

But karma would probably still have come and bitten me in the ass.

And in some twisted way, I didn't fully regret opening up to Ashton. I didn't regret how much I liked—no, loved him. I had the opportunity to really get to know someone as funny and kind as him.

When the alarm sounded, I couldn't help but groan. It took everything in me to hold back the urge to throw that alarm out the window. After about five minutes of stalling, I rolled myself out of the comfort zone known as my bed.

It was Friday, which meant the last day at Lincoln Bay, and it was much more depressing than anyone would've thought.

When I caught a glimpse of myself in the mirror, I almost jumped. It was probably a bad sign when I nearly screamed at my own reflection.

The dark circles around my eyes were more noticeable than the day before. I resembled a raccoon more and more each day. My hair was like a bird's nest, and it probably shouldn't have been that way. *Whatever.* I had no one to impress.

After brushing my teeth and splashing some water on my face, I stumbled toward my closet, the residual effects of my concussion still making my head throb a little. Because the sun decided to shine rather brightly on this oh-so-wonderful morning, I grabbed a random red T-shirt and yoga pants and threw them on.

I didn't even know how I had acquired so many T-shirts. The stack grew larger every year, but I had no memory of buying any of them. So many events had free T-shirts that I took the opportunity to stock up on my wardrobe.

It was a huge deal on my end. Other girls spent so much on buying clothes, and my wardrobe was free. I considered myself winning.

As I stepped toward my dresser, I threw on my glasses. I had forgotten how much more comfortable glasses were compared to contacts.

Well, at least there is one perk to this crappy situation.

I didn't have to fear being blinded from poking my eye every day.

Knowing that I had to somewhat tame this mane of mine, I raked a brush through my tangled hair. When most of the knots had come out, I pulled my hair into a bun that sat right on the top of my head.

Not giving my reflection a second glance, I left my bedroom. Trampling down the stairs, I ran a hand over my bun, making sure it was nice and tight in order to withstand the day. Although my hand didn't get very far because one of the tangles seemed to catch my index finger. I fluttered my fingers a little, hoping to pull my hand back with as little pain as possible. My face scrunched when I accidently yanked a few strands of hair out. Damn. The stupid things I did could've easily gone viral on YouTube.

But for now, I was going to school and hating every bit of it.

I considered my leaving a favor to both me and Ashton. He wouldn't have to deal with my face anymore, and I wouldn't have to be reminded constantly of my idiocy. *It was the right thing to do, right?* Either way, I didn't deserve to be with him.

I slung my bag over my shoulder while taking a bite out of my apple. Looking at the clock, I would be about ten minutes earlier than anybody else. Then again, when wasn't I early? Without a word, I walked toward my beat-up Sedan. Stella had gone home, so I was all alone. The biggest difference between Mom and Stella was how Mom could sleep all day if no one woke her, while Stella was up early, always making herself a cup of coffee.

Following my usual routine—well, usual meaning for the past six months—I drove to Lincoln Bay, got out of the car, and walked into Mr. Blair's classroom for the last time. Ashton wasn't there, but then again, he'd stopped coming early since the day I came back to school. I didn't blame him.

As I walked into the classroom, Mr. Blair's head shot up. "Good morning, Ariel," he greeted me.

"Good morning, Mr. Blair."

"How are you doing today?"

"I'm okay." *And totally ready to go back to Easton High. Well, er, not really—no I'm ready to go back.*

"Only okay?" he said, standing up. I nodded. "Are you excited to go back to Easton?"

"I've been counting the days," I joked.

He cracked a smile. "Well, it's been a joy having someone like you in my class."

"It's been great having a teacher like you."

"You always were incredibly polite. And a great student, too. Did you enjoy the classes?"

Taking my seat, I answered, "Well, excluding the fact that I've learned all of this before, it really was pretty fun."

He chuckled, but he didn't really say much after that, so I assumed he was grading papers.

I stared at the seat that would soon be occupied by Ashton. Next to me. He was so close, yet he still managed to avoid eye contact. Now that was a talent.

Ashton seemed perfectly fine, to say the least. Now that he was single, all the girls took that to mean that he was starting to "date" again. They were probably right, anyway. He had no restrictions left. Ashton could do anything he wanted.

I couldn't help but feel a tinge of jealousy when Ashton smiled at them. He clearly had no problems moving on. I was probably only a fling to him, anyway. A ridiculous, depressing fling that he regretted. We were too young to know what love was, but why on earth did it feel so real?

"Are you confident in your presentation?" Mr. Blair asked, trying to create conversation again. It was probably out of sympathy, though.

"I mean I'm still a bit fuzzy on the project itself, but I guess I'm ready."

"Don't worry. It's basically a learning experience/experiment. They want you to have a taste of everything for your high school life. Plus, it's hard to imagine that

Mr. Kinsey won't give you a good grade. As long as you tried your best."

"Thanks." *Good job continuing the conversation, Ariel.*

Silence.

"Ariel, you are a strong girl. I can't wait to hear about how your presentation goes."

Before I could thank him for the seventh time because I had nothing else to say, the bell rang, and people began to file in. I watched each individual enter the classroom, none of them sparing a second glance at me.

I had become completely invisible in three days, unless they wanted to make fun of me. It wasn't too bad, though, considering that I'd spent most of my high school years so far living through it all. It was only this semester that people saw me differently, and I had trouble deciphering whether it was a dream or a nightmare.

I really should have been thankful. I'd had six months to re-create myself anyway I wanted to, and it wouldn't affect my grades at all. Six months to meet new people. Six months to step out of my little bubble and explore the uncharted territory of high school. Six months to do whatever I wanted and never get in trouble. It wasn't as wild as it sounded, though.

I still stayed home and watched movies while fattening myself up with pizza and pasta. Now, *that* was paradise.

My eyes traveled from one person to another but landed on Ashton. He was talking to a girl on the cheerleading squad who was trying her best to flirt.

I knew her. She was one of the ones who gave me dirty looks at the soccer games. Ashton didn't seem to be paying much attention to her, though. His lips moved, and reluctantly, she went to her seat which was on the other side of the room. I returned my attention to the windows, a small smile unexpectedly playing on my face.

He took his seat next to mine and suddenly I felt small all over again. His presence just did that. Ashton had said that I must have been so different, but he was wrong. The only difference was that any sort of confidence I had around him, had vanished. Well, also the fact that I looked like an ogre.

Yeah, that too.

I debated whether I should even attempt to talk to him. I twiddled my fingers, something I hadn't done in months, and gnawed on my lip. *You'll never see him again. Just say good-bye.*

No, don't make an even bigger fool of yourself than you've already done.

I pulled out a book that I carried with me, and flipped open to a random page. But I was almost one hundred percent sure someone was watching me. My head didn't come up until Mr. Blair spoke. *Just one more day, Ariel. You can do this. Then all of this ridiculousness will end. It will be okay. Just keep on going.*

When an agonizing forty-five minutes had gone by, and the bell finally rang, I sped out of the classroom before anyone could follow me. *Same old, same old. I mean what was I expecting to get from this project? A happily ever after? That only happens in fairytales. Or really lucky people. Really, really lucky people. Besides, the princesses are always drop-dead gorgeous, and I'm just me.*

The next three classes passed excruciatingly slowly, especially considering that I was trying my best to avoid eye contact with anyone. Luckily, none of the teachers called on me.

Finally, it was time for lunch. Once again, I zipped down the hallway, dodging any possible contact with people. I watched out for Erika, making sure she didn't see me. I kept an eye out, so I didn't bump into anyone who knew my name. *Well, that would be everyone in the damn school, you doofus.* As quickly as possible, I weaved around the massive numbers of people, but it seemed that I wasn't quick enough.

"Ariel!" It was Elliot. Panicking, I started to sprint, creating more and more distance from him. I turned around to see that Elliot was getting lost in the sea of people headed for the different hallways of the school.

I was making sure that Elliot wasn't following me when I slammed into someone and dropped lunch bag. I fell backward and landed right on my ass. Adjusting my glasses, I looked up to see Erika staring down at me, confused.

"Ariel? Is that you?

"Yeah," I said, trying to find a way not to have this conversation. She eyed my outfit with disgust.

"What are you wearing?"

"Clothes."

"But—"

"Listen, Erika. I have to go. Sorry." I ran off without another word.

Behind me, Erika yelled, "Ariel, just some advice, that's not the best outfit you've ever worn."

I ignored her.

Exhaling, I walked to the media center. My heart was pounding as though I had just run five miles. I knew what Elliot would've said to me had he caught up. He would've tried to comfort me and feed me the lie that Ashton still loved me, but I knew he didn't.

Elliot would've said that Flora was worried. That I should talk to her. I already knew that I should talk to her. Of course I should consult my best friend, but sometimes I liked being alone.

When you're alone, nobody can hurt you.

Even if Elliot really did want to talk to me, he would never find me. The library would be the last place he looked. He didn't know me that well.

I tiptoed to the corner where I would be camouflaged in the fiction section and leaned my head against one of the shelves, breathing hard. I drew my knees toward my chest and wrapped my arms around my legs.

I was alone.

It was better that way.

Chapter 25

There were two ways I hated being woken up. The first was with a false promise of food, which was a method my mom liked to use when I had stayed up too late to study. The second was being trampled, shaken, and yelled at by another person while having these amazing dreams I could only hope would become a reality.

Flora preferred the second way, and I had a rather strong urge to throttle her when her voice flooded in my head the second I had opened a letter from Columbia, the first word in which was *Congratulations!*

"Get up! Get up! Get up!"

My bed wobbled due to the uncomfortable pressure of another human being treating my mattress as a moon bounce.

Still being half-asleep, I did the one thing a partially unconscious person would do in this particular situation. I punched her, presumably in her stomach.

It probably wasn't the best thing to do, but it

certainly worked. The wobbling stopped, and I had a split second of blissful silence before a loud groan filled the room.

"Why are you such a heavy sleeper, goddammit?" Flora crawled onto my bed again and shook my shoulders.

I tried to shove her off once again, but her cold hands grabbed my wrist before I could successfully do so.

"How did you get in my room?" I croaked out.

Frankly, I hadn't planned to have any contact with her until I got back to Easton, but my plans had clearly been shattered.

"Your mother let me in," she said, defensively. "And I'm pretty sure she was relieved to know that her daughter wouldn't spend the day locked in her room reading her textbooks over and over again."

Traitor. "Well, as you can see, I'm not reading. I'm sleeping. And I was having the greatest dream ever before you oh-so-kindly treated me to your presence." I burrowed under my duvet, enjoying the heat that was warming up my chilly hands.

"Let me guess. It's the same 'amazing' dream you have where you get your acceptance letter from Columbia and then you spend the next twenty hours jumping around because you're so excited." She put air quotes around the amazing.

"I didn't even get to open the letter."

For some reason, my voice had dramatically dropped in confidence. It was as though the reality of the breakup with Ashton had just dawned on me once again, reminding me that I was a selfish brat who definitely didn't deserve his love in the slightest.

"You're really taking this breakup bad, aren't you?" Flora's voice was laced with sympathy.

But it was a kind of sympathy that was a hundred percent pointless because it never helped. It was the kind of sympathy Flora gave me at the end of sixth grade when I had gotten my first and only C on a biology quiz, and, at the time, it had felt like the worst day of my life. It was the kind of sympathy Flora hadn't given me since that awful day in sixth grade, and I didn't like to think that I had sunken so low that Flora felt the need to use that same pity as she did when she saw me wiping my tears in the girls' bathroom.

"I'm fine. I just need to survive a few more days, and this ridiculousness will all end."

"I hate to break it to you, but it's not that easy, Ari."

There it was again.

And it drove me crazy.

"It has to be. The project has ended, so everything else has to end with it."

Flora yanked my pillow away and my head bounced on the mattress. "Ariel, this isn't one of your goddamn SAT books. You have to stop pretending that you're fine when anyone with eyes can see that you're clearly not."

And just like that, I was mad.

"Well, Flora, what am I supposed to do, huh? Yes, I'll admit, I'm not the happiest I've ever been, but it's not like there's anything that I can do about it."

"Ari—"

"No. Look, I knew Ashton and I weren't going to work out the second I laid my eyes on him. I knew it wasn't going to end well. I also knew I should've told him earlier, and even if he wasn't mad, there would still have been no chance we would work out. We were together for what, four, maybe five, months? That's not that long, you know. So please deal with the fact that I'm not with him anymore. I'm dealing with it."

"No, you're not. You're sitting and pitying yourself. And because you're you, you're shutting everyone else out. Look, I'm not going to pity you if that's what you're thinking. But do you genuinely believe that throughout your entire relationship, you knew it wouldn't work out?"

"Y-yes."

"Why are you lying to yourself?"

"It feels better than remembering how Ashton thinks I was a mistake."

"He was mad."

"We're going on different paths."

"I know for a fact you believed that you two had a chance."

"I don't need your lecturing, Flora."

"I am your best friend, you know. Isn't this the time when best friends are needed most?"

"I know what you're thinking and hell no. We are not sitting on the couch and watching *The Notebook* while I eat a tub of ice cream and cry in your arms."

She laughed. "That sounds awful, if I'm being honest. What I mean is that you don't have to be okay right now, but you shouldn't sit in your room and be sad. That's such a waste."

"Thanks for the advice, wise guy."

She didn't answer me for the first ten seconds.

"You know what I don't understand? How is it possible that you have almost no faith in love, when your parents were high school sweethearts?"

And, for the first time, I answered her question with a serious and honest answer.

"They valued love over success."

"And what exactly do you value?"

"I just can't wrap my head around the fact that they chose something as risky as love over a successful and steady future."

"Can I ask you something?" she said softly. I nodded. "How did being with Ashton make you feel?"

I really didn't want to go through this again. I could've lied to her, but then again, there was no point in doing that.

"G-good."

"Better than when you were home alone memorizing SAT words?"

I couldn't see where this was going.

"I suppose," I said suspiciously.

"That, my friend, is why your parents chose love."

Her worlds replayed over and over again in my brain, and I didn't notice I was crying until a droplet of water fell from my face onto my right thumb. I hastily wiped the tears away, hoping that Flora didn't notice.

But of course she noticed, and she pulled me forward so that her arms encircled around my shoulders. It was a short hug that lasted for about five seconds, but it was one that I definitely needed.

"That was intense." I wiped another tear from my eye, a small smile growing.

"Yeah. That definitely woke you up. Just so you know, it's okay to have ambition and be in love simultaneously."

"I—"

"By the way, Ashton's not taking it all too well, either," she interjected.

"What?" I froze.

"You know. Ashton. He's not taking it well, either."

"He'll be fine. I did him a favor."

"Why?" She seemed genuinely confused.

"I wasn't the type of girl he should've been with anyway."

"How do you know?"

"He thinks I'm a fucking mistake, Flora. That's how I know."

"Have you ever wondered why his past … flings haven't worked out? You have to understand that the poor guy has been through a lot, and when the girl he loves suddenly tells him that she's leaving, he doubts everything," she said.

"Aren't you supposed to be supposed to be supporting me, not taking his side?"

"Okay, I admit, he's a dickwad for saying that but you really have to look at his perspective."

"Look, I'm over this conversation. Can we talk about something else?" I looked at Flora with the poutiest face I could muster.

"Ari! He still loves you." She grabbed my shoulders, shaking me.

"No, he doesn't. We're seventeen. We don't even know what love is." I poked her hands, hoping to loosen the pressure she was forcing on me. But she didn't move her hands. I think she even pushed down harder.

"Oh, please. Are you really that clueless?"

"No—"

"Even your mom thinks that you're in love with him."

"She's always been a hopeless romantic," I said.

Flora thumped the back of my head, and I reached and held the back of my head with my left hand. With my free hand, I went to slap Flora, but she caught my arm before I could make contact.

"Ow!" I pouted.

"You say that as if being a hopeless romantic is a bad thing." She folded her arms across her chest.

"I think we've had enough of Abuse Ariel Day. Why don't we go get some food?"

"Let's go to the mall today," she said randomly.

"No, thank you."

"Come on. Elliot will be there."

"Just because you're boyfriend is going to be there, doesn't mean that I want to go. Frankly, being a third wheel doesn't sound like the most appealing offer I've ever received."

"He's your friend, too," Flora whined.

"I'll go with you another day." I waved a hand dismissively.

"No, come with me today."

"Tempting, but I'm going to have to pass."

"You have to go."

"Hey, I have an idea," I began. Flora's eyes lit up. "Let's go to the library. I need to return some books. Or we could go look at some camera lenses."

And just like that, all emotion drained from her face. She stared at me blankly for a few seconds. I cracked a smile at her sudden change of heart. It was too hard to be serious around her.

"You are ridiculous."

"I will take that as a compliment, thank you very much."

"Come on, please?"

"No. I want to go to the library."

"You are going. I bet all you've been doing for the past couple of days is mope around and read. I bet you eat in the library just to avoid Ashton and Elliot at school, too." She commented. "And, I bet you've gone back to wearing baggy T-shirts, sweats, and glasses. Let me guess, you don't wear makeup anymore, and now we're back to day one, aren't we?"

"Your point is …?"

"Oh shut up, Ariel. You know that if I was there, I would have found you in seconds and dragged you out of that library corner."

"That's kind of creepy." I cringed at the thought of actually being dragged out of a library.

"Stalling," she sang. "I really should be mad that you've been ignoring my calls, but you're hurting, so I'll let it go just this once." She playfully punched my shoulders, giving me a smile. "I really think you should come along."

"I'm not sure—"

"Please?"

Flora could do this skillful thing where she could just cry on cue. It was something that could pressure anyone to do something she wanted. And now, she was using her power on me. It wasn't a full-on sob, but her eyes were glossy.

Why couldn't I have that talent? All I had was the ability to bend my thumb back really far. When I was younger, I was so proud of that. Now, crying on cue sounded so much more awesome.

"Fine," I grumbled. "But you have to buy me dinner, and I'm only staying for an hour."

"Deal. Now let's do something with that hair," she said. I scoffed.

"I never said that I would change. I think I look mighty fine, by the way."

"Ariel," she whined. "Please just let me pick out an outfit for you? You know I love you when I say that you look like you've just been mauled by a bear and then buried alive."

World's best friend award goes to Flora Reynolds.

"Well, doesn't that boost my self-confidence?" I began. "And fine, but you only get to pick the clothes. I get to do my hair and face however I like."

"You are incredibly stubborn."

"Hey, that's a compromise."

"Elliot!" Flora squealed, dragging me across the street.

It was like she increased her speed by ten when she spotted Elliot. Oh, how lovely it would be to be the third wheel today!

"Over here!" Elliot shouted, waving his hands in the air.

I looked up, surprised.

Not because of Elliot, but because of the boy who was standing behind him but just in my view.

Ashton was really standing there in the flesh. He was on his phone, so he hadn't noticed me just yet. If I ran away now, he wouldn't even have known I was there. Flora must have read my mind, because her grip on my wrist tightened.

Damn you, Flora.

"Flora, I have to pee," I whispered.

"Oh well. Hold it." She smirked. I attempted to pull my hand out of her grip, but it was no use. She'd gotten really strong these past months. Or I was just weak at the moment.

"Hey there, Ariel," Elliot said.

I faked a smile.

"Hi," I said, looking down.

I felt a pair of eyes watching me, and I didn't have to look up to know it was Ashton. I fixed my glasses awkwardly, trying my best to hide behind Flora.

"Hey there, Ashton," Flora said. Ashton just nodded, not taking his eyes off me. Or maybe he was looking at Flora, and I was behind her. I couldn't tell.

There was a rough silence, and when I finally decided to look up, Elliot and Flora were exchanging looks. He shrugged his shoulders, and Flora scolded him with her eyes. I didn't dare glance in Ashton's direction. I just couldn't face him.

The awkwardness was palpable. I could almost have reached out and grabbed the awkwardness.

"Well, let's go in, shall we?" Elliot proposed. Flora looped her arm through mine and tugged me to the entrance.

I stood on the very left, the farthest away from Ashton.

I knew I looked out of place.

The blouse and jean shorts Flora picked didn't direct the attention away from my raccoon eyes. People were probably wondering why someone like me was walking with them. I wondered that myself. *Oh, right. It's because I looked like that once. Yeah, for six months.*

Flora unlocked her arm from mine and skipped over to a stand with earrings. Not bothering to catch up to her, I stuffed my hands in my pocket.

I just stared at the laces of my beat-up old Converse.

"How are you, Ariel?" Elliot popped up right beside me.

Awkwardly, I took a step away from him. It was strange because before this, I always knew what to say to people I didn't want to face. I always found a way to excuse myself politely. Here, not so much.

"Just peachy," I replied carelessly.

"You and Ashton both." He rolled his eyes.

"What does that mean?"

"You're both so sarcastic when you're sad, and I'm the lucky one who deals with it,"

When I turned around, I found Ashton a few meters behind me looking at the mannequins placed in the front of a store whose name I didn't know. I turned back to Elliot.

"He looks fine to me."

"The key word there is 'looks.'"

"He's fine."

"He still loves you," Elliot blurted out.

"No, he doesn't. Let's change the subject. It's getting awkward."

"You just like to avoid people. You think that he hates you, don't you?" He kept going as if I hadn't said anything.

"He does."

"No, he doesn't."

"Please shut up."

"Don't believe me? Go talk to him now."

I shook my head. I wanted to tell Elliot that I had already tried. And the answers Ashton gave me made it obvious that he didn't like me anymore.

"I most certainly will not talk to him."

"I have to go check on Flora." Elliot tapped his wrist even though there was no watch. "Oh, Ashton," he hollered. "Do keep Ariel busy while I go check on Flora."

My eyes widened, and I slapped Elliot's arm. "Why would you do that?"

"Stop hitting me already," He whined, holding his arm.

"Then stop being such a douche bag."

He just ignored me and walked over to Flora. Elliot whispered something in her ear, and she nodded. Then I felt a presence beside me. Ashton.

As I looked at him, it felt as though nothing had changed. He was still that terribly handsome guy, but now his feelings toward me changed.

"Hi," I mumbled.

It was at a volume where there was a chance he heard it and could have ignored me, or he could have just not have heard me at all.

"Hi," he replied.

I rocked back and forth on the balls of my feet. After tearing my eyes from Ashton, I noticed that Flora and Elliot were nowhere to be seen.

"Flora and Elliot left," I informed him. He raised an eyebrow as he looked at the earring stand where my best friend had once been standing.

"Bastards."

"I know how you feel."

"Elliot is going to pay for this."

Silence. Annoyingly quiet silence.

"Do you, um … do you want to walk around?" I proposed but soon regretted it. "I mean you don't have to—"

"Sure," he said. And like that, I stopped talking.

"Okay."

And like that, we were walking in sync, but it was still nowhere near comfortable. His hands were stuffed in his pockets as were mine. We were standing probably five feet away from each other.

To a stranger, we wouldn't even have looked like friends, let alone a couple. We looked like two people who were coincidentally walking the same speed and direction in the mall.

Just one big coincidence.

"Hey, Ariel?" Ashton asked tentatively.

My head shot up and somewhere deep inside of me, I was hoping that he would sweep me off my feet, say I love you like in the movies and— bam, we would be a couple again. But that wasn't reality.

"You have a piece of grass in your hair."

I ran a hand through my hand a couple times and muttered a quick, "Thanks."

"No problem."

I thought that would be the end of our conversation, but he continued, and when he did, something tugged at my heart a little bit.

"I like your glasses," Ashton admitted.

"Thank you." Wanting to preserve the conversation, I kept going, "They sure feel better than the contacts."

"I'll bet." Ash said. This felt nice. Just to be on speaking terms with him. Of course it was only a short conversation, but it felt nice. "You know, in my opinion, you didn't have to wear makeup to look nice."

"What?"

"I mean, you look beau-fine without makeup." Ashton caught himself.

"Thanks, but I beg to differ."

"You would have been just fine without makeup." Ash offered a smile. I suppose this was his chance to see my real exterior. He must have been really disappointed by what he saw. "It wouldn't have changed how I saw you."

"Thank you." I said even though I didn't believe his words in the slightest.

We talked for what felt like an hour and it felt nice just being on speaking terms.

Acquaintances were good. In fact, acquaintances were great.

Knowing that I owed it to him, I told him he could ask any questions about the project. He seemed happy when I said that. He even smiled his lopsided smile.

"So you're like supersmart?" Ashton wondered.

"I guess if you want to put it that way." Supersmart wasn't what I called myself, but I guess that was a possible synonym.

"I knew you were smart, but damn, girl," he said admiringly. "So that's what those thick packets were?"

I nodded. "Yeah."

"So these six months have kind of been a freebee?"

"Well, you can put it that way if you want. I still had the packets and videos. Plus I still had to take tests."

"That's awesome. Man, I should have made you do my homework."

"You could've tried but it wouldn't have happened."

We were still nowhere close to being a couple again, but I didn't mind. It wasn't like I expected that. I didn't even expect a friendship.

"That explains why you're such a dork."

"Hey! I'm not a complete dork," I complained.

"Oh, please, I saw the face you had when we were partners for that essay."

"Sorry that I don't like working with people."

"Introvert," he coughed.

"Hey!"

"Not to mention how easily you blush."

"I don't blush easily." I put my hands on my hips.

Suddenly, Ashton leaned over so his lips were centimeters away from my ear. "You're beautiful, just so you know."

Okay, I did blush. *How could you not?* Maybe he was right. I angled myself so Ashton couldn't see my face, but I knew that it didn't matter when he stifled his laughter. After a bit, we calmed down, and we were just strolling around the mall.

"Case closed." Ashton ran a hand through his hair.

"Fine."

"I just have one question left." His eyes met mine, and I practically swooned.

"Shoot."

"Before, did you believe, you know, that we'd still be together after you left?"

Just like that, I was speechless again. My feet felt like cinder blocks, and I wasn't able to move. Ashton didn't seem to mind, because he stopped as well.

"I mean, in the beginning I was skeptical, but yes, I really believed we could stay together."

"Really?"

"Yes, I promise. Crazy considering I had no faith in love before I went to Lincoln Bay and met you."

"Same."

"I really do love you, you know?" I blurted out but instantly regretted it when I realized what I had said. *Too far. Too far. Too far.* "I mean, um … well, never mind."

"Ari—"

"No … um, it's fine. I'm sorry I said that. It probably made you uncomfortable," I said.

He didn't need to know that. Ashton must have been well over us by now. I was making a fool of myself.

"Ariel—"

"I think I have to go. Ashton, look, I'm really sorry for everything. Don't worry about me anymore. You can hate me forever because I deserve it. And this is good for you because you never have to face me ever again. This is good-bye, I guess. Thank you for everything and seriously, you're really talented at soccer. I can't wait to be able to see you playing on my TV. And um, I'm really sorry."

With that, I ran away like the coward I was. I was a helpless coward. He didn't need me in his life, and I just needed to believe that I didn't need him.

I could have sworn I heard the padded thumps of Ashton running after me, but this was the one time where I was too fast. When I got outside, I sat on a random bench behind a bush and buried my face in my hands.

That might have been the end, but I still couldn't help the little jolts of electricity on my skin when he smiled that goofy smile. Ashton's real smile. The smile that I would never see again. The smile that I lost the privilege even to look at. And I had a minuscule feeling that I'd be okay. He had let me see part of his life, and I was thankful for it.

That night, the sky was so clear I couldn't help but grab my camera. When I first touched it, my only thought was *God, I missed you.*

I crawled out the window and sat on the same part of the roof I had spent so much of my time—and just a little bit of Ashton's time—on. It felt so good to be holding my baby again. I leaned back so I was lying down and flipped the on switch.

A small red light flickered and then my eyes were glued to the camera as I zoomed in, trying to focus on the full moon with faint stars blinking around it. I found the perfect angle, which took me a good twenty minutes, and then I began the never-ending cycle of taking too many photos, then deleting most of them.

I flipped the camera off and let it sit on my stomach. My eyes fluttered shut, and for that moment, I felt invincible.

Chapter 26

I stood in front of Easton High, strands of stray hair blowing in the light breeze.

I had imagined my return so much differently.

I had imagined being happy. Being pleased that I could return to my old self. But for some reason, something in the pit of my stomach was telling me that I didn't want that. But to a regular student from Easton, I looked like I hadn't changed at all. And physically, they were right. Okay, I had decided to wear a black blouse and denim shorts so I suppose I did look a bit different. But it wasn't a large enough change that people would care.

Emotionally? Well, let's just say I was working on it.

Walking through the halls, I nearly forgot which hallway to go through. It was a reminder of how much had happened in a mere six months.

Six months in one's entire life time didn't seem long at all but it was definitely six months to remember because exactly 182 days ago, my life certainly was not the same.

Six months ago, I had a life of no complications except for the occasional AP physics test.

Other than that, which I had spent an unnecessary amount of time studying for, nada. No boys and certainly no drama.

Now, I was pretty sure my life could be a reality show. A really crappy reality show, of course, but nonetheless, a reality show.

Last night, I finally understood. I understood that Ashton and I weren't meant to be, but I would never regret it. He was going to move on, and so would I and it would be oka—

Oh, who the hell am I kidding? I'm not Buddha. I miss him. A lot. I don't understand. Maybe in some lucky situation, we'd last. We'd have a happily ever after. Ah, if only we were that lucky.

I didn't realize how oblivious I was to my surroundings until my face came in contact with a wall. My nose scrunched up, and I shook my head, trying to get rid of Ashton's perfect smile, which was invading my brain. I took a deep breath and stepped into Mr. Kinsey's classroom for the first time in six months.

"Ah, Miss Winters, it's great to see you," Mr. Kinsey said, standing up from his desk. No one was in the classroom, since class didn't start for another half hour. It felt like reassuring to see him there. He hadn't changed a bit. Same old style. But I hadn't expected him to change, anyway. It was only six months. "Mr. Blair has said many great things."

"Good morning, Mr. Kinsey. It's great to see you as well."

"So how've you been? I absolutely cannot wait to

hear that project of yours." Mr. Kinsey really did seem intrigued.

Much more ecstatic than I was.

"I've been doing pretty well." I held up my plain gray flash drive and fiddled with it between my fingers.

"Anyone coming to watch today?"

I wish. "Nope, no one's coming today." I tried my best not to frown.

"Oh, well, that's okay. Did you enjoy your time at Lincoln Bay? I heard from many of the other students that they really had a great time."

"It was okay. It was definitely an experience."

"How was being someone new for six months? Exhilarating?"

"You could say that." I stuck the flash drive back in my pocket and pushed away a strand of loose hair that was practically poking my eye.

"Has anything changed?"

"More than you know."

Possibly more than I ever wanted to.

"Well, that's wonderful. I see that you're still early as always, though. I was beginning to miss my morning friend." Mr. Kinsey sat down at his desk and clicked something on his computer. It hadn't even been ten seconds, and he was standing up again. "Now, if you'll excuse me, Ariella, I'm going to go to the copy room and get the rubrics for today's presentations."

When Mr. Kinsey stepped out of the classroom, I decided to take a seat in the back row, for once. Fiddling with the hem of my top, that I had no idea why I chose instead of a T-shirt, I looked around the classroom. It was the same as when I had left. There were still the same

French posters around the room, since Mr. Kinsey also taught French.

The language of love.

Gross.

There was just this rude awakening that Easton High had just kept going as it always had. My leaving didn't have much impact on the school. But I felt okay. It'd be fine. Everything would be fine. That was just a chapter in my life that would take a little more time to heal. Eventually everything had to be okay. I had a whole summer—

Oh, fuck being okay.

"Ariel," someone said, panting.

When my head snapped up, my jaw practically disconnected from my mouth. I was probably making a fool out of myself by staring at him like he had two heads.

With his hand shoved in his pockets, he stared at me, smiling.

I rubbed my eyes. He was still there.

I blinked. He was still there.

I shut my eyes for five seconds. He was still there.

Either my mind was playing some serious games on me, or the real Ashton Walker was standing before me.

"Hey you," Ashton said, his voice like a flow of perfection. He looked great. Really great.

And that's all it took for me to crave him all over again. Two words. Six letters. And it was kind of sad, really.

But thank God I'm not wearing an oversized T-shirt.

"Hi," I stuttered.

"How are you?" Ashton was wearing navy blue

jeans with a plain white top, but somehow it worked better than it should have.

"I'm ... okay." I ran my fingers around my bun, suddenly feeling way too self-conscious for my well-being. When I noticed that the conversation was about to die, I panicked a bit. "How are you?"

His eyes were even clearer, since the sunlight peeking in. "Horrible."

I frowned. "Well ... what's wrong?"

"I miss you," he declared so blatantly that I had to check my ears to see whether or not they had deceived me. "And I didn't realize that you were about to slip right through my fingers until your best friend, oh so generously, slapped some sense into me after you left. Literally. My face still hurts." Ashton walked over to where I was sitting.

I was too shocked to laugh.

The butterflies had returned in full force.

"Huh?" I immediately stood up. It was also a habit, I suppose.

I pinched my arm to make sure this was real but it backfired on me because I pinched a little too hard. I pouted and rubbed my arm, forgetting that Ashton was even there. The corner of his lips tugged up.

"Owwww."

"Did you just pinch yourself?" He took a step closer, and, if I'd wanted to, I could easily have held his hand. But that would have been totally inappropriate.

Completely inappropriate.

"Maybe."

"Just listen for a second. I'm sorry, I was so pissed. Honestly, it wasn't that big a deal when I think about it. I overreacted and I wanted to punch a wall, but Flora beat me to it. But instead of a wall, it was my face. You have one … special best friend," he explained, but I couldn't move. "But then it dawned on me that I have made quite a few mistakes myself but you still forgave me, and that girl I *love* was about to walk out of my life forever."

"That … that was present tense," I informed him as though it was a typo.

"I know."

I held my breath. "You've done nothing wrong. I'm the one who's sorry."

"Of course I have. The point is that you forgave me in a heartbeat." His hand touched my forearm, making my heartbeat go out of control. If I just leaned in a couple more inches, our lips would touch. "I thought I had more time to cool off, but before I knew it, it was your last day, and if I didn't do anything then, I would never see you again."

"I'm sorry," I said.

"Don't be. I should be sorry. Falling in love with you wasn't a mistake. It's just the people in my life had a tendency of unexpectedly disappearing, and I guess I just got this idea that because you won't be in all of my classes, you're going to like run away with another guy or something crazy." Ashton's arms gently reached around my waist, enclosing me in a warm hug.

My eyes got watery as I really let it sink in that he was there. He was really standing there, when I thought that he would never see me again. "That'd never happen. I don't blame you for saying that. I should've told you earlier. I wasn't honest. You had every right to hate me."

Ashton pulled back, wincing. "I never hated you. Don't you ever think like that, okay?"

"I'm sorry."

"Stop saying 'sorry,'" he said, offering me a smile.

"Sorry—oops, I meant I'm not sorry," I stuttered. The sound of his hearty laugh made my heartbeat quicken. "But that would be a lie, because I really am sorry."

"Same old Ariel, right, gorgeous?"

"Right."

"I really missed you, you know?"

I grinned, wrapping my arms around his torso. The heat emanated from his body, warming mine.

"You did?"

"It's only been two weeks, but it sure didn't feel like it."

"I missed you too." I spoke into his shirt.

"Oh, and this is for you." Ashton said, pulling a slim box, the length of my hand from his pocket. "Open it. I only put it in the box because it'd get crushed in my pocket without one."

I lifted off the top, revealing a single amaryllis.

"You remembered this?"

"How could I forget?"

And like the girl who could never take a compliment, I blushed. "How did you just get one? Don't you have to buy a whole bouquet? I never knew that you could just buy one flower."

"Just don't question it."

"Why can't I?"

Ashton rolled his eyes. "Because you're ruining the moment."

"Don't I always?"

"Okay, never mind, you've already ruined it."

"It's what I do best. Now, don't take this the wrong way, but why are you here?"

"Well you based your project on me, so shouldn't I get to at least see you present it?" Ash wiggled his eyebrows at me. "I want to see what you think of me."

"You actually want to see it?" I gasped.

"Yes. It's all about me, isn't it?"

"Self-centered idiot," I said.

"I haven't changed either, you know?"

"I've noticed."

"Good." There was a small silence after that. But for once, it wasn't too awkward. And I liked that.

"I-I love you." I took a step back, stunned that I had blurted it out. "I mean you don't have to say it back—"

"I love you more than I thought I could ever love a girl. And if you don't mind, I still intend on taking you back to that cabin in the summer. Only if you want to, though."

I could feel the grin on my lips. He slowly leaned in, but I shook my head, resisting the temptation to pull his lips against mine.

"What are you doing?" I cocked an eyebrow.

His jaw dropped. "Huh?"

"You can't kiss me. We're not married. Yet." I broke out in a grin.

"Ha-ha, you're so funny."

"No I'm completely serious."

"Well, I don't think you mind too much if we break the rules."

Then his lips were on mine. For a few seconds, I remained shocked, but I recovered as my arms wrapped around his neck, pulling him closer. I stood on my tippy toes because I was just plain short. When he pulled away, Ash leaned his forehead against mine, breathing heavily. His lips grazed mine. This was pure bliss.

"God, I missed you."

I leaned in for another kiss, but the warning bell rang. Unlocking my arms from around Ash's neck, I took a step, blushing furiously. Ashton passed me as people began to file into the classroom. It didn't matter how much I liked him; PDA just wasn't my thing. I swore to myself that I would never be the type of couple that made out on the streets.

I watched as at least ten people walked into the room. I didn't recognize most of them from Easton, so obviously they came from other schools. All to see the presentations their friends had created, and I had to admit that it was pretty cool.

I sat down, feeling a warm, fuzzy sensation in the pit of my stomach. When Ashton sat at the desk next to mine, his hand automatically linked with mine. I sat up straight as Mr. Kinsey walked back into the room with a stack of papers.

"Good morning, class and friends," he greeted us with a grin. "Can you believe that it's been six months? I definitely see a lot of changes, and I can't wait to hear all about your experiences. So, let's just dig right in. Ariel, care to start it off?"

"I would love to," I said, standing up from my seat and facing the class.

I was met with the eyes of the people who now seemed so different. For one, Matt looked extremely healthy. I suppose all that football training had made an impact. And he looked happy. Before, he'd always feel self-conscious because of the people who made fun of him. Well, he certainly shut them up.

I patted my pocket for the flash drive and scurried toward Mr. Kinsey's computer. When I pulled up the slideshow filled with pictures, I got ready to press Play. I had timed everything perfectly to make sure the pictures would change at exactly the right times as I spoke. Now, all I had to do was do everything I'd practiced.

Ready … and action.

"Good morning. As you may know, I'm Ariel." I started. *It sounded a lot cleverer in my head.* A few people giggled. "And as you all know, I'm not exactly the most social person out there." I didn't have to turn around to know that the slideshow had flipped to a picture of me in sweats, with my hair up, and my signature big glasses.

"So one could imagine how furious I was when I found out about this project. That'd definitely throw me off track. Ironically, my topic was popularity, and I guess I really did have it coming." I glanced at Mr. Kinsey to see him scribbling down something on the rubric. "What makes the guys tick? Why do the girls act like that? That's what I had to find out for six months.

"Originally, I had hoped that my Aunt Stella would think that the project was crazy and that I'd be told to stay at Easton, but she didn't think that at all. So, with the help of my best friend, Flora, I transformed. She helped me get a brand-new wardrobe, a new hair style, contacts, and a lesson on how to use makeup. And I will admit that I felt really pretty. Surprising, right? Ariella Winters actually looking pretty? That would be a miracle." Mr. Kinsey laughed. The pictures changed to me sitting on a swing with Flora at the park. My hair had been curled, makeup was done, jeans and blouse on, and it had eventually became one of my favorite pictures.

"But it happened. So take your surprise, multiply it by ten, and that's how surprised I was. One thing I noticed was that, with all these new things, came a new sense of confidence I had never experienced before. Still, I inched myself into Lincoln Bay, trying to avoid as much attention as possible." Then I put up a photo of me pointing to the sign that read Lincoln Bay High School outside the school. "Everyone noticed me, to say the least. I mean everyone. And in my brain, I thought everything was just the same. They were obnoxious and full of themselves, and the girls were just so annoying I couldn't concentrate. It took everything I had not to roll my eyes every five seconds." People around me giggled.

"Fast-forward a little bit, and, to my surprise, I had made a friend. He was the principal's son, so he already knew my motives. He was actually a really nice person who guided me around to make sure I wasn't getting into trouble." I put up a picture of me grinning next to Elliot that day at lunch. "But that didn't change the fact that I had no clue of what I would be writing about. All I could say was that a boy was really nice to me. And I didn't really have a huge urge to try to bond with the girls about their boy troubles.

"Then I met a boy. Like, really met. At first, I wanted to lock him in a box and mail him to Australia because of how obnoxious he was. And luckily enough, he was the boy my schedule was matched to. We got assigned a project together that involved out-of-school hours.

"I know what you're all thinking. I'm so strong for dealing with that. I know. I pat myself on the back for dealing with it too." I physically patted myself on the back. "You're probably also wondering how I did it. I don't even know the answer to that.

"Something changed, though. When we were alone, he was like this foreign thing I had never expected. He was nice, funny, and real, and I thought I was dreaming. We became friends. He was someone I genuinely wanted to get to know.

"He had suffered a loss a few years back. He lost someone who had been truly important to him. The one person whom he had really loved was gone. So what happened? He surrounded himself with people, never getting too close to anyone except for his best friend."

There was a photo of me and Ashton sticking out tongues out as I pulled his beanie over his eyes.

Every single person in the room was silent, waiting for me to continue. "In a sense, I like to think that we're sort of alike. No, I have not lost a loved one, but our actions are very similar. I save myself the trouble of having to interact with many people, isolating myself. He surrounds himself with people who praise him, but in a sense he still isolates himself. It's just different types of isolation.

"After that moment, my entire perspective changed. Yes, some people are exactly who they portray themselves to be, but most people aren't. Most people have a story. There's a reason for their actions, and I'm pretty sure that this project was made to teach me that. Everything is different behind closed doors, and I know that now.

"After that, I cannot even begin to tell you the great numbers of things, good and bad, that got thrown in my path, but I do want to end with this. I, myself, even though I don't look that much different, changed. For one, I'm not going to judge you when I don't know your full story. As I walk through the halls, I no longer see the jocks, the popular group, or the theater geeks. I see a bunch of people living their lives, each with their own unique story.

"It's amazing how another individual is able to impact you to the point where sometimes I can't even think clearly without having them pop up in my head. Who would've thought, eh?" My eyes locked with Ashton's. I could see a smile etching onto his face. I guess that meant I was doing okay. The slideshow changed to a picture of me with my thumbs up. Elliot had taken that picture during school.

"Now, I am so much stronger and smarter than I was six months ago. Maybe it's not book smart but not everything crucial is learned through a textbook," I said. Feeling the need to joke around, I added, *"Yes, I, Ariella Winters, was wrong, and I'm admitting it.* Someone should really record this and put it online because I can assure you all this will most likely never happen again.

"Even though there were times I wanted to just hide away forever or shove someone down a hill, I would never take it back. I would choose this path just because of how much I've grown. How much wider my mind is when speaking to strangers. So I've learned a lot of things, really. Everyone may not be what they seem to be. Being social can actually make you a better person. Who would've thought, right? Never again will I place a stereotype on someone I don't fully know. As much as I might want to, I will force myself not to do so, because where that has got me this time, is absolutely incredible. Thank you for listening to my popularity project."

The final photo being of me smiling, my face taking up most of the shot, appeared on the screen. Everyone clapped politely, and instinctively the first thing I thought was, *I better get an A+ for this.*

I saw Mr. Kinsey nod approvingly. "That was

wonderful, Ariel. See? This project really did serve a purpose. Matt? How about you go next?"

Matt stood up, and when we made eye contact, I gave him a subtle thumbs-up. He smiled in return. I made my way back to Ashton with a wide grin on my face. He returned the gesture. Ashton winked, which made me turn beet-red in front of everyone in the room.

For the rest of class, we listened to the other presentations. Ashton had interlocked our fingers, and I took in every second of it. I had come to the conclusion that I wanted us to last forever, and if I hoped and kept on fighting, maybe we would.

But even if this wouldn't last, even if I wouldn't be able to make this last, the "now" just felt so nice that eventually, I stopped letting myself think ahead. Truth is, I had no idea what would happen. And I was finally okay with that.

In the end, I just stopped thinking ahead of myself. Instead, I let myself fall deeper in love with Ashton every second because I could. And for once, instead of fighting it, I let it happen, and I have to say, it didn't feel too bad.

Acknowledgments

It has officially sunk in that I will never, ever, be able to articulate how truly grateful I am for this opportunity to bring Ariel, Ashton, Flora, Elliot, and a bunch of other characters into this world. I could go on and on about every single reason I'm so thankful, but instead, I'm doing you all a favor and squeezing all the love I can into a couple paragraphs.

First and foremost, I am so lucky to have the parents that I have. Mom, you've always believed in me even when I'm the most unreasonable and moody person in the world. You've stayed by me no matter how irritating I am—and trust me, I can be a nightmare—and you've never been anything less than supportive. Dad, I still remember the day I e-mailed you that six-page short story I was so proud of. I was anticipating a billion compliments about how much my writing had improved, but instead, you surprised me by saying that if I wrote something longer and with a decent plot, we'd get it published. Everything I do is possible because of you guys, and I will be eternally thankful for having both of you in my life.

Jessie, I know you probably don't think that you've done a lot for me in this process, but know that, without you, this book probably wouldn't exist. You were the one who really opened me to how cruel yet amazing the world is. You've kept me grounded my entire life. Whenever I'm too oblivious or too selfish, you've always had that tough love I needed to keep me in check. I know that, no matter what, I will always have my sister by my side, and I can't thank you enough for everything you've done for me.

And to the rest of my family—I am so sorry that I'm not writing pages and pages about how much I love you all, but you've all played a part, whether you know it or not. Grandpa, Grandma, though you can't read English, I love you both to infinity and beyond. Uncle, Annie, you guys are some of the coolest people I know. Jalen, Sophie, and Olivia, though you all aren't old enough to read this book or even read a sentence, for that matter, when you do, which will probably be at the age that I am now, I want you three always to believe in yourselves. Sometimes, it may seem hard, or completely impossible, but keep a smile on your faces, and it'll be okay eventually. When you three grow up and finally read these few sentences, know that I will always be there for you. Rosie, my beloved cat, you will never be able to read or comprehend this since you're a cat, but you're my best friend. I know, I know, I sound like a crazy cat lady at the moment, but I don't care. You are the best cat any gal could ever ask for, and if I had the ability to provide it, you'd be living in your own cat palace. There are so many more people I want to thank that it's truly overwhelming so I'm sorry if your name isn't here. I love you and thank you.

Everyone at Author House who has given so much to help me shape this novel to what it is now, thank you. Joel, you have helped me in so many ways. I don't think I would've made it out sane if you hadn't been there. Alan, you could've easily not given my book a second glance. But you did and I am so thankful.

And finally, to every single person who has read my novel, I am so thankful. I hope this sweet little story made you smile because honestly, that's really all I wanted when I began writing. To make people, even if it's just one person out of the seven billion out there, smile. I have grown to love Ariella and Ashton so much, and I can only hope that you do, too. Though it may not seem possible, Ariel and Ashton have helped me through so many tough times. These two and their story kept me looking up. This book means so much to me, and it is thrilling yet terrifying to be able to share it with the world. I am grateful for every single one of you. Thank you, thank you, thank you.